Evaline: A Feminist's Tale

by M. Sheelagh Whittaker

*To Adele,
with affection.

Sheelagh*

Published by Departure Bay

Copyright © M. Sheelagh Whittaker 2016

Print edition

ISBN: 978-0-9954696-3-1

All rights reserved. This book may not be reproduced in any form, in whole or in part, without the written permission of the author.

This is a work of fiction. Names, characters, businesses, places, events and incidents are either the products of the author's imagination or used in a fictitious manner. Any resemblance to actual persons, living or dead, or actual events is purely coincidental.

"Lady, I pray you, if your will it were,"
Spoke up this pardoner, "as you began,
Tell forth your tale, nor spare for any man,
And teach us younger men of your technique."

> Geoffrey Chaucer, *Canterbury Tales*, "Prologue" to *The Wife of Bath's Tale*

This book is dedicated to those who, I hope, will enjoy the read.

To Faith, for having it.
To William, *my* miglior fabbro.
And to all of my children – you know who you are.

Contents

Foreword by Dr. Faith Gildenhuys 9

Perspective
Chapter 1: Active Retirement? 14

Dawning Awareness
Chapter 2: An Inauspicious Beginning 23
Chapter 3: I Am Woman… 25
Chapter 4: Hear Me Meow 27
Chapter 5: Not Exactly John the Baptist 31
Chapter 6: Oh Reading! Joy of My Desiring! (with apologies to J. S. Bach) 33
Chapter 7: Another Point of View 35
Chapter 8: Developing a Syllabus 38
Chapter 9: Changing the Game 42
Chapter 10: A Lot to Swallow 45
Chapter 11: The Apprehension of Confusion 49
Chapter 12: New Horizons 52
Chapter 13: Cry Wolf 54
Chapter 14: In the Footsteps of Marie Antoinette 56
Chapter 15: The Right Qualifications 59
Chapter 16: Positive Thinking 63
Chapter 17: Becoming a Consultant 65
Chapter 18: A Felicitous Event 70
Chapter 19: Degrees of Surprise 73

Chapter 20: You Can Get Anything You Want 76
Chapter 21: Bodily Fluids 80
Chapter 22: The Way We Were 83
Chapter 23: Back in the "Olden Days" 89
Chapter 24: Hot Puppies or Hush Babies? 91
Chapter 25: A Difficult Decision 98

Tests of Character and Endurance

Chapter 26: And the Seasons, They Go Round and Round 104
Chapter 27: Manners Matter 107
Chapter 28: The Pearson Paradigm Finishing School 109
Chapter 29: Ups and Downs with the Twins 113
Chapter 30: Rear-View Mirror 115
Chapter 31: Mommy's Sayings 124
Chapter 32: Even in the Midst of Life… 126
Chapter 33: Fifty-One Ways to Leave Your Lover 132
Chapter 34: Kubler-Ross Revisited 135
Chapter 35: Travel and Sundries 140
Chapter 36: Hard Work Is Its Own Reward 143
Chapter 37: A New Field to Conquer 147
Chapter 38: Halfway Down the Table is the Place Where I Sit… 150
Chapter 39: Down There on the Floor 152
Chapter 40: Free to Be… You and Me 154
Chapter 41: Glasnost and Perestroika 157
Chapter 42: Arbat Street 163
Chapter 43: A Picture is Worth a Thousand Words 166

Chapter 44: In the Alternative 168

Chapter 45: A Private Affair 172

Chapter 46: Miss Congeniality 175

Chapter 47: Choppy Waters 181

Chapter 48: Blows to All Our Hopes 185

Chapter 49: Boardom 190

Chapter 50: Management is the Art of Getting Things Done Through People 194

Chapter 51: Traces of History 197

Chapter 52: A New Tack 199

Chapter 53: Honoris Causa 201

Chapter 54: Redaction 204

Chapter 55: Beyond Words 206

Chapter 56: Voices in the Wilderness 208

Chapter 57: Testing… 212

Chapter 58: Wonderful to Relate 214

Chapter 59: Innocents Abroad 217

Chapter 60: Brief Interlude 221

Chapter 61: Making Choices 224

Chapter 62: The Occasional Merits of Cul-De-Sac Technology 228

Chapter 63: Tidings of Comfort and Joy 232

Chapter 64: I've Got a Gal in Kalamazoo 235

Chapter 65: Just When You Thought Everything Was Under Control 240

Chapter 66: The Not-So-New Broom 244

Chapter 67: A Turn Out of the Sun 247

Chapter 68: Chilled to the Bone 250

Chapter 69: An Unexpected Honour 254
Chapter 70: No Particular Impediments 260
Chapter 71: With Apologies to Tom Wolfe 263

Consolidation of Experience
Chapter 72: A Change of Scene 271
Chapter 73: "That Will Do, Pig" 274
Chapter 74: A Whole New World 277
Chapter 75: A Handbag? 280
Chapter 76: A Phantasmagoric Good-bye 283
Chapter 77: Sometimes it's Better to be the Underdog ...286
Chapter 78: A Different Kind of God 289
Chapter 79: Authenticity Rules! 292
Chapter 80: Beauty and the Bard 297
Chapter 81: Fade to Grey 300
Chapter 82: Who Am I Anyway? 304
Chapter 83: Are There Still Battles to be Picked? 306
Chapter 84: Let Me Not to the Marriage of True Minds… 310
Chapter 85: Let the River Run 313
Chapter 86: There She Weaves By Night and Day, a Magic Web… 315

Master Class
Chapter 87: Brutal News 319
Chapter 88: Bearing Witness 321

Acknowledgements 324

Foreword

Is the central question of this novel a bit passé today? After all, we've come a long way, baby, and sisterhood is powerful. Around the world women are in top positions – or at least near the top – so what can one woman's story, real or imagined, tell us that we don't already know? *Evaline* reminds us that feminism is just as much or more about a lone woman's struggle as about a movement. With humour and irony, Sheelagh Whittaker describes the perils, pitfalls and triumphs of negotiating the corporate world while at the same time dealing with a husband and twins and school bake sales. Like her irrepressible forbear, Chaucer's Wife of Bath, she tells us about pain and pratfalls on the way to establishing a singular identity – which, in the last analysis is what feminism is all about.

Evaline has luck on her side but her will to succeed is strong. She is clear-eyed about her goals and is careful not to be seduced by her own sense of self-worth. She tells an interviewer about studying for an MBA from INSEAD Business School in France:

"I have known some remarkable and special men who were able to get interesting and powerful jobs simply on the strength of their own intelligence and demonstrated capability. Those guys were able to bypass the need for advanced university degrees and specialist professional qualifications because they were obviously talented and full of potential.

"But the ability of the workplace to assess women in the same way hadn't yet been developed. No one would hire an untried woman with a bachelor's degree in arts to be a highly paid consultant, as we did in the case of a clever young man from Yale not long after I joined Pearson. All of us, both male and female, accepted – even believed – that clients

9

couldn't be expected to take a woman's inherent capability on trust; she needed to have the credentials to back her up.

"So a lot of my intention in going to INSEAD was to get the credentials that I would still need to be taken seriously as a professional. And, as it turned out, it worked pretty well exactly as I had hoped."

Evaline is not always a pillar of strength. She copes, just barely, with a sudden and profound tragedy. Once, after confronting a sexist superior in the boardroom, she goes home to dissolve into tears. However, the main source of her power is a quick wit, not necessarily steely determination. During a regulatory review, Evaline has to improvise a part of her budget on the spot, realising that she has left a significant expense out.

"I was wondering if you could direct me to the item in the budget where you've provided for the support of The Duke of Edinburgh Awards of which you seem so proud."

"Thank you, Mr. Chair," Eva responded before anyone else on the team, like the CFO designate, had a chance to answer. "We are very pleased that you've taken such careful note of our intentions in this regard, and I would like to direct you to the line entitled 'Travel and Sundries' in your budget document for the cost allocation that you are looking for."

"'Travel and Sundries?' That's a strange place to budget an expenditure for athletic awards," said the Chair, suspiciously.

"It certainly is, Mr. Chair, but you know how these things go. The accountants have so many bizarre rules and categories, and sometimes they tell you to do things that just don't seem to make sense to anyone but themselves."

In 1778, Fanny Burney published *Evelina or the History of a Young Lady's Entrance into the World.* The novel in letters describes the orphan heroine's moral, social and sexual development, with comic and satirical glances at eighteenth-century London society as seen through the eyes of a seventeen-year-old. By today's standards, it is tame stuff, ending predictably with Evelina ready to marry an impossibly good and handsome nobleman. But, stripping away the local concerns, the twenty-first century reader finds much that is recognizable in the situation that Evelina finds herself in.

Burney describes Evelina's negotiating London society and the marriage market, which evaluate a woman's value fairly crudely. In *Evaline,* Whittaker describes how a contemporary woman must find her way on her own in a world in the face of similarly daunting obstacles. In both cases, there is no single villain, just a society dominated by men who feel entitled. And the men who support Evaline do so with sympathy but it is clear that they are powerless to materially affect her road to success. Leo and then John are often outside Evaline's life for one reason or another. Burney's Evelina is cherished by Mr. Villars but is, like Whittaker's characters, physically removed from his ward while she is in London.

Perhaps Evaline's aloneness is the source of a surprising touch of poignancy in *Evaline.* Though surrounded by children and sometimes by colleagues, she understands that, despite her achievements, she faces whatever dangers lurk on her own. When her twins visit her office boardroom, one of them asks,

"Where do you sit mom? Do you sit at the end near the wall screen or near the cloakroom door?"
"I sit in the middle, facing the big double doors," replied Eva.
"But you're the boss. Why don't you sit at the head of the table? That's where bosses are supposed to sit."

11

"Remember when you were little and you didn't want to do what you were told, you used to cross your arms and say, 'You're not the boss of me.' Well, you were right. I'm not really the boss of anybody; people just let me pretend to be the boss sometimes for a little while."

"So why do you sit in the middle?"

"Well it may sound silly, but I like to sit in the middle of the table facing the door so that when a disgruntled customer with a submachine gun comes to wipe us all out, I'll at least see him before he starts shooting."

As is so often the case, Evaline deflects the focus on her vulnerability through humour, but the incident reveals a great deal about how she views herself, self-deprecating about her position and the tenuousness of it and her life. Her insight into situations displays depth of character and we are charmed by her ability to find her way through challenging situations, big and small. How she deals with mismatched shoes and a terrorist bombing in London tells us much about how women come to terms with life's unpredictability.

Dr. Faith Gildenhuys

Perspective

Chapter 1: Active Retirement?

Evaline looked absently down at her feet, stretched out in front of her on the floor of the limousine. Then she looked again, her focus sharpening as her brain registered an inconsistency.

The toe of one of her business-like court shoes seemed definitely more rounded than the other. In fact, it looked as if one shoe actually had a round toe, while the other toe was quite sharply pointed.

She bent forward, pulling her feet closer in order to see the shoes more clearly in the light of what so far was quite a watery London dawn. It was even worse than she had thought: one shoe was navy blue and the other was black. Investigating further, she was slightly reassured to see that the style of heel of each shoe was at least roughly similar.

"So much for getting dressed in the dark," she muttered to herself, hoping nobody had noticed. "At least it was radio, not television."

Thinking ahead to her next meeting, Evaline quickly reached into the capacious black leather handbag which doubled as her briefcase, felt about amongst the assorted papers, emergency snacks, keys, lipsticks and money holders, pulled out her phone and called her husband.

"Hi, John. What did you think?" Then she added quickly, "I wasn't too impressed myself," hoping to ease his way into the gentle constructive criticism she was sure he already had in mind.

"You sounded a bit nervous, which isn't like you, Ev," John answered softly. "But you got better as you went along. The other interviewee was clearly more experienced on radio than you are and more voluble, but you did get in a good word or two."

"I'm afraid I came across as more strident than funny," Evaline looked at her feet. "But I was happy with the bit about the distinction between race and gender. Lately it's been nagging at me that people talking about diversity in the workplace seem to think that gender and race are exactly the same kind of thing. But how many people of mixed gender do you know, I ask you?"

"Only a few, but those I did meet dressed exquisitely," replied John. "And speaking of funny, you weren't hilarious, but you certainly made your favourite point that there will only be true gender equality when there are as many incompetent females in positions of authority as there are incompetent males. It won't make you popular, but it does have natural justice on its side."

Evaline sighed, absent-mindedly rubbing her finger along a scuff in the red leather of her favourite address book. "Natural justice would be nice, but right now I probably would settle for matching shoes. I just looked at my feet for the first time today and I seem to have unintentionally left home black and blue – at least from the ankles down."

"I've told you that I don't mind if you turn on the light to get dressed for these early interviews. Do they at least look like they come from the same manufacturer?"

Evaline reached down and slipped her shoes off to look at their labels. "No – the black one is Bally and it has a stacked heel, and the other says Russell and Bromley and the heel is leather-covered and a bit worn looking."

"Where are you going? I'll meet you there with two other shoes and you can pick the three you like best."

"Um... I'm going to 23 Great Peter Street, and I'd prefer the Bally if you can find it. Otherwise the navy blue R&B would be OK, but I'm wearing a black suit so I'd still look a little strange. Too bad I'm not both a fashion icon and a businesswoman like Christine, so people would think it's deliberate if I wear navy shoes with a black suit."

"Which door should I meet you at?"

"How about in the foyer near reception? If you bring the shoes in a plain brown bag people will just think I forgot my lunch."

"Okay, love, see you there. Want to bet on whether my tube will beat your limo?"

15

"Nope."

"You know sometimes I get bored of all this," Evaline yawned, balancing on one foot as she checked the black pump in her hand for consistency.

"Bored of what? Getting up early, dressing in mismatched shoes, being interviewed on radio, or going to meetings? And by the way, just because Christopher used to say 'bored of' instead of 'bored by' or 'bored with' doesn't give you licence to use that weird grammatical construction forever. People who don't know your son used to say that when he was four might think you're just poorly educated."

"I'm bored of *all* those things; early rising, haphazard dressing and being interviewed on hackneyed subjects – especially those in which so many of the victims of unfairness seem to be in favour of it." Evaline paused, and then she continued: "It's a theme day today – women's lack of progress towards equality – which could be interesting if I hadn't been talking and meeting about the topic for more than 40 years. Oh, and by the way, I think unusual grammatical constructions add spice to my way of speaking. Furthermore, you can get a perfectly good education on the Canadian prairies as long as you don't care if, for the rest of your life, sophisticated people the world over will laugh at how you say things."

"By changing countries you have at least broadened your array of mispronunciations," offered John. "And enhanced your ability to order from strange menus, I might add."

"Might you? I may know a courgette from an aubergine, and the tax year end of at least three different jurisdictions, but some days I wish I'd changed personal crusades. When it comes to attitudes towards women, every new country I visit seems worse than the last. The change of landscape is interesting, though, and I do like the variety in cuisine," Evaline conceded.

"Stand up straight and let me look at you," ordered John, brushing a stray hair off Evaline's shoulder. After his exacting career as a photo journalist, John naturally looked at his world, including his wife, with a clear, critical but artistic eye. To Evaline's ongoing delight, his own wardrobe evinced the same dedication to quality and subtle but interesting colour choices.

"You'll do. Just be careful what you fulminate about. Even though it's only 8:30 and this is a breakfast meeting, I suspect you've already said enough for one day."

"Don't worry about me," Evaline muttered, "I won't get heard here today no matter what I say. The heading of the press release is already written in gentle bureaucratic phraseology. What I think it should say, however, is '*After years of hand-wringing, the percentage of women in executive ranks almost crawls to double digits.*'"

"How about '*Self-righteous North American feminist derides British for pathetic lack of progress on big jobs for girls*'?" suggested John.

"I'd do that if it would actually make a difference, not just a headline. Otherwise I'll just come off sounding like an older Sarah Palin with Canadian vowels. Come to think of it, I have been a hockey mom..."

"Only one season, and besides, you wear contact lenses. Now, just go in there and behave with the unshakeable confidence of a woman who knows she's finally wearing matching shoes. I'll see you at dinner."

John and Christopher were both engrossed in their computers as Evaline came through the door. She smiled, inwardly congratulating herself and John, not for the first time, for insisting that Christopher use his computer in the front room. Of course, British Telecom's ancient system had helped, as their wireless router didn't emit a strong enough signal to reach to his room in the back and down the stairs. Anyhow, she really liked having their 16-year-old nearby – even if he was concentrating on school work. She also liked to think that his proximity to his parents kept some of the evils of the internet – particularly those directed at adolescent boys – at bay.

"So, Big Girl's Shoes, how was the rest of your day?" asked John.

"It got better. I had a lovely lunch with David and Matthew at Scott's, where I saw Michael Caine and his wife at a table across the room."

"Michael Caine? Who's he?" asked Chris, briefly distracted. "One of your business titans?"

"Not exactly – more of a celluloid titan, if you know what celluloid is."

"Oh, an actor then. Have I seen anything he was in?"

"Well, he was *Alfie* before Jude Law was born, if that helps."

"So is his wife a hot blonde like Sienna Miller?"

"Older and darker," said John, "but the camera really liked her." He turned to Evaline. "What were the boys up to today?"

"Handicapping the Conservative leadership contest," said Evaline. "I love to listen to their opinions. Matthew thinks David Cameron is…"

"Oh, Mom," interrupted Chris, "you have some phone messages. A guy who said he was from an executive search firm called, said you'd recognise the name of the firm, rhymes with 'bender'. And a lady who wants you to play bridge on Thursday. Their numbers are by the phone."

"Want to bet which one she phones first?" John asked Chris.

"Nah, it's a sure thing: the bridge lady."

"Maybe I wouldn't," sniffed Evaline to masculine laughter. "Anyway, what's for dinner?"

"Roast chicken with stuffing," said Chris. "Can't you smell it? And dad went out and bought your favourite Waitrose *tarte aux framboise*."

"Sounds delicious. I'll go change my clothes," said Evaline, unbuttoning her blouse as she went. "And then maybe I'll call the bridge lady…"

"Make sure you put on two slippers from the same pair," called John as Eva headed towards their bedroom, eager as always to change out of her work clothes into something more comforting.

It was after ten the next morning when Evaline decided to return the head-hunter's call. Even though it had been her turn to get up early with Chris, ensuring that he had a wholesome breakfast and some semblance of parental presence in the room while he ate it, she was still quite slow off the mark, dawdling over coffee and reading the new *Vanity Fair* before she was willing to seriously consider starting her day.

There had been a time when she would've returned a call from a recruiter at any hour of the day or night, provided it wouldn't have made her seem too eager, but she was less concerned these days.

Since retiring from flat-out engagement with the working world, Eva had discovered that all those years when she thought she was "living to work" she was actually just caught up in a complex attempt to try to prove her ability and resourcefulness – mostly, as it turned out, to herself. And if she had entertained any notion that her prowess had genuinely mattered, or that the people she was working with had actually grown attached to her, they had been conclusively dispelled by what she thought of as her "Mark Twain moment" – an erroneous report of her death.

Over the years, Evaline had truly liked and admired every one of her assistants. Even after she retired she had remained in close contact with her clever Scottish helpmate, a woman called Flora. She and Flora had met for a lunch date one autumn afternoon and Flora had immediately launched into what she considered a hilarious anecdote.

By coincidence, early that morning the comptroller of the firm where they had last worked together – a man called Lew whom they both quite admired – had come into Flora's office wearing a very serious expression.

"I have some very sad news," he reported. "I've just heard from our colleagues in America that Evaline Sadlier has died."

Flora had tried to look stricken. She'd said, "Oh dear, what a terrible shame. And she and I had agreed to meet for lunch today. Now I don't know who will buy my lunch." While she and Flora had laughed and laughed about the mistake and speculated for some time on how it could have come about, Eva actually took the incident quite seriously to heart. Even Lew, with whom she had a working relationship of mutual respect, seemed to have found news of her untimely death to be more newsworthy than devastating.

The recruiter's call, once returned, followed a familiar pattern. He and Evaline established acquaintances in common, shared a little gossip, then he asked a few questions designed to ensure that Eva's credentials were still valid and that she wasn't suffering from sudden-onset dementia, before finally moving on to the purpose of the call.

He turned the conversation, only a little awkwardly, to the amount of new regulatory oversight provoked by the global economic crisis. Then he asked Evaline if she would consider membership on a board of experienced CEOs and regulators dedicated to improving public confidence in the integrity of corporate financial reporting.

The mandate sounded interesting to Eva, and she had a lot of admiration for those members of the proposed board whom she already knew. But years of experience with this type of feeler had made her increasingly cautious.

"I find your description of the position quite tempting," she told the recruiter, "but I need to ensure that there would be no conflict with commitments that I have already. Would you mind emailing me the board charter and meeting schedule before we discuss this any further?"

Both parties hung up pleased that they had executed the initial moves in this particular ritual dance without any missteps.

"How did your call go?" John asked later.

"Okay," said Evaline. "The board has a very timely and worthwhile task. With my background I'd find it a bit of a challenge, but important. I suppose it would be an opportunity to 'give back to society', but sadly the timetable sounded like it might well clash with what I'm doing already, so I don't think this one will work out."

"Ah," said John, nodding. "No discussion of a hefty retainer, then."

"No," sighed Evaline, "when the call ends with no mention of money, you have to conclude that it's because there is very little money to mention."

"And, anyway, who needs money when you already have a senior's bus pass?" asked John.

"Who, indeed?"

Dawning Awareness

Chapter 2: An Inauspicious Beginning

Even a sympathetic observer would have considered Eva's post-undergraduate attempts at adult life rather poor. First of all she married her high-school sweetheart in a cloud of white tulle and lace and got herself a job as a trainee buyer of ladies' fashions and accessories at Woodward's Department Store. She quite liked the manager of Ladies Dresses – a dapper man with a flattering manner and a well-trimmed moustache – so she participated fully in the shock and mourning that followed his sudden death at the hands of the husband of one of his better customers.

She happily acquiesced when her True Love suggested they move to Toronto to better his career prospects, quickly finding a new job in fashion merchandising and busily decorating their two-bedroom apartment near the Islington subway stop with stylish modern Danish furniture. As a crowning touch, Eva placed one of her favourite wedding presents – an ingenious wrought iron candle-holder that held a spray of a dozen very fine, very long, coloured candles – at the centre of their teak dining table.

Proudly lighting the many candles one evening in anticipation of dinner with friends they had made in the apartment below, Eva leaned too far forward and set her hair on fire (nothing serious, just singed). Undaunted, the next day she moved the modern candelabra to the windowsill where it could catch the rays of the sun. A few days later she came home to find a pathetic array of wilted melted candles.

Later she would come to feel that "singed" and "wilted" were adjectives that applied quite broadly to her relationship with Mr True Love.

The new friends from downstairs were a Vietnam War draft dodger and his wife, both of whom thought it was appropriate dinner conversation to regale their hosts with tales of how many items they heard being dropped on the floor whenever Eva was in the bathroom.

"How do you know it's me?" Eva asked.

"We know," they replied in unison, looking meaningfully at her husband.

"Being a draft dodger must be boring," Eva announced that night as she prepared for bed, having dropped several hairclips, the toothpaste and her plastic drinking glass during her turn in the bathroom.

"Want to know what I really think?" asked her True Love. "I think we're boring."

And somewhat to Eva's surprise, she agreed.

So they split their wedding presents (she insisted he take the candle-holder) and went their separate ways. Eva was invited to stay with a girlfriend who was working on her Master's in Food Science at Cumberland – a pretty agricultural college not far from Toronto – while True Love took one of her few good friends to the Supremes concert with the tickets he and Eva had bought to celebrate Eva's birthday, and then reported to Eva that after the concert the two of them had returned to the apartment near the Islington subway and made love on the marital bed.

Chapter 3: I Am Woman...

As it turned out, Cumberland, a formerly sleepy agricultural college that had been appropriated to double as a dynamic young arts college for the wave of baby boomers who wanted to be "people in motion," was the perfect incubator for Eva's emergence as a feminist.

The first milestone on her journey was reached in Maisie Allick's living room. Eva, newly hired as a member of the college admin staff, had been invited to participate in a female "consciousness-raising" session. Earlier that autumn a number of the professors' wives, female lecturers, librarians and junior administrative staff of Cumberland University had solemnly decided they should get together to participate actively in the women's liberation movement by forming an awareness group and, happily, Eva had been included.

Maisie – a faculty wife with Ivy League poise – had volunteered to have the initial meeting at her large home on the perimeter of the campus. The furniture had been pushed back so that the acolytes could sit comfortably on Maisie's thick carpet, and her husband, who preferred to be known as *Dr. Allick*, had retreated to his campus lab to continue his search for ways to improve the tensile strength of soy bacon.

The group's terms of reference had been drawn from the popular press: *Ms. Magazine* and a book about women's health and sexuality called *Our Bodies, Ourselves*. However, the members of the group, a bunch of budding middle class radicals, were tentative and a bit overwhelmed by the audacity of their mere association, so the use of either mirrors or speculums at the meetings was not even considered.

Eva was simply thrilled to have been invited to join. She had landed a coveted administrative post in Student Services after working for some months on special projects for the university vice president, and it was a relief to have permanent work. To many, being hired for that particular job was a major coup, since her predecessor had been a highly regarded young man who had gone on to even greater things in the institution.

There had also been a change of roommates: with her new sense of security and independence, Eva gave off an air of self-containment that led to her attracting and winning the love of Leo, a popular student leader. For her part, Eva had been drawn to Leo's revolutionary attitudes, which seemed so unlike her own. She also liked his resemblance to John Lennon of the Beatles, right down to the wire-framed glasses and black leather worker's cap – although she later learned that Leo felt he looked more like Strelnikov from the movie *Doctor Zhivago*.

Leo proudly carried the exotic name of Leopold von Richthofen, and was indeed from an offshoot of the branch of the family that featured the WWI German fighter pilot known as the Red Baron. That both Leo and Eva were at a small Canadian university with a history stretching back fewer than ten years did nothing to dampen their enthusiasm or diminish their mutual esteem.

These were heady times. Flower power and Haight-Ashbury may have begun losing their vogue, but the debate about women's liberation was just beginning to gain the attention of young women who wanted much more out of life than they saw their mothers were getting.

Chapter 4: Hear Me Meow

"So, is tonight the bra burners' get-together?" asked Leo over a dinner made from a Chef Boyardee home-made pizza mix – one of Eva's specialties.

"I think our bras are safe tonight," replied Eva. "But I did do the pencil test yesterday to see if I could embrace bralessness this summer."

"I would certainly embrace you braless," quipped Leo.

"Oh Leo," sighed Eva, "I'm on a mission to elevate my level of feminist awareness and you're reduced to making silly, suggestive jokes."

"I wasn't being suggestive – I was stating a fact. Anyway, tell me about the pencil test. What does it involve? Do you pencil names like 'Flopsy' and 'Mopsy' on your breasts and see how long it takes for them to wear off?"

"Flopsy and Mopsy?" Eva sputtered, "I would think 'perky' and 'well-rounded' would be more apt."

"Ah, my sweet, you know I think your beauty is the fuel of myth. You have a décolletage that could launch a thousand Fokkers."

"Hmmm..."

"You still haven't described the test to me. Is it difficult?"

"No," laughed Eva, "you simply put a pencil beneath your bare breast and see if it stays there or drops to the floor. If it drops to the floor, you've passed and can go braless. If the pencil stays, trapped in your abundance of flesh, then going braless is likely a bad idea."

"And did you pass the test?"

"Yes."

"Ah, so 'perky' it is after all."

Eva laughed as she ran out the door and across campus towards Maisie's house.

Excited by the prospect of the meeting, she was one of the first to arrive. Somewhat to her dismay, she noticed that many of the women were coming in with plates of chocolate chip cookies or date squares in hand, although she found the sound of Helen Reddy's song *I am Woman* playing softly on the stereo in Maisie's living room strangely reassuring.

"*I am woman, hear me roar*
In numbers too big to ignore
And I know too much to go back an' pretend
'Cause I've heard it all before
And I've been down there on the floor
No one's ever gonna keep me down again."

The lyrics made Eva smile and cringe a bit at the same time, but she was willing to suspend her critical standards in order to embrace an anthem for the women's liberation movement. She recognised that someone who could get teary-eyed, as she routinely did, during Bobby Gimby's Centennial song *Canada* had already demonstrated pretty forgiving standards of musical discernment.

"Maybe something more soaring and beautiful will emerge later," she thought, "but Helen Reddy will do for now."

Once most of the seekers of heightened consciousness had arrived and settled, cross-legged, on the floor, one of the organisers announced that it was time for introductions – but with one stricture:

"You can't use any information about your husband or your boyfriend or your father to introduce yourself."

This left several women, at least initially, at a loss for words.

Others fared admirably, with Maisie proudly pronouncing that while she was known by the name of Maisie, her very favourite and preferred choice was "Mommy." The number of sighs in the room metered the envy others were feeling that they hadn't thought of this first. That their reaction was unfeminist registered with only a very few.

As she waited her turn, mentally rehearsing what she was going to say, Eva was particularly interested to learn how Paula Frederick would choose to introduce herself.

On Eva's first day on the job at Cumberland, a cheerful, thirtyish woman with a pleasant face and stocky build had walked into the office and sized her up in a forthright way.

"Well, you're pretty enough," Paula had said to her, "and they say you're smart. Let's see if you can keep your spendthrift boss in line." Then she turned and left, calling over her shoulder, "It'll be great to have another woman around."

When her turn came, Paula had no trouble omitting her husband from her personal introduction – although his supportive presence in the background was implicit. "My name is Paula Frederick and I am both a Cumberland grad and a manager in the Food Services department. I love my job even though the hours can be long and events often run late. And I am really glad that we women are finally getting together to get ahead."

Recently returning to work after the birth of her third child, Paula had been the catering manager at Cumberland for several years. The oldest of seven, she clearly loved being involved in the lives of so many people, and used her boundless energy to keep her job and her family running smoothly.

Eva, among the last to introduce herself, was perhaps unaware of what her choice of personal details revealed about her. "My name is Evaline Sadlier, but please call me Eva. Evaline has always sounded to me like the name of a mature woman, and I'm pretty sure I'm not there yet. I've recently started to work in Student Services and I love my job already. One of my first tasks has been to hire my own secretary – a woman called May who is clearly more capable than I am. I really hope that I can do well and learn a lot."

(In truth, Eva had struggled with herself over the selection of May as her secretary. May seemed old – at least 45 – and looked like a schoolteacher from the 1950s, with tight grey curls and cat's-eye spectacles. Fortunately, someone in the personnel department had recognised how valuable Eva would find May's maturity and gently helped to steer her choice that way – a practical kindness that she would later remember with gratitude.)

Eva quit speaking, looked around, smiled shyly at the group, and the task of self-introduction moved along to the woman on her left.

The "de-manned" introductions at that first meeting took quite a while, and when they finally ended an expectant hush fell over the group as a few women seemed to wonder what they should do next. How do you even begin to tackle a problem as new and large as women's liberation? And who had the courage to act as their guide?

By sheer coincidence the student organisers of the campus speakers series had scheduled a remarkable gift to the nascent feminist group. In the week immediately following their inaugural meeting at Maisie's place, Betty Friedan, author of *The Feminine Mystique*, was coming to Cumberland to speak. Those present at Maisie's agreed they would all attend and take notes about suitable topics for discussion at future meetings. And they would meet again in two weeks' time to begin the real task of consciousness-raising.

Chapter 5: Not Exactly John the Baptist

Friedan's east-coast intellectual, Jewish and radical – but somehow rather humourless – message of female emancipation made her corn-fed audience at this Canadian agricultural college shift uncomfortably in their seats. But she was the genuine article: a real pedigreed feminist.

Poor Betty. By the time she'd reached the fourth tier college-speaking circuit, even she was getting a bit bored with her version of "the way, the truth and the light." All the same, like any good prophet, she stood up and proclaimed her message with as much energy as she could muster – though frankly it wasn't a lot. Still, a significant minority in her audience listened with care and admiration to her every word, and then gathered around afterwards in order to have her autograph their well-thumbed copies of her book.

No matter how road-weary and worn out she may have seemed, Betty Friedan's very presence among the group served to legitimise their feelings of vague malaise. So, by the time the women got together again at Maisie's house they really were ready to begin the revolution. It's just that they weren't exactly sure how to go about it.

As a way to focus their dissatisfaction, the Cumberland Consciousness-Raising Chapter (as they now called themselves, with a slight change from "Group" to "Chapter" to add a tone of seriousness) decided to begin by chronicling all the injustices they suffered in their lives – either past or continuing – which were directly attributable to the actions of men.

The list was lengthy, if repetitive. Broken down into themes, the complaints, in ascending order of importance were: He doesn't help buy groceries; He doesn't help with the housework; He doesn't watch the children, change diapers, get up in the night to calm the crying child or go to parent/teacher meetings; He's always playing golf, poker, hockey with the boys; He watches football all day Sunday and every holiday; He doesn't pay attention to me and my numerous grievances; He doesn't take me seriously.

There was no mention of sex. Not gender, but sex.

Eva, whose relationship with Leo was still relatively new, was only able to contribute a whinge or two in the "football watching" and "doesn't do laundry or housework" categories. And she couldn't help feeling that, while all this sharing of grievances was probably reassuring, it wasn't exactly "I am woman, hear me roar" – more like "I am woman, hear me whisper nervously… if you can." Still, it was evident that the women genuinely felt closer to each other as a result, and if the occasional male faculty member did hear about a fellow academician's domestic eccentricities from the adjacent pillow that night, it just couldn't be helped. As Eva was to experience throughout her life, good gossip usually trumps sisterhood.

The Consciousness-Raising Chapter voted unanimously to meet again in two weeks to continue their journey. It was also agreed that the next meeting would be in the big common room of the graduate student residence in order to make the point that women had every right to commandeer space on campus for meetings about women's issues.

Chapter 6: Oh Reading! Joy of My Desiring! (with apologies to J. S. Bach)

Going to meetings with other women and attending after-hours speeches were new experiences for Eva. By nature she was quite reclusive, and her lengthy exclusive relationship with her high-school sweetheart had done little to make her more social.

Eva had had a rather solitary childhood, the result of both circumstance and choice. Her mother, Kay, had preferred to work 'outside the home' once Eva was in kindergarten, and for her part, once Eva had mastered reading she barely noticed that her classmates had mothers rather than housekeepers to go home to. It helped that her father subscribed to the Book of the Month Club and her much older brother Dean was a bookworm too.

Reading was the joy of Eva's existence. To call her a bibliophile was to put it a bit lightly – suggesting something much more superficial than the hyperconnectivity with books that she actually felt.

The result of her preoccupation with reading was that Eva experienced a form of panic when faced with a stretch of time – even as little as five minutes – with nothing to read. Fortunately, instructions on a pill bottle or a leaflet could suffice at a pinch, especially if the written content was repeated in more than one language so she could spend time puzzling out the unfamiliar words.

Eva's absorption in reading often led people to think she wasn't paying sufficient attention to what was going on around her. They were only partially right. She was capable of retrieving a spoken sentence or two from her unconscious mind while reading, and of coming up with an answer to most questions directed her way.

Before meeting Leo, Eva had found Lawrence Durrell's *The Alexandria Quartet* in the Cumberland University Library, and she credited Durrell's representation of four discrete yet overlapping sets of human experience as the source of one of the most important insights of her reading life: the realization that there are no absolutes in human interaction.

While reading the book entitled *Mountolive* in Durrell's *Quartet,* Eva come upon this statement:

> *For those of us who stand upon the margins of the world, as yet unsolicited by any God, the only truth is that work itself is Love.*

She committed the sentence to memory as well as writing it out on a small piece of paper and taping it on the wall above her desk. For a long, long time that sentence served as her creed.

Chapter 7: Another Point of View

The organisers of the speakers series presently served up their next thought-provoking attraction: Xaviera Hollander, "the happy hooker."

Cumberland's student government, including Leo, had taken the job of selecting from the list provided by the speakers' bureau very seriously. They wanted to be perceived as providing good value to the community, and they had been particularly surprised and pleased that year by the array of choices. Overall, they felt confident that they had selected speakers to reflect broad interests...

As he explained to Eva, it was in his role as a steward of the fees expended by the student union that Leo made a point of arriving early on the night Ms. Hollander was to speak, resulting in seats in the very front row. Leo's focus, as he claimed, was ensuring the union got what they paid for.

"Happy," as Eva thought one might most appropriately call this speaker, demonstrated that she knew how to provide real value for money, even just by speaking. She entertained the packed house with a cheerful, almost wholesome monologue about her career in providing fun and sex for cash.

For her part, Eva watched Xaviera with an intensity that bordered on fixation. No doubt Leo was secretly hoping that Eva was trying to pick up some pointers from Happy about how to please a man, when in fact Eva's fascination was, to Leo's ultimate disappointment, considerably more clinical than that. She was trying to figure out how someone like Xaviera managed to pursue her chosen career without contracting some terrible disease, or without throwing up at the prospect of some of the things that she was asked to do by her clients.

Eva's interest could have been described as generic: like many women, in the face of an actual practitioner she found

35

herself trying to understand commercial trade in sex by looking for answers. "What's the real difference between us?" she wondered. "Could I do what she does for money? And, if so, how much?"

Happy's appalling gospel of the joys of prostitution was really, of course, a much more powerful argument in favour of women's lib than the more intellectual and carefully crafted arguments of Betty Friedan. In Happy's world the transactions between males and females were certainly well defined.

In addition, the appearance of "the happy hooker" actually speaking on campus at last made it possible for the consciousness-raising crowd to touch, albeit rather lightly, on the subject of sex.

They approached the topic very cautiously, not quite from behind but at least from the side.

Some time at the third meeting was taken up welcoming new members, and then there was a brief recap of the previous meeting's dreary litany. After that the meeting was opened to comments.

Here was a room full of educated women without a single one among them who could honestly claim a working knowledge of the *Kama Sutra*. With many of the group reduced to almost adolescent speculation about the "insights" offered by Xaviera, those few who had actually read *The Joy of Sex* were immediately accorded advanced standing and potentially even graduate student status.

And then, haltingly, came the little voices, the insecurities, the tiny betrayals. Whose fault is it when interest fades in response to PhD orals (his, of course) or childbirth? Eva, though still in the early stages of her relationship, had fresh, stark memories of previous scenes of tears and long nights lying beside a cold and unyielding back, but she wasn't ready to share them. Listening to the embarrassingly similar experiences of other women just made her sad. While the conversation was perhaps at times titillating, it was ultimately almost boringly repetitive. The session broke up on a subdued note.

Eva never did become comfortable with the sexual confidences of others, despite being on the receiving end of some fairly remarkable confessions. She certainly had libertine leanings – or at least interests – and had developed an enduring prurient appetite for stories about the proclivities of movie stars, politicians and various executives – including some of her knowledge or even acquaintance – but she really didn't like to talk about personal specifics, not even with her closest friends.

Chapter 8: Developing a Syllabus

As an accompaniment to her personal consciousness-raising journey, Eva undertook a self-assigned course in feminist literature. She started with Erica Jong's *Fear of Flying*, whose simple, cheerful notion of guiltless sex struck her as brash but shallow.

Next came Simone de Beauvoir's *The Second Sex* with its nature/nurture argument that females are not born but made, which Eva found intense and intellectual but not all that much fun to read. *The Woman Destroyed*, also written by de Beauvoir, seemed to Eva much more tragically powerful, although not much discussed by feminists – perhaps, she wondered, because the woman is in fact emotionally destroyed by the man in the book.

Eva found a lot to think about in Robin Morgan's *Sisterhood Is Powerful*, and it became, for a time, her favourite reference. Meanwhile, early editions of *Ms. Magazine* jostled with Burt Reynolds' harmless and charmless centrefold in *Playgirl* on the coffee table in the apartment she shared with Leo.

It took some time for the next meeting of the consciousness-raisers to be organised, and in the interim, much to her delight and surprise, Eva was appointed by the college president to Cumberland's first ever Employment Equity Committee. As she remarked to Leo over one of her macaroni, Kraft slices and tomato soup casseroles, "They were looking for a girl in the administrative ranks to appoint and they found me."

Other appointees included a well-dressed, well-spoken, black female professor of mathematics; a star professional football quarterback who taught animal husbandry in the off-season; and a member of the personnel department.

The terms of reference of the Employment Equity Committee were unclear. Its first meeting, mistakenly scheduled on a day when the football hero was out of town for a playoff game, could most kindly be termed inconclusive on all fronts. At the second meeting, with all members in attendance, it was agreed that the question of terms of reference should be referred to the president and the senate of the college. The personnel department was asked to facilitate this referral.

While an early form of shuttle diplomacy between the faculty association and the university president concerning those terms of reference was ongoing, the *pièce de résistance* of the speakers' series came to town: author, scholar and spokesperson for the women's liberation movement, Germaine Greer.

Greer's book, *The Female Eunuch*, was highly topical and she used it, as she so often did with any reason to appear in public, as her invitation to be outrageous. Erudite and articulate, Greer was a highly entertaining speaker, a genuine university woman's kind of feminist. Eva found her book truly, continuously interesting and for the most part well-reasoned – maybe a bit radical and extreme, but she also saw it as an important part of her self-designed feminist syllabus.

"Sometimes I get the feeling that Germaine Greer has embraced sexual liberation less as a principle than simply to be provocative," Eva told a slightly bored Leo over his chipper tuna casserole. (He had agreed to accompany Eva to hear Germaine speak, although he was certain she would not measure up to Xaviera Hollander in entertainment value. He decided, however, he might learn something new about women's sexuality – particularly the clitoral orgasm he had read about while leafing through one of Eva's books.)

"What's wrong with provocative?" asked Leo. "Seems to me that one way to get people thinking differently about the role of women is to shake them up a little."

"I guess so," said Eva, thoughtfully. "And yes, that *is* the heart of the problem, isn't it? How do we get so many people, both men and women, to think differently enough about the role of women in society that we don't have to argue or struggle all the time even for recognition of our right to equality?"

"Well, your question is a bit of a challenge for a man whose intellect has been fuelled solely with your remarkable tuna casserole. Still, I'm willing to work on it, although I think the issue of whether the administration will allow condom machines in the women's washrooms on campus has first call on my time and attention tomorrow."

"It surprises me that you don't recognise that the two problems are related," smiled Eva. "Perhaps I should have put more tinned peas in the casserole..."

In her own way, Germaine Greer, at least as she presented herself, was a lot like Xaviera Hollander: shocking, engaging, sometimes very funny, and like Happy she provided really good value for a speakers' series investment. At Cumberland, quite justifiably, she had been met and feted by a serious group of feminist female academics who could not believe such a luminary had come to speak at their remote little university. (In fact, as someone heard her complain to her arranger, Germaine could hardly believe it herself.) But there she was, and the female faculty were simply thrilled just to have her in their midst, and ready to give her a lot of latitude in her speech and in the sycophantic questions that followed.

An Australian Cambridge-educated radical feminist speaking at a small Canadian arts and agriculture college could be forgiven for feeling superior to her audience, but Germaine had the grace not to act as if she did. Her gospel of liberation, her message to her audience to free themselves from the bonds of their socialization, was received seriously – even studiously – by her audience. Some actually took notes.

Eva was very glad to be present that night. Still trying to find her own position on the issue of women's liberation, she reasoned that every new line of argument that she read or heard would help her towards a unique, personal point of view.

Sadly, though, that evening Eva was distracted during the sometimes meandering discussion of the obvious powerlessness of the female eunuch by the pain of a freshly received, psychic wound of her own. That day, while purging the filing cabinets at work, she had found a document that appeared to reveal her predecessor's annual salary. Trying not to leap to conclusions, she checked the figure with a trusted source who responded sympathetically.

"I wondered what you'd think if you knew about that."

"That" was the grim fact that during the time he'd held "their job," Robin, a younger man with charm and intelligence but inferior qualifications, had been earning a salary fifty per cent higher than Eva's.

The injustice of it seared. Even just the thought of it brought Eva close to tears.

Chapter 9: Changing the Game

The next consciousness-raising session, which took place on a lovely spring day, involved going off in twos or threes to see if, in small, almost private groups, the women could more easily come up with ways to improve their prospects – or at least those of their (as yet mostly unborn) daughters.

Eva went off with Paula, who seemed to be managing her own growing family and the college catering services with genuine ease. Though not holding out very much hope that they would actually come up with ways to make things more equal for women, Eva was sure, at the very least, that Paula would have some good campus gossip to share with her. She also hoped she could encourage Paula to begin to consider her as a close friend.

It didn't happen. Paula, with three small children – one still in diapers – was too tired to do more than plod along the country path they were on, surrounded by delicate spring flowers and cheerful weeds, and Eva, feeling abashed, talked too much about nothing in particular while sneezing and sniffling from all the pollen.

On their return to the group, which had defiantly arrayed itself on the faculty club steps, they found that a general sense of discouragement had cast a pall over the whole enterprise. Finally, though, Billie, a lively redhead with pigtails who was working on her doctorate in veterinary science, spoke up.

"There aren't any protocols to help us out here, no commandments, no acts of parliament, not even any motions in the university senate. It's certainly clear to me, as I'm sure it is to you, that nobody is going to ride up to this college and simply hand the womenfolk recognition and top jobs and good pay. But that doesn't mean we don't really deserve those things or that we should give up trying. It just means we have to accept responsibility for our own destiny.

There's no way around it. We're just going to have to pull ourselves up by the hair on our legs."

Listening to Billie's exhortation, and admiring her for it, Eva felt that she had seen the future.

A few weeks later, Eva went to her boss with a carefully constructed argument that she deserved to earn as much as her predecessor.

Having to talk to Eva about something as personal as a raise clearly made her boss, Fraser, almost pathetically uncomfortable. He shifted in his seat and looked out the window as he reminded her that it was virtually impossible to get approval for out-of-cycle raises.

"It's not that I don't want to give you a raise, Eva," he said, his gaze sliding off her eyes. "You know I think that you're doing an excellent job. But we're partway through the year; full-time student equivalent estimates have been filed, budgets have been set, and I have no room for adjustment."

Eva had anticipated this argument – she was, after all, personally in charge of departmental budgeting, one of Fraser's weaker skill sets – and she had carefully rehearsed her answer with Leo the night before.

"I'm very sorry," she said respectfully, staring directly at Fraser until he had no choice but to look her in the eye. "I understand the difficulty you'll have in getting me a mid-cycle raise. But I've given the matter a lot of thought and I feel that you should have considered the possibility of a problem such as this arising before you chose to take advantage of my lack of knowledge about the college pay structure in offering me such a low initial salary for the job."

Eva paused for breath and gave Fraser what she hoped was an understanding smile.

"It wasn't my idea," he said bravely. "Personnel told me that women in executive assistant roles on campus earn even less than the amount they suggested I offer you."

"But I'm not your executive assistant – Joanna is. And she's senior to my secretary, just as you are senior to me," said Eva, perhaps a little too firmly and directly. "I've thought this over very carefully, and I truly regret to say that if I don't receive a significant raise in pay I will have to resign and find another job."

Upon delivering the last part of her speech, Eva turned and walked as calmly as she could out of her boss's office and down the hall to the women's washroom, where she sat in a cubicle reading the fourth volume of *The Alexandria Quartet* until she felt calm enough to re-emerge.

The seeming intransigence of her own position had really frightened Eva, but she meant it. As she had explained to Leo (over a delicious dinner of minute steak and tinned Green Giant corn niblets): "If I threaten to quit I really have to mean it. Empty threats make you weak and steal your credibility. I don't want to give up my job – I love it – but what happened here was unfair and I absolutely don't want to live with that."

After an anxious few weeks, Fraser approached Eva tentatively with a compromise – an immediate raise of 30 per cent and the opportunity to attend a seminar at the UCLA in organizational development. After obtaining more information about the OD seminar, Eva graciously accepted the offer.

She was able to contain herself until Leo arrived home that evening, but he had to sit through a complete rendition of "I am woman, hear me roar," before he was allowed to sit down to his dinner of slumgullion – a hamburger, noodles, tomato soup and Tabasco sauce concoction that Eva's grandparents had relished during the Great Depression.

"I knew how hard it was for him to tell the president that he needed to give me a raise, so, in fairness, I had to go part way. And the seminar sounds really interesting."

Leo, the experienced student politician but not necessarily the superior strategist, agreed.

Chapter 10: A Lot to Swallow

To book her place at the seminar, which turned out to be offered at UCLA's Westwood campus, Eva phoned the California number on the brochure and had the good fortune to have her call answered by the assistant to the Dean of the Business School – a cheerful sounding woman called Mary Wainwright.

Eva immediately liked Mary, and while the management of this particular seminar was not Mary's direct responsibility, she undertook to help Eva get properly registered and booked into the Westwood Hotel at the university's special rates.

The focus of the course was team building, and a rather famous professor called Newton Margulies was conducting the three-day event. Even Leo was envious of the opportunity.

On learning that she had never travelled to LA before, Mary suggested that Eva arrive on the Saturday before the course began on Monday. Since the reservation at the hotel would not begin until Sunday night, Mary offered to meet Eva at the airport and invited her to stay overnight at her home before shepherding her to the Westwood the next day.

It was an innocent time. Even Fraser felt that Eva had been lucky to encounter such a helpful person on the staff of the business school – a fact that seemed to provide sufficient character reference – and Leo was happy that Eva would have a female chaperone.

Eva recognised Mary immediately, all warmth and red hair and freckles, as she walked into the flight arrivals area. Each had provided the other with a description of herself for identification; Eva's being that she would be wearing a red-and-white polka dot scarf, but their immediate kinship made the polka dots redundant.

They bundled her bags into Mary's car and joined the majority of the population of Southern California on the freeway. Eva was busy staring out the window as Mary outlined their afternoon and evening.

"I was hoping to stop by the pet store for a mouse or two, then I thought we could go to a restaurant along the Pacific Coast highway where they have wonderful seafood and great views. We'll go for an early dinner so that it's still light. I know you must be feeling the time difference, and that will give you a chance for an early bedtime.

"Tomorrow I thought we could join a couple of my girlfriends for a trip to see the Queen Mary in dry dock down the way."

"Sounds great to me," said Eva, wondering what the mice might be for. "And dinner will be my treat, of course, after all you're doing for me."

The pet store was in a nearby quaint one-storey brick shopping mall, with a baker and a bookstore on either side. No fan of animals, Eva went into the bookstore to browse while Mary went in search of mice.

"No luck," said Mary as she joined Eva at the bookstore. "There's been a run on mice, if you can believe that, some sort of school project, and they won't have any more in for few days. It's too late to go anywhere else, so let's get going to the restaurant. Do you like California wine?"

"I'm not a very experienced wine drinker," admitted Eva. "Spritzers are usually my choice and you don't get much wine flavour with those. But this is an adventure and I'm certainly willing to try something new."

The dinner and the view were spectacular, and the compatibility of personality and attitude the two women had immediately sensed held true. Eva was relaxed and tired as they headed for Santa Monica.

"Why were you looking for mice?" she finally asked as they drove along.

"Oh, my pet boa constrictor hasn't had anything to eat lately and he must be getting hungry."

Suddenly alert, Eva asked, "You have a pet boa constrictor? Where does it live?"

"Oh, the students in my last scuba class – you remember I told you I teach scuba diving on weekends – bought him for me as a joke for an end-of-course gift. They thought I'd return him but I found I kind of liked his muscular charm. Don't worry, he lives in a big cage in the apartment. You'll see him."

"Where do you keep the cage?" Eva asked in a tight little voice, desperately trying to sound casual.

"Well, my apartment is small so he lives in the living room. And he sleeps mostly."

"I thought I was sleeping in your living room?"

"Yes, but don't worry. The sofa doesn't quite touch the cage when it's pulled out and he's only ever escaped once, and that was when someone accidentally left the cage door unlatched."

Leo came to pick Eva up from the airport the following Thursday evening. They hadn't been in touch since she'd set off due to the exorbitant long-distance charges levied on calls across the continent.

As they drove toward Cumberland, Leo asked, "How did it go? Was Mary as nice as she sounded? Was the course interesting?"

"The course was excellent, Mary turned out to be a really good new friend, and I survived a hungry boa constrictor."

"You survived what?"

Eva went on to describe, with hysterical laughter fuelled by fatigue and the free drinks she had downed on the plane, how when they got to Mary's apartment there was a large wire cage against the wall in the living room with a dark shape in it. Eva was directed to the bathroom while Mary made up the sofa bed, plumping up the pillows and turning down the lights before directing Eva into the bed (entry on the boa-free side). She wished Eva good night and was gone – into the bedroom with the door closed.

Suddenly alone with the boa, Eva was at a total loss as to how to react. Could the boa stick its snout through the bars and bite her toe? Do boas even bite – or do they suck? Or do they squeeze you until you're unconscious and then slither at you with that famous loose jaw of theirs open like a dark cavern?

Trying to stay calm, she wondered if it was possible to sleep all curled up in the top part of the bed farthest from the snake. Less calm, she wondered if she was going to die in a small rented flat in Santa Monica. If she turned on the light would that wake the creature? Is light attractive or frightening to boa constrictors, and how could she find out?

Finally Eva erected a small barricade at the foot of the bed with her suitcase and the two pillows and the blanket Mary had left for her, then she curled up at the top of the bed and fell into an exhausted, fitful sleep.

She woke with a crick in her neck to see Mary standing over her with a cup of coffee in hand.

"I'm so sorry. I didn't realise The Creature, as I call him, would make you so nervous. He's not even full-grown, only about six feet long right now, and you're really only in danger if you smell like a small furry animal," Mary laughed.

The rest of the trip was a comparative breeze.

Chapter 11: The Apprehension of Confusion

Safely back at Cumberland, Eva's work life resumed its comfortable rhythms, which now included the workings of the Employment Equity Committee.

The agenda for the next committee meeting, prepared by the representative from Personnel, only contained two items:

1. *Discussion of terms of reference*
2. *Hailey Job Assessment Study Results (for information only)*

The committee's terms of reference were still mired in discussion between the Office of the President and the university senate, who were wrangling over which principles of equity were to be applied and whether those principles should be applied equally to tenured and untenured academic staff, and to some or all of the non-academic staff. There was also disagreement over which category the library staff should be placed in.

The head of Personnel, Tony DeMarco, had requested the opportunity to make a special presentation to the committee on the findings of the Hailey Job Assessment team.

According to communiqués from the president, the Hailey job assessment involved benchmarks and correlations with other similar institutions and would provide the university with reassurance that its remuneration system was both fair and defensible. The assessment system was expected to be a useful tool for the administration, both in negotiations with the faculty and government funding agencies. Of course, virtually all of the recipients of those communiqués were fully aware that the real purpose of the job assessment process was designed to raise performance expectations and reduce costs.

"There will be no losers in this process," began Tony before the interested committee. "Those who are found to be overpaid, as revealed by their position on the grid, will not receive a salary reduction. Those individuals will simply be 'red-circled.'"

"What exactly does that mean?" asked Chad, an athlete to whom circles and crosses usually meant football plays.

"Those who are red-circled will receive no salary increases until inflation and the natural progression of the salaries of others at their level catches up to them, or until they are promoted," replied Tony, almost as if by rote.

"That's a bit grim," muttered Eva.

Carefully ignoring her, Tony continued: "There are also, of course, individuals whose current pay falls well below that which their Hailey assessment says they ought to receive. Unfortunately, we will not have sufficient funds in the budget for the next several years to deal with that problem. Those individuals will be 'green-circled' so that they can be closely monitored and, of course, they will receive regular annual raises."

He then distributed charts and graphs replete with red and green circles to the committee to show overall results by job category.

"While you're looking these over, let me assure you that in almost every instance we achieved anonymity for the people in each job category by grouping three or more incumbents."

"This analysis certainly is interesting," interjected Dr. Edith Rivers, the committee's academic appointee, "but might I ask you why, in particular, you asked to present these findings to the Employment Equity Committee?"

"Yes... well... um... regrettably the results have revealed a small problem of what may be perceived as bias, and the president and I agreed that the committee should be properly apprised of the facts before anyone begins to challenge the findings."

"Bias?" asked Chad.

"Yes. You'll notice on the page entitled 'Gender breakdown analysis' that the majority of 'red-circled' employees are male and the preponderance of 'green-circled' employees are female. We are a little concerned that this information, taken out of context, could cause confusion."

"So, concerned about confusion arising from the clear evidence of bias in pay levels favouring men, are you?" asked Edith dryly.

Eva laughed, Chad looked at his hands and Tony had the wit not to respond to that comment.

Always a quick study, Eva had immediately noted two points of personal interest among the charts and graphs. The first was that, despite the assurances of anonymity they had just been given, there was only one incumbent in her own job category. The second point was that, even after her recent raise, there was still a green circle around her position, making it evident to all that she was still seriously underpaid according to Cumberland's now codified standards – and yet, due to the university's stated financial realities, she stood to receive nothing more than mere cost of living increases in the years ahead.

Glancing at his watch, Chad announced that he had to get to the stadium by 4 o'clock for practice, and the meeting abruptly ended.

Chapter 12: New Horizons

"I think I should get an MBA," announced Leo over a dinner of Shake-and-Bake chicken, potato puffs and frozen peas. "I feel under-employed as a revolutionary in a small, mostly agricultural college and I'm not making much progress on this thesis of mine. I'm beginning to think I should try to make my mark in the business world instead of becoming a dusty old academic struggling to keep from being marginalised by newer and better thinkers."

"Yes, you're better than that, Leo," said Eva, generously offering him the last Bisquick scone from the basket. "You have energy and new ideas. Although I have to admit that there does seem to be a lot more of your thesis in the wastebasket than still on the desk..."

She went on, warming to her theme, "Too bad solitaire isn't a marketable skill. The spots on our cards are almost worn away from the hours you've spent on that sofa contemplating a conclusion to your second chapter. You know, a change of direction really is worth thinking about."

Eva ignored Leo's indignant stare and continued, "The other day, when I was delivering those English essays that I'd marked for what you so disparagingly call 'pin money', I took the opportunity to tell the august – and rather attractive – tenured professor that I really envied his vocation. I said I'd love to be able to think and talk about literature all day. But do you know what he said?"

"No, what?" said Leo, ever the conversational tennis player. "That he found such an aspiration charming in a young lady like you?"

"No, silly. He told me that he believes getting a Ph.D. in English destroyed his ability to enjoy reading novels for the fun of it. If that happened to me I don't know what I'd do. Maybe kill myself."

"I really don't think that would happen to you, Eva, but that doesn't mean I think you should get a Ph.D. in English either. I suspect Dr. Rather Attractive doesn't have your gift of compartmentalization. He probably finds that he can't turn off his critical narrative, even when he's reading for pleasure, whereas I think you can."

"You're right," replied Eva. "Anyway, tell me more about this MBA. Have you thought where you might go?"

"I've given the matter considerable thought – especially when I was supposed to be conceptualizing chapter three of my thesis over in my carrel in the library. It looks like Western, York, McMaster and UBC are all good possibilities in Canada. The American schools are awfully expensive. But I was wondering about somewhere like INSEAD in France; it has a reputation as one of Europe's leading business schools and it would take me back to my roots."

"Oh. Well, reading *Peanuts* for all those years may have misled me, but I thought the Red Baron parked his Fokker in Germany."

"Don't be a smarty-pants. My family has a proud European heritage. And my mother's French, you know."

"I know," said Eva. "I can hardly wait to meet her. She'll probably be delighted to have a conversation with someone who speaks a version of French unique to the Canadian prairies. I'm told my accent is particularly memorable..."

"But her English is quite good, as are her German and Russian."

"Would I meet her if we went to INSEAD?" asked Eva.

"We?" Leo looked surprised. "I, um, hadn't thought of us *both* going to study. I thought you might find a job – maybe teaching English."

"Forget that," said Eva firmly. "And I certainly don't want to spend the next several years green-circled. Looks like I probably need to get an MBA too."

53

Chapter 13: Cry Wolf

Before leaving Cumberland, Eva and Leo attended one last speakers' evening, to hear Farley Mowat, author of a nature-under-enlightened-observation book called *Never Cry Wolf*. Not in reality much of a nature lover, even at the safe distance of a book, Eva was only mildly interested in Mowat, but Leo had attended the feminist lectures with her and it seemed only fair for her to go along to this one with him.

As it turned out, the balding, bearded, semi-famous naturalist and author provided an amusing contrast to the speakers who had preceded him. Mowat came to talk to the assembled students and faculty about his sympathy for wolves, and to everyone's surprise his personal behaviour was somehow strangely in keeping with his subject. He insisted on a having a pitcher full of vodka with him on the podium and proceeded to pour helpings whenever he felt the need. His speech was as devoid of inhibition as might be expected in the circumstances.

Leo's student leadership role meant that he and Eva were invited to the reception for Mowat after his talk, by which point in the evening Mowat didn't have any small talk to offer and was clearly anxious to leave. While others were circling the cheese tray, he came up behind the winsome companion who had arrived with him and cupped her breasts with his hands, with a "stop me if you have the nerve" smile directed towards anyone looking their way. Unperturbed, the young woman, who clearly did not find his behaviour novel, removed his hands and shifted to his side.

"Getting tired?" she asked him fondly.

Eva found the casual humiliation of Mowat's female friend upsetting, and she and Leo left the reception soon afterwards. Their official departure from the university took place only a few weeks later.

Despite the struggles over her salary, Eva always thought of her position in Student Services as her first real job, and one which she loved. She had at last glimpsed the kind of work she would like to do, and she had become convinced that a business degree would help her find another, even better, job in the future.

Farley Mowat's crude and sexist behaviour, Billie's admonition to "pull ourselves up," and Eva's own nervy threat to quit if she didn't get a raise, turned out to be the most enduring memories of her time at Cumberland.

Chapter 14: In the Footsteps of Marie Antoinette

Leo had had the foresight (and the spare time) to take his GMATs – Graduate Management Admission Tests – when the exams were being held on the Cumberland campus. Eva, at that time still employed, had needed to work that day. This meant that Leo had to drive Eva, never a confident driver, over to McMaster University in Hamilton to sit the standardised business school exam early on a cold winter Saturday morning.

Eva had feared that lack of sleep, caused by the dual anxieties that she wouldn't wake up in time or that a surprise blizzard could make roads impassable for the early-morning drive, would considerably reduce her notional chance of a good score. However, they were both promptly accepted for the INSEAD Business School MBA programme in Fontainebleau, starting in September, and immediately began to make excited preparations.

The countryside around Paris was shimmering with August heat when they arrived, jetlagged and disoriented. Once they'd checked in to L'Hotel Napoleon, "au coeur de Fontainebleau," they fell, exhausted, onto the inviting duvet-covered *lit matrimonial*.

Happily, despite the persistent heat, within a few days the couple was relaxing with canapés and wine, toasting their prospects from the comfort of a shady table in the hotel's back garden.

"Thank heaven for 'connections', as the British call them," said Eva. "Your parents' friends are so generous – a gîte *and* a car! – and they were extremely tolerant of my frightful French accent."

"Yes," agreed Leo, "we sure were lucky. I can't believe they apologised for the age of the car!"

From their apartment in Munich, Leo's parents had made some calls and their dear friends, Yves and Nicole Tremblay, had picked Eva and Leo up at the hotel the day after their arrival and driven them around the countryside to see some places that were on offer to let. Finally Yves had driven them to their own home in Vulaines-sur-Seine where, after a refreshing beer, Nicole had diffidently shown them a little building on the property that they sometimes rented out to tourists.

The Tremblays expressed some concern about how comfortable the gîte might be in winter, with just a fireplace and a space heater, but Eva, in particular, loved its rustic charm, and both she and Leo loved the rent. It was well within their budget – all the more so with use of the ancient Citroën in the yard thrown in for free. The slightly musty furnishings and rickety chairs did not dampen their enthusiasm.

Vulaines-sur-Seine was an easy commute to the INSEAD campus, and even the fact that, as residents of the *commune*, they would qualify to be called *Vulaignots* seemed somehow thrilling.

Eager to move out of the hotel, Eva and Leo spent the next couple of days sweating while sprucing up the cottage and getting the Citroën, quickly nick-named Rouille, into roadworthy condition. The heat was overwhelming, but the cottage was surrounded by large trees and they hoped that once they'd moved in they could just relax and try to keep cool.

The gîte had been a coach house before it was converted, and it still had some surprisingly rustic features – such as only one sink for all purposes, and a shower with a very tentative stream of water.

"This is a great adventure," Eva and Leo kept reminding each other as they scrubbed and swept and sweated and sneezed. And it was. There they were, in a home replete with genuine French provincial atmosphere, just a short drive from INSEAD and not terribly far from Paris.

They were so caught up in their new life that they almost missed the news that Richard Nixon, President of the United States, had finally resigned as a result of the Watergate affair. Yves and Nicole invited them over to watch the rebroadcast of Nixon's speech, with French translation, on television. ("A little confusing to say the least, especially when Nixon seemed to be speaking French in a woman's voice, but Nicole's quiche and *salade verte* were delicious," reported Eva to friends later.)

The aesthetic of the gîte, with its stone walls, slate floor and almost monochromatic colour scheme of pine, greenish beige and cream was just to Eva's taste. She loved the quaint hardware in the house and the fact that their really quite new mattress was supported in the bed frame on a lattice of rope. She even loved the old water pitchers with their matching chipped bowls – at least after she had adjusted to the idea that they were intended for daily use, not just decoration.

Leo asked Yves where to get the best chocolate croissants and set off nearly every morning in Rouille to buy fresh croissants and a baguette.

A great fan of the movies, Leo thought that Eva and he were like Audrey Hepburn and Albert Finney in *Two for the Road*. Eva, while thrilled to be cast as Audrey Hepburn – a woman she at least liked to imagine she slightly resembled – felt that the more difficult potential parallels in the two stories (for example the seeming inevitability of mutual ennui) were probably best left unexplored.

Chapter 15: The Right Qualifications

Attending INSEAD was both exhausting and exhilarating. In addition to a rigorous business curriculum, students were required to achieve a level of proficiency in three languages. While Eva struggled with her German, she was becoming steadily more fluent in French. Fortunately, the school charter allowed students to write their assignments in English. All the same, they both made a real effort to become more international – or "cosmopolitan", as they liked to describe themselves.

The curriculum demanded of Leo and Eva a previously unencountered volume of mentally challenging or sometimes just plain gruelling work, but there were also plenty of opportunities to drink and laugh and talk. And the food was memorable.

Leo, an amateur musician with an introspective bent, became very interested in the intricacies of operations research. As he explained to Eva, the elaboration of coded instructions for the computer reminded him of instructions in musical scores.

Eva focused on economics and finance, mainly because she had never studied either subject before and she found them much less reliant on rote learning and much more prone to the vagaries of human nature than she had anticipated.

Their course schedules kept them going in different directions most days; a situation they strongly agreed was for the best. As a result, Eva became study pals with Bram Rose – a slim, intelligent man from Paris with a way with numbers and a mysterious fiancée who was never seen but often felt. Bram and Eva had a comfortable rapport and waited companionably in the computer room late into the night, hoping a terminal would become available so that they could share the use of the university's mainframe computer to run the programmes in BASIC that they had written as assignments.

There were lots of team assignments, and Eva found herself working with a varying array of characters. She grew very fond of a Portuguese called Carina: a slim, dark-eyed woman with a fine brain and an unflappable manner. Less than 10 per cent of the class was female, but they found themselves treated very equitably. Workload proved to be a great leveller.

Leo enjoyed solitary workouts in the gymnasium on campus, pondering his assignments as he relaxed in the steam room. Just before they left Canada he had purchased a copy of *Zen and the Art of Motorcycle Maintenance* by Robert Pirsig, and he read and annotated his copy during quiet intervals.

Over the months, Eva and Leo came to know many of the secrets and quirks of their classmates. Some were brilliant and some were feckless, but it was hard not to concede that working with their fellow students was likely a pretty fair rehearsal for real life.

The largest and most hotly debated class assignment focused on presentations about whether or not it would be possible and practical to have a Europe-wide currency. Issues of national identity and the dangers of trying to harmonise divergent European economies resulted in impassioned discussions, with the Germans and the English sometimes resorting to name-calling and increasingly frequent references to World War II. From a North American point of view it all seemed intellectually fascinating, but somehow not so emotionally engaging. Instead, Eva found that she felt considerably more anxious about the rising tide of Quebec separatism that was threatening the unity of her homeland. Emotionally she was strongly committed to a bicultural Canada, and on a more practical level she had not put all that effort into learning French only to live in a unilingual country.

INSEAD's reputation and the eclectic make-up of its MBA graduates meant that on-campus recruitment for post-graduation employment was intense and rewarding. Despite the joys of France, both Leo and Eva were eager to return to work in Toronto, and they each received some tempting offers. Eva chose to go to work for a consulting firm which specialised in the public sector. It was called The Pearson Paradigm ("with a capital T for 'The'," as she laughingly told her friends and family), while Leo joined a specialist high technology magazine start-up called *Synapse*. They were on their way.

Decades later, Evaline was asked by an interviewer what influence her time at INSEAD had had on her career. After some thought, she replied that INSEAD and the MBA had given her a widely recognised credential that helped her tremendously in finding an engaging and challenging job.

"I have known some remarkable and special men who were able to get interesting and powerful jobs simply on the strength of their own intelligence and demonstrated capability. Those guys were able to bypass the need for advanced university degrees and specialist professional qualifications because they were obviously talented and full of potential.

"But the ability of the workplace to assess women in the same way hadn't yet been developed. No one would hire an untried woman with a bachelor's degree in arts to be a highly paid consultant, as we did in the case of a clever young man from Yale not long after I joined Pearson. All of us, both male and female, accepted – even believed – that clients couldn't be expected to take a woman's inherent capability on trust; she needed to have credentials to back her up.

"So a lot of my intention in going to INSEAD was to get the credentials that I would need to be taken seriously as a professional. And, as it turned out, it worked pretty well exactly as I had hoped."

Chapter 16: Positive Thinking

From the very first minute, Eva loved working for The Pearson Paradigm. Privately, she had believed she was neither smart enough nor worldly enough to qualify for a management consulting job at Pearson, and she was convinced that she was hired only because she'd kept her mouth shut during the interviews with all the partners and had let them do all of the talking. It hadn't been her intention to do so, nor was it her natural inclination. It just turned out that she couldn't get a word in without interrupting the flow of her interviewers, and she decided interrupting was more dangerous than seeming quiet.

Regardless, she now had a business card that read:

Evaline Sadlier, Consultant, The Pearson Paradigm

And as far as she was concerned, she had nowhere to go but up.

Hurrying to work in the morning on her walking route through the rough margins of downtown Toronto, she frequently muttered to herself: "*Tous les jours a tous points de vue je vais de mieux en mieux.*"

"What did you say?" asked a colleague who caught up with her on the pavement near the office one day.

"I'm practicing Coueism," she replied. "I encountered it in France, although I realised right away that I'd heard much the same mantra years earlier. My dad had a book by Norman Vincent Peale called *The Power of Positive Thinking* and it really is the same thing by another name."

"And what is it?"

"They call it positive autosuggestion – the ability to convince the subconscious that a goal is achievable."

"Okay. So I ask you again, what are you muttering? It sounds foreign."

63

"It's French. But in English what I'm saying is: Every day in every way, I keep getting better and better."

"Oh. Well, I hope it works. Pearson can always use the help."

"So can I," Eva whispered to herself, very quietly. In English.

Working at TPP, Eva imagined herself to be an apprentice to the contemporary craft guild of consulting. When she was twelve years old she had encountered the true story of the lives of the Gilbreth family of New Jersey in a book called *Cheaper by the Dozen*. Reading the book, Eva was particularly struck by the way the parents, Frank and Lillian, both of them time-and-motion study experts, had applied the precepts of their profession to the raising of their large family.

At INSEAD, while learning about Frederick Taylor, originator of modern management consulting, and his book *The Principles of Scientific Management*, Eva had encountered a case study applying scientific management to bricklaying. The study had been written by Frank Gilbreth – "The actual Frank Gilbreth!" as she had exclaimed to Leo. That the clever child-rearing described in *Cheaper by the Dozen* was an offshoot of scientific management seemed especially meaningful and encouraging to Eva.

A few months later, when Eva's brother, Dean, came to Fontainebleau for a quick visit, they fell to talking about how civil engineering – and in particular the execution of great engineering projects like the railways across North America – had pioneered techniques such as time-and-motion study and critical path analysis and modern consulting. When Dean mentioned that Lillian Gilbreth had still been teaching at MIT during his own time there as a student, and that he'd even been able to audit some of her classes, Eva felt really quite envious.

"Now *there's* a woman worth emulating," she declared. "A great career, lots of kids... So sad about her husband's early death, though."

Chapter 17: Becoming a Consultant

Eva loved her lowly position at Pearson. As the consultant, she didn't feel she had to seem smarter or better than any of the others; she just had to pay attention and not embarrass the firm in front of clients.

Early on, she acquired a reputation for fast thinking. On her second day on the job she was told to go along with one of the partners to make a pitch for a new assignment. She barely knew what the assignment entailed, but she was told during the brisk walk on the way over that she would be expected to do the initial research into the structure of the industry under study and then confirm or correct the partner's preliminary thinking about the immediate challenges facing the potential client.

"I can do that," she affirmed quietly to herself.

The presentation went smoothly, with her senior colleague communicating just the right elements of experience and enthusiasm for the task. As the meeting was winding down the prospective client looked over at Eva in a friendly way and said to her:

"I understand you are quite new to Pearson. How long ago did you join?"

Smiling brightly, Eva replied: "Thank you. Yes, I am quite new. I'm still completing my first year at Pearson and I've loved every minute of it."

"Every minute," snorted Liam, her colleague, as they left. "Thank heaven you didn't have to tell them those wonderful minutes could still be counted in the hundreds."

Because it was management consulting, and she was at the bottom of the hierarchy, Eva had to put in a lot of hours just to keep up. Even though she was working hard, she retained her somewhat deferential inclination to offer up lots of information in discussions but leave others to draw the clusions. It was soon made clear, however, that this approach was not going to succeed at Pearson.

Excited to be included in a dinner with two partners while on an out-of-town assignment, she was surprised and unprepared when one of them – an innovative thinker called Charles – turned to her and asked: "What do you think the client should do here, Eva?"

Eva tap-danced around the question, trying to turn it back on the partner to answer. Her hard-won confidence did not yet extend to offering opinions to partners on what they should tell the client.

"This won't do, Eva," interrupted Charles, kindly. "Diffidence is fine is some situations, but at Pearson it's your job to have an evidence-based point of view. If we just wanted research, we'd hire a researcher. You are the one who's closest to the raw data and that puts you in the best position to draw a preliminary conclusion. You need to develop a hypothesis as early as you can in the assignment so that you can test what you're learning and see if it holds up."

On reflection, in the privacy of her hotel room, Eva realised that she had been taking refuge in the naïve assumption that no one was particularly interested in what she thought, and so she didn't have to force herself to draw conclusions. While she would have liked to argue that she was just being humble, she secretly feared that she risked being exposed as lazy. Whatever the case, she knew that her mental lassitude had to end.

As the months passed, Eva accumulated more and more genuine experience and felt less and less need for filler in her personal profile. As number two or three in a fast-changing array of teams, she tried to watch and learn, emulate and innovate; all the while working to strengthen her ability to anticipate what might be expected of her.

As one of the more emotionally remote partners, Stephen, described it: "You have two meetings' grace before you need to know more about the industry than the client, and just three before you must demonstrate enough genuine insight into his business that he feels your opinion is worth paying for."

Eva quickly developed what she called her "wide net" approach to learning about an issue or a company. First, she would get all the available print information from any source she could enlist – industry associations, think tanks, green papers, annual reports, news clippings, trade magazines... the works. Next she would spread out all the information around herself on whatever nearby flat surfaces she could find and read indiscriminately until a pattern began to emerge from the numbers, products, statements and people involved. Then she would sleep on it – sometimes quite literally.

In those pre-internet days, pulling together information from diverse sources was labour-intensive and time-consuming, filled with telephone calls and visits to reference libraries, but the information digestion process was still the same: Read and learn and hear everything you can, then relax and think about it all and see what surfaces.

As she struggled gathering and assimilating information, she challenged herself to come up with something thoughtful like the old quotation from Durrell's *Mountolive* that she could tape on her cubicle wall. The result was a blend of Wordsworth and her own observation:

> *If poetry is emotion recollected in tranquillity, then insight is raw data organized by the subconscious.*

She felt quite pleased when, coming back to her desk from the coffee room one morning, she noticed Charles, one of the more intellectual partners, stop, read her quotation and nod approvingly.

In Eva's early days in consulting, work on industrial strategy was the most coveted goal of top tier consulting firms. While The Pearson Paradigm sometimes had to take whatever work was offered just to keep the firm afloat, an industrial strategy assignment was the kind of work the founders still dreamed of. So when Bram Rose, now working in a division of the French government concerned with *collectivités d'outre-mer* (overseas communities), convinced his boss that Pearson should be hired to develop a strategy for the French islands of Saint-Pierre and Miquelon, just off the coast of Newfoundland, Eva's star in the Pearson firmament rose quickly.

However, the assignment itself made Eva nervous.

"At INSEAD they let us write our assignments in English," she pointed out to Charles. "I can read the documents and do the interviews, but I can't write a strategy in French that would be fit for real French people to read. They would laugh us off the islands."

"Don't worry," Charles assured her. "We know a good French translator who will help with all that. You focus on what the population of the islands should be doing as an alternative to fishing for cod. Maybe you can come up with something for the fishermen in Newfoundland and Labrador too, while you're at it."

It would have been fun if she hadn't been so anxious. With a total population of around 6,000 people, Saint-Pierre and Miquelon operated in a kind of rustic exile from metropolitan France, fishing and sending the occasional hockey star to play for the honour of *la patrie*. It seemed obvious from the start that the only enduring economic hope for the islands lay in some form of perpetually renewing connection with the sea and tourism – and the remote outside chance of an offshore oil or gas discovery.

The islands' officialdom, such as it was, welcomed Eva and her teammate – a young French Canadian called Jean Sirois who had recently joined Pearson – with excessive hospitality. Fried, boiled, smoked, even maple-sugar cured… if there was a way to cook fish, Eva and Jean sampled it.

Following their visit, the strategy document – carefully written, laboriously translated, bound and delivered to Paris in person by Eva – was appreciated for the quality of its research and the obvious care behind the formulation of its recommendations. Bram assured her that the success of the assignment had enhanced his reputation at the ministry.

What the Pearson partners knew for sure was that the strategy was endorsed and, on that basis, a second runway was funded and constructed at the Saint-Pierre airport. Eva's assignment was included with pride whenever a list of the firm's qualifications for further work on industrial strategy was attached to a proposal, and Eva received an unsolicited raise of $5,000 – which really seemed like a lot of money at the time.

Chapter 18: A Felicitous Event

"Felicitations," said Carina, long distance from Sao Paulo, when Eva phoned to tell her she was pregnant. Their friendship, forged in the pressure-cooker of INSEAD, had remained strong despite their geographical separation.

"Felicitations – what a great word!" said Eva later when reporting the conversation to Leo.

"It's a wonderful word. It would also make a perfect name. Let's call the baby Felicity!"

"Yes!" agreed Eva, "It captures everything about her circumstances. But what if it's a boy?"

"It won't be a boy. A boy would have a good sense of timing, and any smart baby boy would know that this is not his moment."

Eva and Leo had been back in Canada for some time now, and their new jobs had proven to be just what they had hoped. Though a baby had always been in their plans, and they were both rapidly approaching thirty, they hadn't yet given much thought to working out the ideal timing. So when the baby took matters into its own hands they actually felt relief, among other emotions. One important decision had been made for them.

Surprise and delight were dominant for a while, but then they had to get down to practicalities: How and when should they tell people, and how was the baby going to fit into their lives? Of course the baby, although only at the cell-dividing stage, already knew the greater truth – that Leo and Eva were the ones who would have to do the fitting.

They had agreed to have Eva make her call to Carina at Globo TV, where she worked in Sao Paulo, as a trial run.

"Even if she puts it on the TV news, no one else that we know can speak Portuguese," reminded Leo.

"I actually find it quite hard to believe that our incipient baby would *not* top the international news," replied Eva, tilting her nose into the air with mock indignation.

"I would have to agree," smiled Leo. "And, you know, there are some circles where the prospect of another von Richthofen would be newsworthy – although they do still prefer them to be legitimate."

"Marriage is so passé," said Eva.

"Try explaining that to my mother," replied Leo, just a little nervously.

For her part, Carina had been very excited and even claimed to be jealous. After some thought, she phoned Eva back to offer some wise advice.

"You want this baby," she told Eva. "Don't let the reactions of others diminish your joy.

"It's you that will have to feed it and raise it and send it to school, so don't let someone who won't bear any of the weight of the child's upbringing burden you with disapproval.

"I can hardly wait to see you 'all belly' at our class get-together in July."

Carina had set the tone. After waiting cautiously until the three-month point had passed and the threat of miscarriage was greatly reduced, Eva and Leo gleefully told their families and friends about the baby. And they followed Carina's advice by not giving anyone a forum to express doubt or concern about their unmarried status.

Leo's mother, Greta, with whom Eva had formed a close and loving bond while living in France, was allowed to express a gentle regret.

"It isn't the situation I would like for my own daughter," she ventured.

"I understand," responded Eva, gently patting Greta's hand. "Now, tell me, did you breast-feed Leo?"

Eva's mother, Kay, smiling determinedly at her husband, said: "Times have changed and so must we."

The partners at Pearson, committed to a kind of intellectual liberalism that gave them no choice but to welcome the pregnancy of one of their promising juniors, waited patiently for Eva to firm up her plans. When Eva suggested that the baby, due in late December, deserved a lengthy Christmas holiday and a nanny by Easter, they were privately relieved.

One of the partners, a former Ivy-Leaguer called Cal, in a moment of heady relief, asked Eva if she might really prefer to be away for a month or two more. Then, realizing the risk he'd taken with one of the firm's assets, he looked stricken.

"Oh, no," replied Eva, secretly amused. "This baby wants a mother who's out there fulfilling herself in the marketplace, not staying at home blenderizing cauliflower and reading trashy novels… although, now that I think about it, that does sound like fun."

Feeling the need to defend his own stay-at-home wife – even if the act of defence was against his self-interest, not to mention that of the firm – Cal couldn't resist patronizing Eva.

"It isn't all leisure you know, staying at home with a child and being a homemaker. It's an important job with responsibility for the smooth running of a household and the happiness of your entire family at stake."

"I'm sure it is," replied Eva in a conciliatory tone. "It's just not the job that I trained or applied for."

Chapter 19: Degrees of Surprise

As Eva explained to anyone who would listen, she didn't work right up until she gave birth just because she wanted to be a ridiculously dedicated working mother. She did it because otherwise she would have been bored witless.

As the natal day drew near, Eva felt that in her case the expression "large with child" had taken on heroic dimensions.

"Am I really supposed to be this enormous?" she asked Dr. Ford.

"You do seem a bit on the large side," he replied. "I am finding that my healthy mothers are having bigger and bigger babies, but you've gained 40 pounds and that does seem quite a lot."

"It sure feels like a lot, too," sighed Eva. "And the kicking and general upheaval going on in there makes me wonder if I'm housing an entire play group."

She did try to follow a 'glide path' in approaching the birth. A week or two before the due date, Eva booked off work. Despite her girth she managed to thoroughly bleach and scour their cosy one-bedroom apartment and lovingly wash and fold all the new one-piece baby suits and receiving blankets in neutral shades of yellow, green and white that she had carefully acquired. Leo and Eva had talked about moving into someplace larger, but since they planned to keep the baby in the bedroom with them initially, they had decided to stay put – at least for a while.

Her nesting completed, Eva turned her attention to the pile of novels she'd been saving to read between napping, baby-changing and feeding. As soon as she finished the third book – a sweeping Irish romance – she lost her composure, struggled to her feet and lumbered across the room to call Liam at TPP to ask if there was anything she could do to make herself useful around the office.

"Well," said Liam, "we could certainly use you to edit reports for clients."

So, in Eva went and there she remained, editing, until her contractions were strong enough for her to call Leo and ask him to meet her at the hospital.

During the birthing process, one of the resident doctors commented to Eva that she was being very stoical.

"Oh! What do you mean by that?" Eva felt that a possible compliment was worth hearing about in more detail.

Surprised by her question, the resident replied: "Well, many of the mothers moan or cry out during particularly strong contractions."

As if to illustrate this, a howl was heard from next door.

"Does that make it hurt less?" asked Eva.

"Some women believe that it helps, though there isn't any proven medical basis that I'm aware of."

"Then why would I do it?"

The resident went away to help someone who might better appreciate his insight into the birthing process. Later, when he heard shouts from the direction of Eva's room, he smiled to himself.

But there was a different reason for those shouts. After Eva had obediently and fairly quietly pushed out a very red-faced little girl, the obstetrician, standing ready to deliver the placenta, suddenly blurted out: "What's this?"

"What's what?" asked Leo, who had insisted on being present at the birth.

"It seems there's another baby's head here," said Dr. Ford, as a second child began to make its way out of the birth canal.

"Twins?!" Eva asked, horrified.

"Yes, twins," Leo and the doctor answered in unison.

~~~~~

For the rest of her life Eva would measure degrees of surprise on a scale in which "Yes, twins" was a ten, and her own crying during the singing of the national anthem was a one – that is, totally predictable. An eight was a real shocker, and a nine would leave the victim just short of a faint.

Over the years, both Eva and the twins were to encounter plenty of people who simply could not believe that you could carry twin babies unwittingly and without even the doctor detecting their presence. Of course, as ultrasound came into wide usage and both the gender and the actual number of passengers on the baby train became automatically knowable, the unexpected aspect of the twins' arrival just seemed all the more mysterious and hard to believe.

Chapter 20: You Can Get Anything You Want...

For his first few days of life, twin baby boy didn't have a name. He didn't seem too fussed about that situation, and while his parents were extremely fussed, their fussiness was focused on other things, like how to feed and clothe, much less raise, two children simultaneously – in a one-bedroom apartment.

When she had finally re-gathered her wits, Eva phoned Carina from the hospital, keen to be first to tell her that the baby they had been talking about was now twins.

"Jesus Cristo!" said Carina. "How big are they, singularly or collectively?" she asked, ever the MBA grad.

"Felicity, also known as Baby One, is 5 pounds, and Baby Two came in at 5 pounds 2 ounces. So if you bundle them together, as they in fact were until quite recently, you have one hefty 10-pounder. No wonder I seemed to have gained a lot of weight. Now I just need to gain the wisdom and patience to see me through the years ahead. I haven't been allowed to keep them in the room except at feeding times because the doctor says they have jaundice. This morning I was allowed to totter down and look at them, decked out in little sun glasses and diapers, lying under a sun lamp to help lower their bilirubin. They looked like a couple of extremely youthful hedonists lolling on the Riviera."

"Meanwhile, how are *you* feeling, big mama?" asked Carina.

"Ah," sighed Eva. "My main reaction is fatigue. I just feel soooo weary. Leo's been great – especially since he's had his own share of adjustment to handle too – but I do seem to need a lot of propping up. And not just physically. The same set of questions keeps cycling through my brain but getting me nowhere. Why didn't I realise there were two babies in there? Why didn't the doctor notice? Where are we going to put two of them in our apartment? How can we afford another crib, another layette, another buggy? How much help will we need? When can I please go back to work? It seems like sleep is the only thing that stops all the worrying, but when I wake up it just starts all over again. What was it you used to say to me? 'That which does not kill us makes us stronger'?"

"Yes," confirmed Carina, "but I didn't think you'd take me so literally. And, frankly, I don't think Nietzsche had twins in mind when he wrote that."

After discussion, negotiation, threats and tears, Baby Two was named Theodore, or Teddy – a choice inspired in part by claims of Steiff connections in Leo's family.

"All he needs is a button in his ear," muttered Eva to Carina during a phone call a few weeks later. But in truth she liked the name Teddy much more than she had initially admitted, especially as her little boy grew more and more to match it.

Baby surnames had been argued through by Eva and Leo months previously. Convinced they were having a girl, and fuelled by Eva's determination that the baby share her last name too, they had finally agreed on the hyphenated name Felicity Sadlier-von Richthofen. Members of both families had reservations about this, although they at least had the good sense to keep their views to themselves.

In the privacy of their bedroom, long before the double birth, Eva's father, Nowell, had suggested to his wife that their granddaughter might be in the third or even the fourth grade before she would be able to spell her own name, while in the von Richthofen boudoir there had been some unease that their prospective grandchild would have too *few* names.

Meanwhile, having already put a lot of effort into deciding a last name for their baby, Leo and Eva felt that there having turned out to be two babies was no reason to depart from the already agreed-upon plan of how their last names should be registered.

It was Leo's job to fill in the babies' birth registration forms, particularly since he and Eva were not married and he wanted to be sure that he was properly registered as their father. While his handwriting was almost totally illegible, Leo's printing was studied and precise, and he filled out both forms very clearly, pointedly specifying the hyphen.

With relatives and helpers coming and going at all hours, it was surprising that Eva happened to be alone in the apartment (except for the babies, who were both finally asleep) when officialdom called.

"The public records office phoned this afternoon," she later told Leo over dinner. "The man called to explain, in a very mellow 'sixties' kind of way, that, to quote him precisely: 'Lady, we don't do hyphens.'"

"What do you mean, they don't do hyphens?" asked a confused Leo.

"What I think he was saying, although it took me some time to understand, was that our province's record office does not accept hyphenated last names at the time of registration of birth. He was quite nice about it, but he gave me until tomorrow morning to call him back with instructions; otherwise he's going to go ahead and register von Richthofen as the babies' last name, and Sadlier as their middle name."

"Well, that's not so bad," said Leo, sounding relieved.

"Fine for you to say," Eva fired back. "Your name isn't being relegated to a middle initial – if that. How about we agree instead that, since we aren't married, Sadlier should be their last name and von Richthofen their middle name?"

Leo blanched at the suggestion. "My dad would kill me if I let our branch of the von Richthofen name disappear."

"Well, you could point out to him that killing you would certainly help to ensure that outcome," replied Eva drily. "You could also point out to him that you're still young and might yet find a moderately attractive, pliable woman willing to take your name and have your son. As a matter of fact, you could start looking for her tomorrow."

Leo and Eva, perhaps uniquely, were happy with the compromise they'd worked out. The next morning Eva phoned the mellow guy from the records office and told him how they'd decided to register their twin children.

"Our little girl will be registered as Felicity von Richthofen Sadlier, and our son will be registered as Theodore Sadlier von Richthofen."

"Okay, lady," drawled the records man, "that works for me. I'll just cross out the hyphen in the boy's registration, circle the name Sadlier and draw a line with an arrow on it to put it into the middle name space here on the form. Then I'll cross out the hyphen on the girl's registration, circle the name von Richthofen and draw a line with an arrow on it to move it into the middle name space on her form."

"I think that should do it. And don't forget that the 'v' in von is lower case."

"Is that all?"

"I guess so," sighed the sleep-deprived new mother of twins.

Much later, Eva applied for copies of their long-form birth certificates so that she could obtain passports for the twins. After opening the official registry envelope and looking at the documents she laughed and laughed. By then, she had forgotten the details of her phone conversation with the mellow guy at the registry office, but there on the documents, interspersed with Leo's careful printing, were the crossed-out hyphens and circles and arrows that had been carefully added to comply with regulations.

"How very like Arlo Guthrie's dealings with officialdom in his song about Alice's restaurant," she thought.

Chapter 21: Bodily fluids

Felicity and Teddy were christened, with much ceremony and even more fussing, in the beautiful, flowing antique white garments lovingly chosen by their two grandmothers.

"They look like twin girls in those dresses," Leo muttered to Eva as she tucked the twins into their matching car seats in preparation for the drive to the church.

"Teddy's dress has blue ribbons in the sleeves," whispered Eva, "so there's no risk of confusion."

Having flown in from Brazil, Carina insisted on being godmother to both children. Eva's brother Dean served as Teddy's godfather, although, being colour blind, he was never at any time quite certain which twin he was holding. To complete the picture, Leo and Eva had asked Bram to be godfather for Felicity.

"I guess with a Jewish godfather they'll have all the bases covered," muttered von Richthofen Sr.

When water was drizzled on their respective foreheads, Teddy smiled and gurgled and Felicity looked around quizzically at those present.

"There's an omen," whispered Nowell. Eva's mum just smiled.

The twins' early life seemed mainly to revolve around breast milk, poo, and, of course, tears – quite frequently Eva's. Her arms ached and her breasts hurt from feeding the babies, and she feared her brain would atrophy if she had to watch one more mindless television show while feeding. The only prospect that seemed worse was not having a mindless television show to watch.

At first Leo and Eva put the babies to bed beside each other in the one crib that had been purchased, thinking that the twins would like to continue to be close together just as they had been in the womb. But it soon became clear, from all the kicking and flailing of arms and the expulsion of gastric juices, that the twins had no objection to sleeping separately. So, quite quickly, the inexperienced parents bought another crib.

Confirming earlier indications that they may not be very fast learners in the parenting department, Eva and Leo placed the two cribs together in the living room, assuming that once they were comfortable the two babies would sleep, well, like babies. But instead they were treated to further selections from the *nessun dorma* until Leo and Eva finally understood that *they* were the ones who had to share – not only their room but their bed – while the other baby slept in blissful solitude right beside the vanquished sibling's empty crib.

Having just about coped with the shock arrival of two babies, Leo and Eva were more inclined to laugh hopelessly at their nocturnal situation than to complain. But the kindly joint offer by their parents of funds towards the purchase of a small house in a friendly neighbourhood was eagerly and gratefully accepted.

Once the house was theirs the very next thing they did was furnish it with "help." The nanny they selected from the agency's list was a capable, energetic British woman called Juliet who confessed that her favourite movie was *Mary Poppins*.

"Big surprise," mimed Eva to Leo behind Juliet's back.

In her interview, Juliet had impressed Eva with her 'can-do' attitude, and Leo had been particularly pleased to learn that she had a driver's licence and really liked to drive. Further questioning revealed that while Juliet wasn't a student of scientific management and had never heard of Frank or Lillian Gilbreth, she instinctively had the mass production mindset needed for feeding and dressing more than one infant at a time and would take pride in organizing and teaching the twins.

All the same, it seemed more than likely that help from just one other person wasn't going to be enough. While Juliet was ready to be in charge all during the work day, when Leo and Eva were due home from work she wanted to be gone. The transition from work personae to mommy and daddy proved difficult and chaotic for the couple, so they hired a local high school student to help them out in the evening.

To bridge the hours between when Eva and Leo got home from work and when the babies were fed their dinner, they chose a calm, sensible and warm teenager called Lily. Lily had abundant natural blond hair and a cheerful demeanour, and by the time he could sit like a little tripod, Teddy's preferred place to sit was on the floor between Lily's legs, keeping himself from tumbling over by resting his little hands on her thighs.

"That boy already shows real discernment," observed Leo.

During a partners' meeting at The Pearson Paradigm, Cal, clearly still unsure how he felt about having Eva in the firm, suggested to the others that perhaps she had shown insufficient commitment to her career by having twins. (All the partners had attended the christening, and Cal was still smarting a little from the teasing he'd received from his wife afterward for acting obsequious around Leo's father.)

Instead of leaping to Eva's defence, Cal's partner, Charles, took a different tack: "If I read Eva correctly, she'll be keener now than ever to get out of the house and do an outstanding job for our clients. There's nothing like the opportunity to deal with a lot of diapers and feeding and washing and crying to make some women want to make their mark in the world of business."

"Especially if it's the mother who's doing the crying," thought Eva's secretary, Tracy, overhearing the conversation.

Chapter 22: The Way We Were

Tucking an unruly grey curl behind her ear as she looked up from her regular leisurely Saturday perusal of *The Times of London,* Evaline asked: "John, do you remember how you felt about money when your kids were little and you were working as an art teacher in Saskatoon – you know, back before you met me and abandoned all earthly cares?"

"Do I?" John laughed, "I think the anxieties about money from those days are permanently etched into my guts. I remember so vividly the sense of responsibility that I felt to protect and support my family, whatever way I could. Teachers are never paid very well, so I tried to supplement my income with photography. But when I wasn't taking pictures I was trying to improve our surroundings or increase the value of our house through getting deals and doing most of the work myself."

Reminiscing, he continued, "In retrospect, some of my efforts to enhance the value of that marital home may have been a bit extreme. One Saturday during breakfast it suddenly became clear to me that the wall between the dining room and the living room made both rooms seem unnecessarily cramped, and that the wall had to come down. I didn't even stop to change; I just went for the tools and got started. And by the end of the day it was all done – except, of course, for a few finishing touches."

He went on, "Anyway, yes. I did feel a lot of pressure to make sure that my young family was safe and well fed and warm. As you know, that last of those – the warmth – can be quite a challenge in a prairie winter. But what made you ask that?"

"Oh," said Eva after finally remembering her question, "I was trying to explain to Christopher what it was like when his siblings were young and we were young parents too. He does understand that he got older parents but with the compensation of a slightly higher standard of living. Still, it all seems rather abstract to him, so I was trying to think of a way to make it more tangible."

"He certainly has grasped the 'old parents' part," laughed John. "I remember he was only in year four when he informed me that I was a lot older than the principal of the *entire* school."

"I don't know if that's better or worse than what he told me. A couple of years ago he announced that I was older than any of the fathers of his classmates. Now why, do you suppose, didn't he compare me with the mothers?"

"Don't worry; I'm sure it wasn't just because most of them are yummy mummies with perfect makeup and designer leisure wear..."

"I've had my 'yummy' moments," sniffed Evaline.

"Of course you have, sweetheart," added John consolingly. "And besides, it was a long time ahead of any of theirs."

"Anyway," she went on, choosing to ignore John's comment, "my own memories of early struggles with family finances seem rather prosaic compared to your story. There were no post-breakfast wall removals. Not even close. Leo was certainly no handyman. As a matter of fact, we didn't even own a hammer."

"Probably very wise of him," said John thoughtfully. "You can be frightening enough bare-handed."

"No, seriously," said Evaline. "When I think of those early days what comes most powerfully to mind is the daily challenge of trying to juggle all the expenditures involved – nannies, diapers, taxes, heating oil, a new roof, work clothes, car maintenance. There always seemed to be more going out than coming in. Leo and I had interesting jobs with lots of potential, but our family finances were like a see-saw where a great big lump of debt sat like Pooh at one end and a little tiny income like Roo sat at the other."

"I always think Mr. Micawber's advice to David Copperfield perfectly suits the situations we were both confronting back then," said John. "'*Annual income twenty pounds, annual expenditure nineteen nineteen and six, result* happiness. *Annual income twenty pounds, annual expenditure twenty pounds ought and six, result misery. The blossom is blighted, the leaf is withered, the god of day goes down upon the dreary scene, and, in short, you are forever-floored. As I am!'"*

"Beautifully quoted," Evaline applauded.

"I do especially like the bit about the god of day going down upon the dreary scene," said John. "Debt really can be depressing – such a killer of hope. That's why, at least since early childhood, I've always tried so hard to avoid it.

"But we all have our own approaches," he added. "Wasn't it when Felicity and Teddy were little that you and Leo developed your famous Lifetime Income Smoothing Plan?"

"Yes, and how very properly respectful of you to name it in full. As a matter of fact I remain surprised and a little hurt that it has not yet appeared in some weighty and learned textbook – Samuelson's *Economics*, for example."

"I know," said John supportively, "the lack of widespread recognition for your Smoothing Plan is really unjust."

"Its underlying concept has been a source of great comfort to me over the years. Funnily enough, just the other day I was trying to figure out how to illustrate it on paper. Do you want to see what I finally came up with?"

"Believe it or not, I would," confessed John. "But why were you trying to draw it?"

"I wanted to explain the whole idea to Felicity because I think it's particularly relevant to someone over thirty. But you know how nervous she gets about anything that veers even slightly towards the mathematical. I thought if I could figure out how to draw it in a simple diagram she might find the concept easier to understand."

Evaline hunted down some coloured pens.

"Please pay careful attention. Now, the X-axis that I'm drawing represents the amount of money you have available to spend over your entire lifetime. Let's call that 'ready money'. And the Y-axis represents the years of your life from the moment you leave your parent's home, enter the workforce and begin to earn money. I'll label that 'earnings span'."

"So the end of the Y-axis is when you die?" asked John.

"Roughly," explained Evaline. "That's why this is called *lifetime* income smoothing."

"What about funeral expenses?"

"Do you want to see this graph or not?"

"Please do go on."

"So here at the beginning, say you're 24 years old, you start earning and the line begins to go up like this. Then maybe you get some decent pay increases, your total earnings rise higher and higher and things are looking really good. You even make some smart investments. But then you get older and retire and your annual income drops down to whatever your pension pays, plus your stock dividends and bank interest and some odd jobs that you do. I'll label that line 'income.'"

"Is this pointy bit what they call 'peak earnings'?"

"Precisely."

"Your example person here did okay. Is this you?"

"That's not the point. The most important line on the page is this flat line here called 'expenditure.' This represents having roughly the same expenditure level, or standard of living, your whole life. You never get to feel rich, but you never have to feel, or behave, as if you're really poor either, as long as you believe in your future. The key is that these two areas below the expenditure line, which I'll colour fuchsia for ease of understanding, represent the part of your life when you're spending more than you're making. And this area above the line, which I shall expertly fill in with a Christmassy kind of green, is when you're making more money than you're spending. There now. As Mr. Micawber might have said if he saw my graph, happiness is when the green part is at least as large, if not larger, than the two fuchsia wedges put together."

"That sounds a bit MBA to me," said John, pretending to look worried. "But what if your earnings don't keep going up?"

"That is a potential weakness in the plan, I'll admit. I was lucky; I never had to face that problem. Not only did my earnings go up, but I was always naively sure that they would. However, that was in what the kids call the 'olden days.' Things seem to be different now."

"Didn't it bother you all those years ago to think that you might never have significantly more luxury – a bigger house, fancier trips, nicer clothes, more help, better art – than you had then?"

"Nope. The really great thing about the lifetime income smoothing plan was that I could relax and not worry about my unpaid credit card balances, because I had a rubric to explain it all."

"Although I think I now comprehend the nuances of your plan, I'll confess that I'm at a loss as to exactly where teaching your irresponsible doctrine of feckless spending to your beloved daughter fits with your feminist principles."

"Which part don't you understand – embracing income smoothing or passing it on to another woman? If it's the latter, I'm certainly happy to discuss income smoothing with Teddy, although I suspect he won't need much explanation."

"A bit of both, although fiscal irresponsibility does seem stereotypically 'girly' to me."

"I disagree. I see it less as irresponsible and more as embracing life with a soupçon of risk, which is something women need to be encouraged to do."

"Trust you to see consistency where thousands wouldn't," John sighed. "So, what did Felicity say when you presented her with your plan?"

"First, she said the graph looks like a shark's fin. Then she said she thought you weren't supposed to spend money that you don't have. And she's right, but we did it anyway – and then made up a funny title for our behaviour to excuse ourselves. Felicity gave me her disapproving look when I said that."

"Hi Mum. Hi Dad," called Chris cheerfully as he came through the door.

"Ah, Chris. Perfect timing. We were just talking about the money worries we had when we were young parents. I was thinking about how anxious I was when Felicity and Teddy were toddlers and I wasn't sure how I could pay for the snowsuits they needed. I remember standing in the department store looking at the snowsuits in their size, all disgusting colours like orange and purple, and worrying about how to find the sixty dollars to pay for each of them."

"One hundred and twenty dollars. How much was that in pounds and pence?" Asked Chris.

"About sixty," John guesstimated.

"Oh. That's not much, but I guess it seemed like more in the olden days. What colour was my first snowsuit?"

"Brown, I think," offered John after a little thought.

"British racing green," Evaline corrected smugly.

Chapter 23: Back in the "Olden Days"

Back at work after her "twin" maternity leaves (which were concurrent, not consecutive, as she was eager to point out to the Paradigm partners), Eva felt relieved.

"She makes it sound like a prison sentence," Liam muttered to Stephen over lunch.

Eva readily admitted that staying home all day with the babies had made her feel anxious that she would lose her edge – although, if questioned, she might not have been able to explain what she meant by that. All she knew was that she savoured both the renewed challenge of consulting and her euphoria driving home each night at the prospect of seeing her babies.

With a lot of help and good will, especially on the part of the twins, Eva was able to continue to nurse in the morning and evening without too much discomfort. That is, if you didn't count the anxiety she felt when the absorbent breast pads carefully installed in her bra threatened to leak while she was still at work. Thoughts of the children were particular triggers and best avoided entirely.

With Juliet, Lily, Leo and Eva – not to mention eager-to-help grandparents – all variously focused on keeping Felicity and Teddy happy and healthy, Eva found that she was soon able to pull her work out of her briefcase around eight in the evening and get in a few extra hours. In those pre-laptop computer days, she worked on pads of squared-off paper which she rested on her own lap as she sat on the sofa near the TV. Eva claimed that working on the sofa like a student gave her the illusion that she wasn't really working.

All in all, she couldn't believe how lucky she was.

Leo, meanwhile, was not so happy. While he was delighted with the twins and shouldered a full share of the burden of their care, from diapers to walking the floor at night, workplace politics depressed him. The editor of *Synapse*, the magazine for which Leo worked, had at first been fascinated and delighted by Leo's great name, his European experience and his quirky psychology-based approach to the scientists and entrepreneurs they interviewed. Now, however, readership was not growing fast enough, budgets were being cut, and, in an era where typewriters still reproduced exactly the characters that had been keyed in, Leo was revealed to have a very slapdash notion of spelling.

The editor had taken to greeting Leo in the mornings, in front of the rest of the staff (seven in total), by saying cruel things like "Good morning L-O-E, is your article about new discoveries relating to photons and neuters done yet? Or have you been too b-u-zz-y?"

It was classic bullying. By nature Leo was inclined towards solitary pursuits such as weightlifting at lunchtime, and the more uncomfortable he felt the more he reacted by withdrawing from the social life of the office. Unfortunately this made him more and more of a target.

"Look, sweetie, I really do sympathise," consoled Eva. "With all the writing you have to do it's easy to make a little mistake that looks ridiculous. Remember when I sent out that proposal in which I declared that Paradigm had 'years of increasingly focused and valued experience in the *pubic* sector'?"

"Well I think it's time for me to update my résumé and go looking for a new job," said Leo. "Although nothing that I can include in my list of qualifications could rival the claims you made for Paradigm."

"You did sire fraternal twins. Surely that can be made to sound provocative – especially in the hands of a creative writer?" suggested Eva, trying to lift Leo out of his gloom.

Chapter 24: Hot Puppies or Hush Babies?

Eva was hurrying to her desk, a little behind schedule, when Liam hailed her.
"How're the kids," he asked, somewhat perfunctorily.
"Thriving. They're really picking up on their 'centre of the universe' roles very quickly, considering they've only had a short period of training," replied Eva.
Liam smiled in spite of himself. "Well, I hope you've already taught them to be self-sufficient... although maybe that term doesn't apply if you're a twin," he mused. "Maybe the correct phrase is 'mutually sufficient'. Anyway, I really need you to work on this new project. It's a bit out of our normal routine but I think you might have fun with it. Some lawyer friends of the firm are trying to find an expert witness for a damages case and we thought the task might be just right for you. Why don't you sit down over here and let me explain."

First thing next morning Eva went over to the offices of Cooper and Greene to meet the lawyers and hear what they needed from her. Jack Cooper, a redhead with a deceptively relaxed manner, had been working for the client for some time and had his good ol' boy pitch down pat: "Some years ago our client, Cooking Innovations, saw the potential for a line of products called Cooking of the Old South. Their market intelligence indicated that people in the North were becoming interested in things like pork BBQ and grits and hominy and black-eyed peas. So the small appliance designers at Cooking Innovations set to work and one of their first manufacturing ideas was a deep fryer specially designed for making hush puppies."
"Aren't hush puppies a brand of shoe?" asked Eva.
"Not in the world of Southern cooking they aren't. They're succulent little bundles of cornmeal and onion, deep-fried like donuts and popped into your mouth between

91

good ol' bites of pork rib and some tangy collard greens. Anyway, the new product guys gave the little frying machine a green light, passed the specs to legal to apply for a patent, thought themselves up a cute little name, Hot Puppies, and the market really began to eat them up," he laughed.

"The Southern theme caught customers' imaginations just as they'd hoped, and sales were going well for Hot Puppies until a competitor of Cooking Innovations, International Cooking Machines, began to piggy-back on the popularity of Hot Puppies with their own new product, Hush Babies."

Eva nodded with some interest. While her cooking skills did not stretch to anything even vaguely ethnic, she was certainly at ease with all components of the case as described thus far: food, marketing and the unanticipated arrival on the scene of more than one baby.

Jack continued, "As soon as Hush Babies hit the market we applied on our client's behalf for a court injunction claiming patent infringement in order to prevent International Cooking Machines – or ICM as they call themselves to disguise the fact that they're not at all Southern – from flooding the market with their new product. And we were successful. The only hitch was a specification added to the injunction as granted that, if we were unable ultimately to prove that the product really had infringed on our patent, Cooking Innovations would owe damages to ICM."

His tone changed. "Sadly for our side, very sadly, it all took a while, and when they were all done the court found no infringement of patent, so now Cooking Innovations owes ICM money to compensate for keeping their product off the market for the 18 critical months it took to hear the patent case. ICM is claiming $1.7 million in damages and there's a hearing in three weeks to determine whether their figure is justified."

"That's all very interesting. What do you need me to do?" asked Eva.

"Well, Eva, for us to be able to defend our client properly we first need you to figure out how many Hush Babies would have been sold, and at what price, during the 18 months the injunction was in force, if they had been allowed free access to our market. In other words, how many Hush Babies machines would those scurrilous copycats have sold if they'd been out there competing with our Hot Puppies."

"Hmm," said Eva. "That is really quite a complex problem. I'm going to need a lot of information from your client if you want me to work this one out."

Back at Paradigm, Eva spent many hours thinking about things like channels of distribution and holiday sale flyers. She even spent a precious weekend afternoon, babies watching her wide-eyed from their multi-purpose car seats perched on the kitchen counter, trying to make hush puppies with each of the competing products. Leo pronounced both attempts "gross" and she didn't disagree. After he'd left the room, Eva told the twins that they should try to remember what they were seeing, because they wouldn't see mommy in an apron in the kitchen trying out new recipes very often. Felicity just stared at her and Teddy had already fallen asleep.

At the office Eva endured at lot of teasing about a woman's place being in the kitchen surrounded by puppies and babies, but she took it in good humour. As she told Leo over dinner one evening, "They probably gave me the assignment because it involved small kitchen appliances and sounded like girl stuff to them, but it's actually quite a complicated and interesting problem, and I'm learning a lot about patents and injunctions as I go along. So maybe the joke is really on them…"

Jack was great to work with. He listened carefully as Eva explained the consumer decision model that she had developed to estimate the respective sales of Hot Puppies and Hush Babies if both products had been on the market simultaneously during the critical 18 months, incorporating variables for incentives, customer satisfaction, promotions and "first-mover advantage".

She also worked with Phil Brownley – a major-league accountant who had been hired by Cooper and Greene to complement her testimony with that of his own regarding costs, realizable margins and net profits.

Of course, the other side had hired experts too, and Team Hot Puppies were eager to hear the calculations of missed sales that the other side would be presenting to the court.

Eva was the first in the witness box – an old-fashioned wooden enclosure with no space for a chair, situated at the level of the court but well below the elevated seat of the "prothonotary", as the court-appointed adjudicator was called. She and Jack had carefully rehearsed her testimony, and her charts and graphs of theoretical sales, broken down by market and outlet, were proffered smoothly to the court.

Then came the cross-examination, which didn't feel quite so smooth, with ICM's stern lawyer, Mr. Smith-Graves, challenging first Eva's credentials and then her calculations. There was a brief moment of comic relief when he gruffly asked her about the relevance of the content of an INSEAD course called "Fiscalité et Decision" and Eva outlined the highlights of the course to him in French, then kindly offered a translation, but overall the questioning was severe, demanding and rather stressful.

Eva had been warned by Jack that he would be unable to speak to her, even during breaks, while she was under cross-examination, and, although prepared, she found it a lonely and grueling process. Sensing her discomfort, the presiding officer went out of his way to treat her in a polite and courtly manner, as if she was wearing a pillbox hat, pearl choker and wrist-length white gloves in the witness box. He even offered to have a chair brought in from his office so she could sit down. Eva expressed gratitude for his thoughtfulness but demurred.

Then, late on the second day of cross-examination, to her great dismay Eva noticed that her breast pads had failed her and that her navy blue linen suit was darkening in circles on her chest. Fortunately the wet stains were not terribly obvious against the dark colour of her jacket, and she had wrapped her jaunty red and white polka dot cotton scarf around her neck as she was leaving the house that morning. Taking her chance while ICM's lawyer was reviewing his notes, she loosened her scarf and subtly fanned the ends out over the lapels of her jacket, praying that she was the only one who had noticed that her bosom was becoming increasingly wet.

That night, as she was getting ready for bed, Eva's reporting of the whole incident had Leo howling with laughter. *"That which does not kill us makes us stronger,"* she reminded herself as she put her stained linen jacket into the dry-cleaning pile.

Mr. Smith-Graves had promised that his cross-examination of Eva would be completed the following morning and that the next expert witness, the accountant, Mr. Brownley, could then expect to be called to the stand. Interested in watching his two expert witnesses perform, the Vice President, Sales and Marketing, from Cooking Innovations had come to court, and from her vantage point in the witness box Eva noticed two large brown-paper-wrapped boxes on the floor beside him.

The final questions from Smith-Graves were mostly designed to show that Eva's model for the total volume of sales of both brands of hush puppy fryer appliances grossly underestimated the total number of eager purchasers there would have been for the product.

"Come, come, Ms. Sadlier. A person like you, of all people, should understand how desperately hostesses throughout the country would have wanted to be able to make and serve some delicious Southern-style hush puppies to their eager, nay salivating, guests."

Having been extremely careful in her answers for several days, Eva temporarily let down her guard and said defensively: "I am sorry Mr. Smith, but a person like me would have been very unlikely to use such a product."

"Ah-ha! So in estimating the total market for specialty hush puppy fryers you have generalised from your own attitudes, have you?"

"No," replied Eva, concisely but not entirely wisely. "If I had foolishly and unprofessionally generalised from my own attitude toward the product I would have estimated very few sales indeed."

From her position at the front of the court Eva could see the VP Sales and Marketing looking startled at her revelation, and Jack wince. Only Brownley, busy preparing for his own testimony, failed to look up at her.

"Thank you. No further questions," said the ICM lawyer, looking a little startled.

"I have a few questions for re-direct," said Jack, rising quickly to his feet. He then calmly proceeded to ask Eva a few detailed questions of clarification about her model and her calculations. Finally, he said to her, "Am I correct in assuming that when you were working on the market uptake data for hush puppy makers you had a representative consumer in mind, a person who was particularly interested in trying new appliances and creating exciting ethnic dishes for family and friends?"

"Yes," replied Eva soberly. "As I testified previously, my expert opinion was based on objectively verifiable data on customer attitudes."

"Thank you" said Jack, and he sat down firmly.

"You may step down," Eva was told.

The afternoon was taken up with the dry calculations of margins and overheads by the accountant. At the end of the day, after the VP from Cooking Innovations had left to make his homeward commute, Eva noticed that Brownley had one of the mysterious brown-paper-wrapped boxes in his hands, but the other was nowhere to be seen.

"What is that?" she asked ingenuously.

"Oh, it's a Cooking Innovations Party Grill. It's just out. My wife will really love it – I can't wait until I see her face when I take it home tonight."

"Your wife must really like cooking special dishes for family and friends," smiled Eva.

In retelling the events of the morning to Leo, Eva paused and asked him: "What exactly do you think their lawyer meant when he said 'a person like you'?"

"He meant a female, of course. Don't you know that cooking is for girls?"

"I wish he were here tonight to share this delicious meal of chicken baked in tinned mushroom soup, accompanied by instant mashed potatoes and frozen peas, that I've whipped up for us. Anyway, I'm sorry that I did us out of a free party grill with my smart mouth."

"Why are you apologizing?" asked Leo, genuinely puzzled. "After all, what would you have done with it?"

"Well, we could've given it to Dean's wife, Gibby, for Christmas," replied Eva. "She's a girl and she likes that kind of thing."

Chapter 25: A Difficult Decision

Listening to the testimony of ICM's expert, Dr. Lionel Pryce, was much more relaxing for Eva. The most stressful part of her job was finished and now all she had to do was to help Jack think up questions for cross-examination of the learned academic.

It had been clear from the start that the ICM team considered Dr. Pryce's PhD in marketing trumped Eva's lowly MBA, and therefore his opinion should be taken as authoritative. He was well rehearsed and spoke with confidence about market demand, consumer habits and product superiority. With him in the box were several sheets of computer printout and he referred to them frequently.

Dr. Pryce's strongly held position was that the damages claim of $1.7 million represented an absolute minimum, and that there were many market forces that could be taken into account which would make the amount higher still.

Towards the end of the day, Eva had whispered to Jack that she would like him to ask the court to have all of Dr. Pryce's printouts put into evidence so that she could review them later. Jack looked at her quizzically, but took his chance during the day's wind-up to ensure that copies of all the printouts were handed over.

During their after-hours strategy discussion, Jack asked Eva to focus first on helping him devise questions for Dr. Pryce about his credentials.

A great baseball fan, Eva couldn't help but make a wry comment as she scanned the curriculum vitae she'd been handed. "Look", she pointed out, "here on page 4 under *Other Achievements* Pryce informs us that he played a season of baseball for the Connecticut Tigers. That's a farm team for the Detroit Tigers, you know."

"I might have guessed that myself," suggested Jack.

"So near and yet so far," Eva mused. "He was almost a real Tiger. It must have really meant a lot to him to put it on his résumé."

"That gives me an idea for closing," said Jack.

"What?" asked Eva.

"Just wait," said Jack with mock solemnity. "Right I want you to give me some proper ideas for cross-examination of that résumé – and to explain to me why you wanted those computer printouts."

Jack's cross-examination of Dr. Pryce – whom he accidentally kept calling Mr. Pryce or Lionel – started quite slowly. He began by asking Pryce about his doctoral thesis on *The Interior/Exterior Colour Choice Nexus for High-End Sports Car Buyers*.

"Many cooks in your research sample of buyers?" he asked casually.

"I don't know," replied Pryce. "It was hardly relevant."

"How about women? Surely they were relevant."

"Women generally don't buy high-end sports cars," Dr. Pryce replied curtly.

"So that's a 'no' then?"

"Yes… I mean, no."

Don't smile, Jack wrote on the note pad on the desk in front of Eva as he appeared to be ruffling through his notes. She quickly composed her best poker face.

Having located the multiple pages of the Pryce C.V., Jack looked up and said, "Did you enjoy playing third base for the Tigers?"

"That is hardly relevant," interjected Smith-Graves.

"As relevant as some of the questions you asked this fine lady, my expert," Jack rejoined. "I just wanted to know if your client had enjoyed exercising his prowess as a Tiger."

"Some of the best times of my life," responded Pryce proudly, without giving his lawyer a chance to intervene.

Jack proceeded to engage Pryce in the minutiae of his calculations with frequent reference to his computer printouts. Then he asked, with an air of genuine puzzlement,

99

"What does it mean when it says 'V 9' on your page of computer calculations?"

"Where do you mean?" asked Dr. Pryce.

"Here on the upper right-hand corner of the printout," Jack explained, leaning forward to make sure Dr. Pryce could see where on the page he was pointing.

"Oh, that," said the witness dismissively. "'V' stands for version."

"'V' stands for version, does it? So this is the ninth version of the model of hypothetical sales of Hush Babies cookers that you prepared?"

"Well, you must understand that properly metering all the endogenous and exogenous variables requires a fair amount of fine tuning, and iteration," answered Dr. Pryce, clearly sensing a trap.

"And how do you determine which version is the right one?"

"Like all researchers, we examine the output of our models to test for accuracy and plausibility."

"And then what? Do you pick the most plausible and say 'This is it'?"

"No – it's much more scientific than that."

"How is it more scientific?"

"We have data on analogous sales and the prevailing economic climate and consumer trends."

The cross-examination continued for some time, with the objectivity of Dr. Pryce's models now under serious assault. Finally, sensing some restlessness on the part of the prothonotary, Jack concluded, "Am I correct in assuming, Dr. Pryce, that you have relied on the model labelled V 9 for your testimony?"

"I believe so," answered Pryce, much more tentatively than when he began.

"And how many versions of the model did you run?"

"Fourteen, I think, or maybe it was fifteen." Dr. Pryce looked pleadingly to the ICM lawyers' table for confirmation, but none was forthcoming.

"But you liked V 9 the best?"

"It wasn't a matter of liking…"

"I have no more questions for this witness," Jack informed the court.

With schedule changes on both sides – including a worrisome medical emergency for the prothonotary – it was a week before Eva was back in court to hear the testimony of the ICM accounting expert and closing arguments. Not surprisingly, each lawyer focused systematically on the evidence that supported their own client's contention as to how many Hush Babies would have been sold during the period in question, and how much revenue would have been generated through the profit margins calculated by their accounting expert. Jack, however, finished with a flourish.

Addressing himself directly to the prothonotary, he closed by saying, "As I am sure you have long since concluded, your decision rests on which of the two market analyses proffered provides the most credible estimate of lost sales. Your decision in this case turns on a very difficult choice between expert witnesses. But only you can make that choice. And your choice must be… between the Lady and the Tiger."

To surprised laughter, Jack stepped away from the lectern and sat down.

It was several months later that Team Hot Puppies learned the prothonotary's decision. Much to Eva's disappointment, he had awarded damages of $700,000 plus costs to ICM.

During their wind-up lunch, however, it emerged that, unlike Eva, Jack was very pleased by the outcome.

"But he just cut their claim down the middle," complained Eva.

"ICM was entitled to something for damages, Eva," explained Jack, "and without our efforts they could have got all $1.7 million that they claimed. And, besides, $700,000 is not half of 1.7 million; it's closer to 40 per cent. As far as I'm concerned, the adjudicator picked the Lady. Our client has already called me to say they think we did a very good job."

"So I'll be getting a Party Grill after all then?"

"They weren't quite as pleased as all that," smiled Jack.

Tests of Character and Endurance

Chapter 26: And the Seasons, They Go Round and Round...

There was a lot to celebrate at the twins' second birthday party. Despite some hair-raising moments, both children had made it safely through another year, the family had just moved into a larger house and Leo was only a week away from starting his new job.

Finding the right opportunity had been difficult for Leo, with exciting prospects that tantalised for weeks only to evaporate in a phone call, and offers that turned out to involve far too little money or a home base on the other side of the country.

Leo's new position as a regional executive for the Club of Rome – a global think tank – was virtually ideal. Back at INSEAD he had been strongly affected by the Club's seminal publication, *Limits to Growth,* and had spent considerable time with his professors working to understand and use *Limits'* World3 computer model to simulate population growth and the depletion of the world's natural resources. He had become fully convinced of the urgent need for comprehensive worldwide changes in environmental policy. In Eva's private opinion, he could be a bit of a bore on the subject, but she was hugely relieved that he had at last found a job – and one for which he was so well suited.

For their birthday, Grandma Sadlier had made Felicity and Teddy a pair of nearly life-sized stuffed cotton dolls with big embroidered blue eyes; one a boy doll with fluffy yellow yarn hair and blue checked shorts, the other a girl with yellow yarn braids and a blue checked dress. To add to the confusion that seemed always to follow in the twins' wake, Grandma also dressed the towheaded twins in outfits she had made to match those of the dolls, so it looked at times as if not two but four "twins" were adding to the birthday party chaos.

Felicity had immediately named Teddy's doll More Teddy, and then she named her dolly Sunny. When Leo suggested to Felicity that Teddy should be allowed to name his own doll, Felicity thought for a minute and asked simply: "Why?" Then, without waiting for an answer she ran off shouting, "Cake! Cake!" followed by Teddy, who joined enthusiastically into the call for cake. The doll's name remained More Teddy, or Mo', as it became over time.

After cake, Felicity and Teddy raced in circles, shredding tissue paper from their excess of gifts beneath their feet, charming everyone with their promiscuous hugs and three-word sentences. When they decided to strip off all their clothes and pile on top of each other on their nice new potty chair, Juliet whisked them away for a bath while Eva, Leo, their parents and some friends sat savouring the quiet and drinking champagne toasts to Leo's exciting new job and the couple's newly acquired house.

Situated in a Victorian-era working class neighbourhood, the renovated house had many levels – a feature which met Eva and Leo's need to have a little breathing space when they came home at night. Downstairs there was a large bed and bathroom combination for the nanny, with a laundry down the hall. The main floor, consisting of kitchen, dining and living room and powder room also provided a sound and space buffer that was important for everyone's sense of privacy, while upstairs were rooms for sleep and play for the children, and the family bathroom. Down the hall from the children's bedrooms was a large room with steps up to a loft which held Eva and Leo's queen-sized bed.

Eva could still walk to work from the new location, Leo only had a short commute and the twins were already signed up for the Montessori school just blocks away.

"With this move we've immersed ourselves in Yuppiedom: two jobs, two kids, a nanny and a big mortgage," Eva thought cheerfully as she set off for the first time on her new walking route towards work.

The Pearson Paradigm was also growing and changing. There were now twenty consultants and five support staff – enough people to be called "personnel" and to begin asking for titles and organization charts and systems. The five partners agreed that the consultants needed to be able to measure their progress towards becoming a partner someday, and Eva found herself promoted to the newly created position of "consulting principal".

Having kissed each twin good night for the third and last time, Eva came downstairs to find that Leo had opened a bottle of champagne to celebrate her new title. "Here's to a brilliant future – today consulting principal, tomorrow the world!" he toasted.

Eva smiled contentedly. "It's a start," she acknowledged, "and if my mantra keeps working then I should be able to keep getting better and better."

"That's fine for you to say," laughed Leo, "but from the point of view of myself and the twins, we love you just the way you are."

Chapter 27: Manners Matter

The men who founded The Pearson Paradigm had quite a lot in common. Those who had not enjoyed the benefit of a proper gentleman's upbringing had at least been blessed with the intelligence to emulate the style and manners of those who were. As the firm grew, though, some of the bright new hires were young people from less privileged backgrounds. The addition of two female consultants also continued to change the culture of the firm.

Working in two- and three-person teams as they did at Pearson helped greatly to ensure that everyone learned and understood the need for consistent ways and means of doing things. How they should all look and act, especially with current or prospective clients, was also vitally important – and quite a delicate challenge.

At the firm's regular meetings the partners began to grapple with issues such as dress and manners. It had come to everyone's attention that one of their Ivy League recruits loudly slurped his coffee, and another bright spark, who was a bit unworldly, had two or three jackets and two or three wearable sets of trousers, none of which matched. There was also the quantitative genius with a sweet face marred only, in the partners' opinion, by the fact that her eyebrows were thick, very dark and met in the middle.

Eva was just returning from a rather boisterous marketing lunch one Tuesday when Stephen called her into his office. "Oh, oh," she thought, "too much levity."

But that wasn't it. The partners had decided they would like Eva to take on a little project for the firm in her "spare time."

"It seems we need to add some polish and sophistication to the Pearson team," Stephen began. "First impressions are important in our business, and customers need to feel that they can ask us to accompany them virtually anywhere. In other words, Eva, we think we need some manners and grooming training for the younger consultants, and we want you to be in charge of that training."

"You don't think asking me to do this is a bit sexist?" asked Eva carefully.

"Not at all," replied Stephen. "It's a highly appropriate task for a middle-level consultant who aspires to greater things."

That evening, as the twins ate their macaroni casserole with their fingers, Eva provided Leo with a translation of what Stephen had told her. "He said if I want to get to be a partner, I'd better get on with organizing the etiquette training. So that's exactly what I'm going to do."

Teddy interrupted the conversation with a howl: an elbow of crusty macaroni had lodged in his right nostril and in trying to get it out he'd pushed it up even further. After several unsuccessful attempts by Leo and Eva to get him to close his mouth and blow the piece of trapped pasta out of his nose, and then no success with Eva's eyebrow tweezers, Leo took Teddy to Sick Kids' Hospital while Eva put Felicity to bed. As she read Felicity her current bedtime favourite, *Just for You*, and then waited to make sure her daughter was properly asleep, Eva had ample chance to reflect on how easy it is to fail sometimes, even with the best of intentions.

"I've got to make this project fun," she resolved. "Otherwise I'll come off as a kind of prissy Ms. Manners – not at all the image I'm trying to project."

Chapter 28: The Pearson Paradigm Finishing School

While she felt she shouldn't admit it, Eva actually enjoyed working out ways that her colleagues could be encouraged to think about the contribution good manners and appropriate dress might make to business success. The partners had given her a modest budget to work with, and when she wasn't focusing on matters of "great import" – such as whether the cable company she was working with should include a complex pitch for CPI adjustments in its rate application – she was checking out people who offered to coach business executives in the niceties of the soup spoon and the salad fork.

The woman she ultimately chose for Paradigm's manners training was an appeal court judge's widow who had decided to offer advice on decorum rather than risk becoming a burden to her children or having to take up bridge. Calling herself "a consultant in the fine art of seeming at ease", Mrs. Gentle had convinced her university alumni magazine to write about her service; and Eva, herself a much-later alum, had read the piece with growing interest and enthusiasm. Maybe it was her self-description or maybe it was her name, but something about Mrs. Gentle's offering seemed just right to Eva, and she immediately made an appointment for them to meet to discuss how they might work together.

Meanwhile, convincing her Pearson colleagues – some of whom had rapidly growing families to support – that it was important to make an investment in their appearance also took some planning. She approached Fabio, the manager of Leo's favourite men's shop, with a proposal: Would he consider offering after-hours instruction in how to put together a work wardrobe on a budget, accompanied by a discount to members of the firm who then purchased clothing in his store? When Fabio countered by asking for a minimum purchase guarantee, Eva checked with Leo and then with her father to see if they would help support the arrangement by making purchases of their own. Leo agreed that she could even give him a new suit for Christmas if it came to that, and the deal was on.

Entering into the spirit of his task, Fabio put together a full colour illustrated matrix of clothing choices for the young consultants, with suits, ties, shirts, belts and accessories running down the left-hand side of the page, and style descriptors – simple/conservative, intellectual/preppy or east coast, and restrained bohemian – across the top.

"That should certainly cover it," remarked Eva, reviewing the page and nodding appreciatively to the proud manager. Then she went over to her own favourite boutique and negotiated a discount for her female colleagues.

Eva had also been reading about a new service called "Colours", which claimed it could help avoid costly wardrobe errors by identifying the colours best suited to each individual's complexion and hair colour. Having never fully understood why some of her outfits looked exactly right and others simply did not, the notion of having her most flattering colour choices scientifically codified appealed to Eva.

The Colours brochure promised to launch clients "back into the retail marketplace equipped not only with an understanding of the season – *winter, spring, summer or autumn* – best associated with your personal colouring, but also with a packet of swatches of your best colours to take with you wherever you go." At the risk of being considered more than a touch superficial, Eva added the Colours service to her list of appropriate business dress training aides.

To lay a foundation and launch the programme, Mrs. Gentle ("never Irene") and Eva devised an elaborate European-style dinner for all of Pearson's professional staff, including the TPP partners if they wished to attend, where the menu called for the use of every special-purpose utensil that could be incorporated into one meal. Beginning with Coquilles Saint-Jacques and eating their way through several courses – a cold soup, asparagus, quail… and on to Baked

Alaska – the meal was served by hospitality students hired by Mrs. Gentle and carefully briefed by her on correct service and presentation.

The dinner was hilarious. In the safety of their own company (none of the partners chose to attend) the young consultants felt free to make fun at their own and each other's expense and to ask detailed questions.

"Mrs. Gentle," asked Samantha, the newest recruit, after correctly using her finger bowl, "what was the most amazing moment concerning manners that you ever had?"

After giving the question some thought, Mrs. Gentle replied, "I often accompanied the judge when he had to go overseas to attend legal events and give lectures, and one night we were invited along to a rather special dinner given by the Canadian Consul General in Sao Paolo. The other guests that evening were corporate executives who were in Brazil trying to sell some very expensive telecommunications equipment to the government. I was seated at the right hand of the Consul General, and my husband was seated to the right of his wife."

Looking carefully at her audience, Mrs. Gentle elaborated. "As the dinner progressed, I noticed that the corporate executives tended to start eating as soon as they were served, rather than waiting, as one should do, until everyone else had been served. They also talked with their mouths full and gesticulated with food on their forks. I felt very uncomfortable for them because it was clear to me that they had been poorly raised and were not a credit to our country or even to their own company when travelling abroad. After a while I noticed that the Consul General was mimicking some of their seemingly rude behaviour – in particular starting to eat as soon his food was put in front of him, while his wife would wait until everyone else had been served. Unable to contain my curiosity, I asked the Consul General, in a low voice, why he and his wife were taking two such different approaches to the etiquette of the meal."

Mrs. Gentle continued, "'I am impressed that you noticed,'" the Consul General confided. 'Most people don't. One of our most important diplomatic tasks is to make people, especially our guests, feel at ease. My wife and I have decided that if I follow the manners of those who are the least, shall I say, polished, and she tries to conform to a more traditional high standard, then everyone should be comfortable.'"

"It was a valuable reminder," Mrs. Gentle went on to say, "that manners are intended to smooth social interaction, not to find ways of embarrassing people. If you are the host of an event, it is your job to make people feel welcome, not out of place – even if their behaviour suggests that they perhaps are. Sometimes real skill is required, but it is best to remember that kindness is truly important and also likely to be appreciated and warmly remembered. And the same simply cannot be said for exposing people to ridicule."

"That is a perfect note on which to end our evening," concluded Eva, pushing back her chair.

Chapter 29: Ups and Downs with the Twins

In a moment of total self-delusion about how much time and energy she really had, Eva signed up to sell hot dogs at the school fair from noon to 2pm one Saturday. As she understood it, the hot dog stand was the responsibility of the senior kindergarten parents, and since she had two children in senior kindergarten, her responsibility seemed unmistakably clear.

Leo had agreed to take the twins to get their faces painted – Teddy wanted his face bright blue all over so he could look like a Smurf, and Felicity wanted to look like a real live kitty – and then to the bouncy castle, before bringing them over to buy hot dogs. They had all learned the hard way that the bouncy castle should be *before* the hot dog eating, not after.

The day had already gotten off to a bit of a rough start. First, at around 2am, a tousle-headed Felicity, dragging her ragged comforter, had clambered up the loft stairs and insisted on snuggling down between Eva and Leo in the queen-size bed. An hour or so later, Teddy had arrived, clutching Mo'.

"Let me in," he urged loudly and pushed at Eva until she shifted in the bed.

Leo, now left with no space at all on the far side, picked up his pillow and set off, naked, muttering, "I'll go down and sleep in Felicity's bed."

Since Felicity's room also served as the guest room, she had a double bed to herself – a situation which made both Eva and Leo quite wistful on occasion.

Minutes later, Leo was back at the top of the loft stairs again, pillow clutched in front of his manhood.

"Juliet was in Felicity's bed," he whispered. "Something about scary noises downstairs; she'd come upstairs to feel safe."

"Well, it's likely there were fewer naked men trying to get into her own allotted bed downstairs than there were elsewhere," Eva sighed. "Look," she went on, "I'll go down and sleep in Teddy's bed while you look after the kids. I can't think of anyone who might be in his bed right now, but if a bogey man is there I'll just send him up here to sleep with you."

Only when Eva reached Teddy's bed did she realise she'd forgotten to bring her own, adult-sized pillow and so was stuck with his child-sized one. She'd also forgotten that Teddy liked to sleep with all his little plastic GI Joes arrayed around him. "Goodnight, Joes," Eva muttered as she pushed the small invading force aside.

A breakfast of cinnamon buns and lots of coffee cheered all the adults up, and before long there Eva was, chipper in her long denim skirt and man-tailored white linen shirt, at the booth ready to cook and sell hot dogs.

"Hi, I'm Sandra, Chloe's mother," said the capable-looking woman in a big blue-striped apron, already at work at the stand putting hot dogs in boiling water.

"Hi, I'm Eva, Teddy and Felicity's mom," smiled Eva, pulling her own apron with Botticelli angels painted on it out of her purse and tying it behind her back.

"No you're not," replied Sandra, matter-of-factly. "I *know* their mom. She's blonde, has a British accent and wears a red coat."

"Oh, no. That's Juliet, the twins' nanny. I'm their mother."

"Are you sure? I've never seen you before and I see them with their mother around the school all the time. Maybe you're at the wrong booth."

"Maybe I am," laughed Eva, ruefully, "but since I'm here we may as well get working. I see three hungry customers heading this way."

Chapter 30: Rear-View Mirror

Evaline was beginning to feel that agreeing to this interview had not been such a good idea after all. She'd been waiting for 20 minutes already in the rather lovely, Viennese-style café in Mayfair, and the woman who was supposed to meet her had just texted to apologise that her train was late but that she would be there shortly.

Throughout her years as a working mother and a practising feminist, Evaline had always tried to find the time to accommodate researchers and writers who wanted to listen to her point of view. Sometimes she could quite honestly have described encouraging women to have truly fulfilling lives as her avocation. But, given the chance to sit and think about it like this, she had begun to feel presumptuous for believing that she had anything to say that was particularly unique or even helpful.

The author and academic she was waiting for had particularly caught Evaline's interest because she had described her research as an attempt to "identify and describe the kinds of critical job assignments that can help a woman rise to top levels of business".

"Is there really a top?" Evaline wondered, "Or is each top really just a new bottom in disguise? I'd better not get too philosophical; this author probably doesn't want to hear me ramble about the role of work in a productive and fulfilling life. More likely she just wants to focus on what women can do to improve their chances – like the speed-writing ads used to say, 'Do you want a 'gd jb + mr py?'"

A gust of wind from the open door ushered a smiling, slightly dishevelled blonde in her thirties to Evaline's table.

"So sorry to keep you waiting, I'm Ingrid," she said in a soft Scandinavian accent. "Goodness, I am a wet mess. Let me hang my raincoat up and try to dry off a little."

Ingrid soon returned, speaking quickly. "I really appreciate your agreeing to help with my research. You will be my last interview and I am hoping that I can also test some of my theories on you."

"Relax and catch your breath. I'm delighted to meet you," smiled Evaline. "Would you like a cappuccino? They're very good here. It has actually turned out to be quite useful to sit here thinking about what you're trying to research. My ideas about women and work have been shaped and tested by my own experiences over the years, but I don't often get the time or the opportunity to sit still and just think about it all."

"Yes to the cappuccino. And I can't wait to hear what you have been thinking."

The conversation that followed was rambling but somehow surprisingly efficient. Despite first impressions, Ingrid soon proved very focused and she seemed to have real insight into what it takes to succeed in business. As she explained her findings to Evaline, it was obvious that she had already developed quite a clear and comprehensive description of what a woman might seriously consider doing if she really wanted to reach the top.

At 58, Evaline would be her oldest interviewee, and Ingrid wanted to explore what particular events she felt had made the most difference to her career.

"Can you tell me the first 'really big accomplishment' that propelled you on your way?"

"Well," said Evaline, staring thoughtfully into space, "I guess it was winning the competition for the licence to start Canada's first mobile phone company. This was back in the early 80s and hardly anyone had yet grasped the enormous potential of mobile phones, but it was clear even then that they were going to be what we called 'game-changers'. Some well-known Canadian investors had decided to get together and bid for a licence from the government to create a nation-wide mobile phone company, and they called a partner at the consulting firm where I worked and asked if we could prepare their proposal. The only problem was that the deadline for submissions was February 21st and their initial phone call only came on Friday, February 4th."

Evaline smiled wearily at the recollection. "We were pretty stretched with work already at PP – that's what the junior staff called The Pearson Paradigm – but the challenge was irresistible. Stephen, an extraordinarily bright and capable partner, talked it over with the investors and finally agreed that he would take on the task with me as number two. Then we spent the afternoon in the whiteboard room, charting out all the components of a winning submission."

Evaline remembered it vividly. "Late in the afternoon I went to my cubicle to begin organizing a meeting for Sunday – just two days away – with representatives of all the elements we needed: engineers, lawyers, bankers, computer programmers, product specialists... the works. I also had to arrange for a lot of doughnuts and coffee. When I came back to the whiteboard room to announce that I had all the experts lined up, Stephen broke the rest of his news to me. 'Eva,' he said, 'I'm leaving for a family scuba diving holiday in Saint Maarten tomorrow and I can't change it. I promised my son we'd do this for his birthday and I can't possibly get back before Wednesday night. Until then you're going to have to carry this one on your own. You have a plan here on the board and a rough budget. Just take everyone through it on Sunday. Make sure you give out clear assignments. Use the plan to create an overall framework and a timeline and get everyone going. Don't be worried; I know you can do it.'"

She continued, "It was undoubtedly the most challenging 15 workdays of my life. Lots of bizarre things happened... and kept on happening. In one case, I was on the phone trying to reach an electrical spectrum engineer who had been recommended to me, when I was suddenly told his boss wanted to speak to me. When the boss came on the line he told me in a shocked, shaky voice that he had, just minutes earlier, been informed that the engineer I was seeking had been electrocuted and killed. Looking back at how narrowly focused I was on the task, though, I'm almost surprised I didn't ask the man on the line if there was anyone else whom he could recommend for the job."

Evaline paused and then went on as if it were yesterday: "Including concrete details in our business proposal, such as engineering signal dispersion maps and advertisements for the service, was part of the plan Stephen and I had developed to differentiate our submission from the other applicants. Because we felt it was so important, we even spent time choosing the name for our service – ICan Phone.

I particularly remember a breakfast meeting I'd lined up with the head of a big ad agency – I think it was Vickers & Benson – to talk about designing some radio and television ads. We met at 7:30am in the King Edward Hotel's gracious dining room. The agency head, his name was Richard, was a stranger to me and we began by making polite chitchat over poached eggs. Then he shifted into sales mode, asking me about our target market and our service concept and a lot of other important advertising considerations.

"After only a few of his questions I remember looking him straight in the eye and saying: 'What we need are four radio ads, two television ads and four print ads, in both French and English, for a revolutionary, ground-breaking mobile phone service.'

"He began to do calculations on his napkin, speaking aloud about things like 'creative' and 'research', until I stopped him. 'You have a budget of $40,000 and I need them in five days,' I said. He looked at me stunned. Then he passed me the leather folder containing the bill for breakfast and said, 'Well of course. This is for you.' And he got up and left. The next night, at 1:30am, I got a call at the office from a slightly confused but funny 'creative' who wanted to know what I thought of the radio jingle he'd written. It was actually quite good. Five days later we got the story boards and scripts for the advertisements.

"The days and nights were filled with moments like that, and in the end, at 5am on the morning of Sunday, February 20th, bound copies of the proposal – featuring contour maps and advertisements with a fancy coloured cover that boldly proclaimed ICan Phone – were ready to be delivered. Part of the strategy to make our overall approach unique was to have the applications particular to each region in Canada delivered personally by a member of the application team to the government office in that regional centre. I had been delegated to deliver the copies to Edmonton because I have Western roots, so at 8pm that Sunday I got on the plane from Toronto. I'd wangled a bulkhead seat in economy because I was unwilling to let the applications out of my sight and the whole bundle of them, tied together, could rest during the flight in a storage cupboard whose door was right in front of me. The two men seated to my left may have felt a bit crowded at the sight of me arriving with all that paper, but I was too fatigued to notice. In fact, as it turned out, no sooner was the plane in the air than I took the smallish pillow provided by the airline, tucked it on the shoulder of the man beside me, and lay my head down, muttering, 'I hope you won't take this personally.' I slept solidly through the four-hour flight, the first continuous stretch of more than three hours of sleep I'd had for a week. As we landed I woke up, thanked the man beside me, removed the pillow from his shoulder without even thinking to check for drool, and disembarked. The entire experience was so intense; it was months before I recalled that flight and wondered what that poor man must have thought during all those hours of flying. I certainly hope he didn't need to go to the washroom."

"And what happened with the application?" asked Ingrid, caught up in the story. "Did your investors get the licence?"

"Yes, they did. But, as it happens, it took a lot more time and work before it was finally won. In fact, it wasn't until December that there was finally no remaining doubt that we had succeeded. In the meantime I was so busy that I wasn't aware that my hard work and the occasional bright idea were being noticed by some important business people, and by the Pearson partners. In the spring of the next year they officially asked me to join the partnership."

"My goodness, what a great example of a really big accomplishment that made a difference. And listening to you and your story about the plane trip makes me wonder about the sociology of the workplace. Did you spend much time thinking about the impact of the prevailing culture and the culture of the office on your efforts?"

"Oh yes, we all did. Back in the 70s and 80s when women started complaining about sexist language and its impact on attitudes, some broadcasters went so far as to circulate official lists of correct on-air word usage. That was very encouraging. At the same time, some misguided people, male and female, aggressively argued that a chair is a piece of furniture, not a business title, as if they'd never heard of homonyms. At times I really did wonder if we could possibly succeed in changing the way people speak. But nobody talks about stewardesses any more, and words like hero and actor and waiter refer equally to men and women, as does the term 'guys'. Firefighters and police are good examples too. All that change is really encouraging."

Evaline went on, "I thought maybe the sexist language battle was almost won, but recently I've been hearing a lot about 'unmanned' submarines and 'unmanned' space vehicles, and 'manpower statistics' and 'man hours', and I'm realizing that the big victory I saw was just a skirmish. Now that I'm sort of retired I realise it's not just sexist language that we should worry about – it's the widespread vulgarization of the language as well. And I've been guilty of this myself."

"What do you mean?" asked Ingrid.

"Recently, when I was playing cards with some girlfriends, one of them said something like, 'I was so pissed off,' and another interrupted with 'language, ladies, language.' When I asked her where she got that expression she told me her mother used to say it, especially to her father and her brothers, if she thought they were being vulgar. That quaint phrase, with all its overtones of British class aspirations, made me think about my own lapses into vulgarity. It crept in slowly over the years, but by the time I was in my 50s I suspect that I said the f-word at least once a day, and words like 'shit' and 'pissed off' so often I didn't even notice them. Yet now that I'm under a lot less strain, my guess would be that I might use the f-word less than once a month – if that – and I use those other vulgar terms much more sparingly."

"So why do you think you spoke that way? Were you trying to be like the men?"

"I'd like to say not, but it wouldn't ring true, would it? At some level I must've thought I'd be taken more seriously if I talked 'tougher'. I remember one woman in the company being described as a woman who 'clanged when she walked,' and I was somehow actually envious of her.

"It's all part of workplace etiquette, I guess. Years ago I organised etiquette classes for junior consultants in the firm where I worked. The course turned out to be such a success that my 'graduates' later reported to me that those lessons had been vital at key junctures in their careers. If I had to run the course over again, I would add a session on language because I've come to believe that the consistent efforts of even a few people really *can* change a culture."

Before leaving the espresso-scented cocoon of the Mayfair café, Ingrid asked Evaline if she would mind talking with her off the record about the relationship stresses that can arise from a high-powered career.

"Sure," she replied blithely. "Do you have another hour or two?"

"Well, we all know that every relationship has its inherent challenges," continued Ingrid, "so what I was really wondering was if there were times when it was obvious to you that the stress of your work affected any of your personal relationships."

"Hum… I think if you asked my family they would tell you that I'm a pretty cool character under stress – cold even – and that I act out my neuroses by doing things like being superficially very tidy and making sure that the magazines on the coffee table are all at right angles. Of course, that has also meant that when I really do reach what in retrospect might be called intolerable levels of stress, I can behave in ways that are, let's say, quite memorable. For example, Felicity and Teddy could both tell you in a lot of detail about 'The Day Mommy Got Angry', even though it happened more than 30 years ago. It's a day that lives on in infamy."

Evaline giggled at the memory. "I'd just flown home to Toronto from Ottawa, where I'd been part of a panel at an industry conference. In the airport waiting area I met two consulting colleagues who turned out to be on the same flight. When our flight was suddenly cancelled for mechanical reasons, I shared with them one of my 'experienced traveller' techniques. I suggested that since it might take the airline a while to sort out the rescheduling of our flight, we should all immediately go to the standby desk and get our names on the list for the next flight out. So we did. When the next flight came to board standby passengers, my two colleagues – whose names, it turned out, had been placed on the standby list before mine because I had ushered them up to the desk – were called for the flight. Then it was announced that the flight had been filled and the next would be leaving in two-and-half hours. To my colossal dismay, my colleagues both walked to the gate and boarded without a backward glance. When I finally walked through the door at home that night I was three hours behind schedule. My head was bowed with fatigue, which is probably why I immediately noticed a trail of bright red droplets running across our wheat-coloured carpet, stretching all the way from the front door down the hall to the kitchen.

"'What happened here?' I demanded of the hapless Leo, who was sitting in the kitchen reading the newspaper while the twins did their homework.

'Oh, that,' he replied. 'I found some lambs' kidneys at the butchers – isn't that great? I guess some blood leaked out of the paper they were wrapped in.'

'And how were you planning to get the blood stains off the carpet?' I asked him quietly.

'Oh, I thought you'd know what to do. You're really good at that kind of thing.'

'Really good at what kind of thing?' I raged suddenly, 'Cleaning up after you?'

'Well... no,' stuttered Leo, clearly shocked. 'I meant stain removal. You always tell me to leave that kind of thing to you.'

'Do I? And why would I say that?'

Finally the long-suffering Leo also snapped. 'Don't you come in here late and shouting! We were all happy before you arrived!'

'Well I certainly wasn't happy. And now I'm angry. As a matter of fact, don't you waste your time being angry at me because it will be *impossible* for anyone to be angrier than I'm going to be.'

"The kids wisely tip-toed away and hid in their bedrooms, and Leo grabbed the car keys, stomped out the door and drove away. I went and got my stain removing kit and sat on the floor crying and rubbing away at the blood on the carpet while trying to keep my salty tears from adding to the pinkish mess."

"What happened next?" asked Ingrid, intrigued.

"Oh, after some scrubbing I was able to remove almost all of the blood stains. Then the kids came down and invited me to watch *Dukes of Hazzard* with them – one of my least favourite TV shows ever – and much later Leo came home. The next morning he and the kids went out and bought me two chocolate-covered doughnuts for breakfast and we all went to the Y."

~~~~~

Chapter 31: Mommy's Sayings

Felicity and Teddy, now in grade school, did not like it when either one of their parents was absent. Eva sometimes thought they felt the absence of Leo more keenly, since he was, at least in her opinion, the "fun" parent while she was more the "law and order" parent, but she kept that minor insecurity to herself.

"How do we know what we're supposed to do every day when you're away?" complained Felicity one Sunday evening as she sat on the bed watching Eva pack for a trip to Regina. Leo, cleverly, was in the other room watching football.

"Ya, mom, how do we know what we're supposed to do every day when you're not here to tell us?" embellished Teddy.

"Hum…" said Eva, taking their concern seriously. "I have an idea. Why don't you two make a list of all the things that you can remember that I tell you every day, then I'll go over it with you, and Daddy can help us make it into a tape recording? Then you can play the tape when I'm away and that will help you to remember what you're supposed to do."

"Can I read the list for the recording?" asked Felicity.

"Can I hold the microphone and wear the ear muffs?" asked Teddy.

"Of course."

Mommy's Rules
1. Brush your teeth
2. Don't shriek
3. Say thank you
4. Be nice – it's good
5. Wash your hands
6. Don't talk with your mouth full
7. Ask Juliet
8. Ask Daddy then.

9. Go to bed
10. Get back in bed
11. Don't pinch your brother
12. Don't bite your sister
13. Wear your snow pants
14. No, you can't have two glasses of pop
15. Brush your teeth
16. Flush the toilet, for heaven's sake!

"I heard 'Brush your teeth' go by twice on the tape," commented Leo, later. "Was that intended?"

"Sounds like a good idea to me."

Chapter 32: Even in the Midst of Life...

Conjuring up a new narrowcast channel for the rapidly expanding cable universe was yet another quite unusual assignment for a consultant, and one that really pleased Eva. Her track record with ICan Phone, and her obvious enthusiasm for competitive situations, had landed her the job and she was back in the Pearson whiteboard room diagramming another critical path and trying to come up with a clever name for this particular venture.

Unlike ICan Phone, where the team had to invent the service almost from scratch with only the shoephone from *Get Smart* as a guide, the new television channel was going to have to wedge its way into an already crowded marketplace of specialty channels, each competing for a sliver of audience. The backers had spoken vaguely about lifestyles and fitness and well-being as if together they comprised a market niche clamouring to be filled instead of an already over-crowded, guru-infested stream of exercise shows.

Unfortunately for Eva and her family, most of the planning work for the channel – optimistically named *Vault!* – had to be done in Ottawa. The weekly commute quickly fell into a pattern: serious reading of research and programme ideas and budgets on the Monday flight leaving at 7:30am, and serious drinking of straight gin on the rocks on the Friday flight, landing at 5:30pm. Luckily, on Fridays Eva only had to have enough remaining energy, and sobriety, to make it from the plane to the limo, and then through the front door where Leo and Juliet would have everything waiting for her – especially the twins.

Delightfully individual, Teddy, who looked more and more like a Renaissance cherubim as he grew older, had been revealed by this time to be both musical and gifted at French, while Felicity, who favoured her hair in braids and her legs in sweatpants, steadfastly resisted French until she was allowed to leave the French Immersion class and, at last, join the ranks of those school children that she persisted in describing as speaking 'human'. Felicity's great strength was team sports – especially hockey. Muffled up in her pads, mouth guard and safety helmet, she behaved like what her admiring von Richthofen grandfather called a 'real warrior' on the ice.

Both children were invariably eager to tell Eva about their week and their plans for the weekend, and Eva, mellowed, was delighted simply to sit and listen to them. Later in the evening Leo would recap his week for her and listen to her reports of tense negotiations and little triumphs.

"*Vault!* is a really great name for a new channel," Leo had said enthusiastically when she first tried the name out on him. "I like the implication of leaping into the future or trying to reach a higher level. A simple jump, a pole vault, an architectural vault, a storage vault, a cranial vault, a burial vault – the optional interpretations are wonderful and they all fit interesting types of programming. I think you have a real winner there."

"Thanks," laughed Eva. "Now all I have left to do is organise the scheduling and the budgeting and the staffing and…" Still a bit tipsy from her trip home, she sank deeper into the sofa, ready to watch the news of the day through her eyelids.

It was Leo who suggested the summer holiday at his uncle's cottage near Espanola. He argued that once the family had made the long drive through the Canadian Shield they could luxuriate in the peace and natural beauty of rocks and pine trees and enjoy freshwater swimming for two whole weeks! The idea of being virtually inaccessible, resting, reading novels, swimming and eating blueberry muffins slathered in butter in the morning and potato chips with dip at night, was irresistible to Eva. The promise of a tent for the twins to play in, and even inhabit overnight, sealed the deal.

With the initial application filing for *Vault!* at last in the hands of the regulator, Eva flew home, cold sober for a change, to help pack for the holiday. Leo met her at the door with a doleful expression. The Malthus Group from England wanted to come to Toronto on Monday and meet with Leo and his team to talk about ways that they might work together in spreading the "limits to growth" gospel.

"You go ahead with the kids and luggage tomorrow as planned, and I'll rent a car and drive up on Wednesday night after the Malthus people have left."

"Any chance they might succumb to famine, war or pestilence and leave sooner?" Eva joked, trying to make the best of things.

"Not funny. Although I did hear something about a measles epidemic in Bradford."

A nervous driver at the best of times, Eva tried to argue that she and the kids could wait until Wednesday to go up with Leo. But neither Leo, nor the twins, was in favour of any delay.

"You can get there without me," asserted Leo. "The forecast is for a dry, sunny day and I just had the car in for service."

Teddy tried to be reassuring. "We promise we won't fight, mommy, will we Liss? I'll even sit in the front seat and help you navigate."

"No, I'm going to be in the front seat," said Felicity firmly. "Mom needs me to put the tapes into the tape player for her."

"Are you sure you don't want me to meet with the Malthus people," asked Eva turning to Leo, "and you can drive the car loaded with luggage and squabbling children up the highway, singing sixties anthems from compilation tapes as you go?"

To Eva's great relief, the long drive was uneventful, with hamburgers at a diner in a converted old rail car and a quick look at the Big Nickel in Sudbury. After a relaxing cool swim before bedtime, she and the kids fell into a deep sleep, and then celebrated their safe arrival the next morning by making the promised blueberry muffins.

"When I grow up I'm going to give my children muffins for breakfast every day," announced Teddy.

"I'm not," proclaimed Felicity. "My kids are going to be allowed to have two Strawberry Pop Tarts with extra icing every day."

"Hum…" said Eva. "Why don't you two go see if you can find oars for the rowboat?"

On Wednesday they all made chocolate chip cookies flavoured with orange rind for Leo. As far as Eva could tell, only a few shreds of skin from the ends of Teddy's fingers got grated along with the orange, and they all gave the dough a good stirring.

"Can you ask Daddy to come in and kiss us when he gets here?" asked Teddy.

"Make him eat some cookies first. Then he'll have yummy chocolate chip breath when he kisses us," added Felicity.

"I sure will. And can you two be really quiet in the morning when you get up? Why don't you read your *Archie* comics for a while?"

"Can we eat some chocolate chip cookies to keep us from starving?" asked Teddy.

"Just this once," smiled Eva.

Late in the afternoon, as he was about to leave town, Leo called Eva to tell her he was on his way. They estimated together that if the traffic wasn't too bad and there were no accidents he should be there by 11:30.

"Love you, drive safely," Eva called down the line as she hung up.

Eleven-thirty came and went, as did midnight, and one, and one-thirty. At first perplexed, then worried, now frantic, Eva paced around the cabin, at a loss as to who she could call or what she should do. She had no idea how far along the route Leo might be, so she couldn't think what to tell the police if she called.

At three o'clock she phoned 911, too anxious to wait a minute longer.

"I'm really sorry to bother you, but my spouse hasn't arrived from Toronto," she explained to the operator. "He left more than 10 hours ago and he hasn't called and I know he would call if he could because he knows I'd be frantic. He should have been here hours ago and I can't think where he might be."

Trained to field calls from desperate people, the operator took Eva through a careful series of questions, then asked her to stay on the line. Five minutes later the operator came back to ask her what kind of car Leo was driving, but the now sobbing Eva told her that she didn't know as it was a rental. She thought he had probably gotten it from Hertz, but only if they had the best deal.

After another, shorter, wait the operator returned to ask, "Did you husband wear a wedding ring?"

"Oh, we aren't married," replied Eva, feeling ridiculously wrong-footed about her domestic situation. "But he does wear a ring that I gave to him on his right hand. It's white gold with beading on both sides."

"Now, sit down and tell me more about your spouse," said the operator kindly, "a police car is going to come and pick you up and help you."

Felicity, wakened by her mother's desperate voice on the phone, came out of the bedroom.

"Where's Daddy?" she asked. "And why are you crying?"

"He's been held up," said Eva, pulling herself together. "Why don't you go back to bed?"

Felicity disappeared and then returned in a little while with Teddy, both dressed in the brightly coloured sweat suits that had been purchased especially for their holiday.

"We're going to wait with you," she announced.

Felicity, Teddy and Eva all had strikingly different recollections of the two policemen who came to the door of the cabin in the early dawn, and of their subsequent ride to the hospital. All they could agree was that one was a tall man and the other was a short woman.

In order to get them into the car without too much hysteria, the policeman had told Eva it appeared that Leo had hit a moose somewhere outside of Sudbury and that the car had been demolished. Leo had been very seriously injured and had been taken to the nearest hospital.

The police did not tell Eva then that, according to an eye witness, the car had rolled several times after the impact and then exploded in a ball of flame and that Leo, if he in fact was the driver of that car, had been incinerated. She learned most of that later at the Sudbury Regional Hospital. Even later, Eva learned that the police initially had to rely on his gold ring and the car rental company for identification until they could obtain Leo's dental records.

Chapter 33: Fifty-One Ways to Leave Your Lover

In a macabre way, Eva had been fascinated by the behaviour of Jackie Kennedy at her husband's funeral. Watching John-John and Carolyn, she had sort of understood that for Jackie, lying down and sobbing and refusing to get up or dressed, to brush her teeth or comb her hair, were simply not options. She had young children to look after – not to mention the needs of a grieving nation.

Nevertheless, Eva didn't want to think and she didn't want to feel. She didn't want to cope. She didn't want to be admired for her composure or her carefully chosen wardrobe; she wanted to be a dishevelled, dirty wet bundle of misery.

Leo's parents could barely even grasp, much less confront, the havoc the accident had visited on them. So Eva's parents, Kay and Nowell, supported by Eva's brother Dean, had to take over.

In a moment of dark humour, shared only with Eva, they agreed that at least the sometimes thorny question of cremation had already been settled. Planning for the funeral was also expedited when the von Richthofens made it clear, through their fog of grief, that they expected Leo to receive the Lutheran rites of his birth.

Everyone agreed that Martin Luther's most famous hymn, *A Mighty Fortress is our God,* should be the hymn to open the service. At Eva's instigation it was also agreed that Peter Allen, Leo's best friend from his undergraduate days, would sing *Bridge over Troubled Water* and *Annie's Song,* two of Leo's especial favourites.

Leo had greatly enjoyed the rhymes and rhythms of Paul Simon's *Fifty Ways to Leave your Lover* and he would often wander about the house quoting lyrics like: 'Hop on the bus, Gus' or 'Make a new plan, Stan'. In the early-morning hours of the day of the funeral as she lay awake and talking to his spirit, Eva tearfully reproached him for making the number fifty-one by adding the option 'Try hitting a moose, goose...'

Felicity and Teddy insisted on having parts in the service, and Eva agreed that it was best to let them be involved. Inspired by the now somewhat out-of-date list of *Mommy's Sayings*, they decided to create a list of *Things We Love about our Daddy*.

"The tense might be wrong," observed Eva privately, "but who cares."

The twins had decided to read their list in turns, and when the serious-faced 10-year olds stood up at the front of the church in their white outfits (Greta had decided that black was too old for children) the room hushed.

They read the title in unison. Then Teddy, in a clear but wavering voice read the first line, followed by Felicity.

"He liked chocolate ice cream and beer."

"He liked to watch *Animal House* with us, even when Mom said 'Turn that thing off.'"

"He gave good cuddles."

"He made great cheesy nachos."

They continued to take turns listing Leo's qualities until the only dry eyes in the church were their own.

"Most of all, he told us he loved us and Mom every single day."

Back at the house for the wake, the kids went off with Juliet to watch *Bedknobs and Broomsticks* – one of their favourite videos. Eva sat in the corner of the living room, balancing a cup of tea on her knee and struggling to carry on a conversation with whoever stopped by her chair.

The Pearson partners were out in force and they all expressed their sympathy. Liam, true to character, asked Eva when she thought she might be back at work.

"I'll be back in time for the regulatory hearings for *Vault!*." Eva assured him. It wasn't only the slightly comforting prospect of the distraction of work that

133

motivated her, she realised. She was now the family's sole support and she could not risk neglecting her otherwise satisfying and well-paid job.

With the active and generous assistance of Juliet and the grandparents, Eva did her best to keep the twins' life as much like "before" as possible. It was quite common for her to wake up and discover that both twins had migrated into her bed during the night, but she reminded herself that trying to sleep all together was actually a long-established family practice.

Some nights Eva just sat on the couch in the quiet house, Juliet downstairs watching her favourite sitcoms and the twins asleep upstairs, and cried and cried.

Work – especially in the form of tough assignments – really was a helpful alternative. One evening she caught herself staring off into space remembering the quotation she had once taped on her office wall: *The only truth is that work itself is Love.*

Chapter 34: Kubler-Ross Revisited

"My esteemed sister phoned," called Chris from the back of the flat as Evaline and John struggled through the door with their bags of fruit from the Church Street market and bulky staples from Tesco.

"Which one?" replied Evaline as John muttered "Don't shout" – mostly for his own benefit.

"The one who is currently on the Stanstead bus heading our way with lots of luggage. She wants someone to meet her and help her home."

"I'll go," volunteered John. "It may be my only chance to talk to her alone while she's in town. I'm sure you've planned a high-velocity tour of the thrills of Knightsbridge. All Chris and I will get to share is some weary dinner conversations..."

"Not true," laughed Evaline, unaware that Felicity had, in fact, told a colleague that her upcoming stopover in London, en route to a symposium in Berlin, was going to be a "highlights package of London accompanied by my partially retired but not at all retiring mother."

Relaxing in a sunny café near the Tate Modern, Felicity and Evaline sipped wine and shared their thoughts about life as a young working woman. Evaline found it especially pleasing that she and Felicity had such similar attitudes even though their respective experiences spanned a whole generation.

"Mom," said Felicity at one point, "what actually happened to you after Dad died? Teddy and I have talked a lot about how we felt and what we did, and of course we had each other, but what about you? How did you feel? What did you do to deal with it all?"

"Oh, Listless," said Evaline, falling into one of her old pet names for Felicity. "It was so hard and I was so lonely. I did some really shameful and embarrassing things."

"Ah, Mom, you can tell me. You shouldn't be embarrassed – I'm your daughter."

"That's probably why I ought not to tell you. I really don't want you to think ill of me. It was such a profoundly sad and, from this vantage point, rather ridiculous time."

"Let me pour you some more wine," said Felicity, pulling her chair conspiratorially closer to her mother.

"After your dad died, when I could finally think again, I realised two terrible things. One was that I'd become the sole breadwinner and guardian of the future for you and Teddy. Your grandparents were all a great help – although Grandfather Rolf died not long after your dad – and Juliet was a brick, but I still felt like our whole future was resting on my shoulders. It was really scary. The other thing was that I'd made a big mistake in my relationship with your father: I'd let him be my only close friend. When he died I realised that I had no real friends to turn to, no one that I liked and trusted enough to let them help me deal with all my fears. I'd always liked your "aunty" Paula, but she had her own problems to deal with and I'd never succeeded in getting as close to her as I hoped. And while I love Carina, she was busy with her own life, and in those days Brazil was a long way away."

"I don't see what's embarrassing about all that, Mom. Being frightened and lonely is what I'd expect you to have been."

"Yeah, especially right after the accident lots of people realised that I must've been feeling awfully lost and miserable and they tried, in various ways, to help me. Looking back, the ones who were the most help were the ones who brought food. In times of crises sometimes it's the practical gestures that are the best... there was one rhubarb pie with lovely flaky pastry that I still particularly remember..."

"I remember Mrs. Johnson's macaroni and cheese casseroles. Were they ever good," added Felicity.

"In addition to food, lots of people gave me advice. Some of it was practical – like the friend of my dad's who helped me trade in our two cars for a low-maintenance Buick – and some of it was downright funny. But it was all well-intentioned. A few years before your dad died a woman called Elizabeth Kubler-Ross wrote a book titled *On Death and Dying*, and he and I both read it and talked about it. In the book Kubler-Ross identifies five stages of grief: denial, anger, bargaining, depression and acceptance. If I remember correctly, after the your dad died I was given six copies of that book, not to mention the number of times someone took me aside and gave me a garbled version of the cycle of grief. My favourite was the woman who pulled me aside at a conference to tell me 'all about the sadness cycle', which she described as anger, depression, dealing and happiness. I still wonder what she thought happened in the 'dealing' phase, but I somehow suspected from her manner that she thought it should involve drugs."

Felicity laughed as Evaline continued. "Anyway, despite the sometimes touching, sometimes laughable efforts of others, I didn't always deal with my loneliness in the most virtuous, or even sensible, of ways. After living in a tunnel of misery for about six months, I began to start to act a little more normal, smile more often – that kind of thing.

"That's when men started cautiously approaching me, suggesting dinners or drinks that we both knew were only a prelude to more."

"But you needed to get back into that world again, Mom, and we all wanted you to; Teddy and I even had a secret plan to ask Uncle Dean if he could fix you up with one of his friends, or maybe help us sign you up with a dating agency."

"I didn't know that!" Evaline laughed ruefully. "How far did that plan go?"

"We talked it over with Juliet, and she said maybe we should wait a while and see how well you were able to do for yourself."

"Well, you guys were probably wiser than Juliet in that case, because I didn't do very well for myself. At first I was surprised and uncomfortable when some of the men I knew – even some your dad had known – flirted with me. Almost all of them were married, of course. But as time passed I got lonelier and they seemed to become a little more attractive, and I did some things that I wish I hadn't done."

"Like what?" asked Felicity, leaning forward with increasing interest.

"Sadly, pretty much what you'd imagine. I had one silly rule, which seems pathetic when I look back on it. My rule was that I would not cavort with any man whose wife I knew and whom I might someday have to look in the eye. Talk about situational ethics! And I was so god-damned insecure. All someone needed to do to seduce me was tell me how smart and pretty I was."

"But you really *were* smart and pretty, Mom, although 'cavort' is an interesting euphemism…"

"Yeah, right. Well, who wants to come right out and say it? It was all rather pathetic. It reminds me of my friend Alyse who studied at INSEAD with me. She was rather plump and a bit strange-looking and lacked self-confidence, so she was ridiculously grateful to any man who paid her any attention at all. One time a fairly good-looking but sleazy guy in our *principes de finance moderne* class who was dating one of Alyse's best friends offered her a "quickie' and Alyse, who had an essay due the next morning, reluctantly told him 'no' but then went on to say, 'but thanks for asking.' Did I ever give her a hard time when she confessed that incident! Thanks for inviting me to abase myself – that's what she was actually telling him. But in retrospect my behaviour after Leo died wasn't much better. I never got to the point of saying 'thanks for asking' to anyone, but I sure did manage to sell myself awfully short."

She continued, "There were times when it all seemed farcically funny – at least to me. One day one of my colleagues asked me if I'd like to go to the health club with him at lunchtime the following week. It was a bit surprising, as we weren't particularly close, but I agreed, envisioning eating a healthy lunch while watching other people work out. I should have got the hint when he reminded me the day before to bring along some workout clothes. Of course, I

138

didn't have any, but the morning of our 'date' I put some shorts and a matching T-shirt in my bag, along with my runners. When we got to the club two surprising things happened: First, he directed me to the desk to pay my fee for an exercise day (he had a season's pass), and then he disappeared into the men's change room, saying: 'See you after the class.' The class was gruelling. I was in the back row, trying my best to keep pace, and he was in the front row, serving as an example to us all. After a much-needed shower I met him outside, where he indicated that he'd already bought a takeout sandwich to eat back at his desk and suggested that I do likewise.

"My conclusion from that episode was that he had no ulterior motive; he simply thought I needed to get fit – and he was probably right."

"It can't have been *all* bad, Mom. Weren't any of the guys okay?"

"Oh, some of the guys were fun – sexy even – but the encounters lacked all context. I certainly didn't want to go so far as to be a homewrecker. Though truth be told I was never really tested. No one ever actually offered me that choice."

"Well thank heaven you found John," said Felicity.

"Yes, thank heaven. Now, let's go see what he and Chris are proposing for dinner. My guess is Pizza Express."

"Sure." There was a long pause. "Mom, do you mind if I tell Teddy what you've told me? We used to worry and wonder about you such a lot. I don't feel right not telling him this stuff… please?"

"Oh all right. I guess I figured you'd tell him anyway. So, thanks for asking."

"Anytime, Mom. Anytime," laughed Felicity, visibly relieved.

Chapter 35: Travel and Sundries

The first two days of the regulatory hearing into the details of how *Vault!* could be expected to perform as a specialty channel had gone very well. The team was well rehearsed; the video that had been commissioned to promote the channel was a wild montage of brightly dressed people, young and old, swinging around vaulting horses, clearing hurdles and popping out of craniums with brain food. Eva especially liked how the final quick sequence of gymnasts swinging more and more rapidly on their hands around a vaulting horse morphed into a windmill with six vanes, each vane a gymnastic pixie with one of the figures of the word *Vault!* emblazoned in red on a white leotard.

Just a few financial questions to go, then the interveners' presentations, and the hearing would be done. The *Vault!* team knew that to win the right to broadcast a new channel they must demonstrate a number of ways that the channel would benefit the greater community. One of the many selling points Eva and the team had made much of was that *Vault!* intended to be a prime provider of funding for nominated high schools to assist students in winning The Duke of Edinburgh's Awards – a demanding curriculum of community awareness and fitness that meshed perfectly with *Vault's* professed goals.

The questioning was winding down and there were some final queries about The Duke of Edinburgh's Awards and how the funds would be allocated, when Eva noticed the chair of the hearing, Jake Whaley, rapidly scanning pages in his version of the application binder, clearly looking for something in particular.

"What can he be looking for?" she wondered. "Likely something relating to those awards." Then she guessed: "Oh, no – he's looking for the budget for the awards support and is clearly not finding it."

Quickly but calmly Eva turned the pages of her own binder to the detailed financials. Running her eye down the lists of numbers, she began to feel a little ill. She couldn't see any line item for the awards, or any consolidated line that looked even vaguely plausible or large enough. "We couldn't have left that out of the budget, could we?" she asked herself. A further quick review made it painfully clear that they had.

Knowing that the amount for the awards that they had stipulated in the narrative of the application was $120,000 per year, Eva focused on every budget item significantly greater than that amount. They had designed the channel on the cheap, so there were very few amounts outside of signal transmission and staff salaries that were much greater than $120,000.

As her heart started beating faster, she heard the chair interrupt one of his long-winded colleagues and say: "Thank you, Phillip. I think we've explored that point in sufficient detail. Now I have a question for the team. I was wondering if you could direct me to the item in the budget where you've provided for the support of The Duke of Edinburgh's Awards of which you seem so proud."

"Thank you, Mr. Chair," Eva responded before anyone else on the team, such as the CFO designate, had a chance to answer. "We are very pleased that you've taken such careful note of our intentions in this regard, and I would like to direct you to the line entitled 'Travel and Sundries' in your budget document for the cost allocation that you are looking for."

"'Travel and Sundries?' That's a strange place to budget an expenditure for athletic awards," said the Chair, suspiciously.

"It certainly is, Mr. Chair, but you know how these things go. The accountants have so many bizarre rules and categories, and sometimes they tell you to do things that just don't seem to make sense to anyone but themselves."

"Do they?" said Whaley, sceptical but resigned in the face of Eva's chutzpah. "I must admit it doesn't make much sense to me. Anyway, unless anyone else has a question we'll break now and reconvene to hear the interveners in 20 minutes."

"Not a word," hissed Eva to the CFO as he approached her immediately after the break began. "You only joined the team three weeks ago and you certainly don't know how we budgeted for the awards."

"No," he sighed. "But I fear I'm going to have to find the money from somewhere now."

"Only if we succeed in getting the licence," replied Eva, and went off to get the largest, strongest cup of coffee she could find.

Chapter 36: Hard Work is its Own Reward

Eva's maternal grandmother, Grandma Brown as the family called her, had a homily for most occasions. "If you cry on your birthday you'll cry all year round" was the one Eva liked the very least.

Probably due to all the pent-up anticipation, however misdirected, birthdays were a time when Eva was upset easily. On one particular birthday, when she was quite young and Grandma Brown was visiting the family, Eva did cry. Grandma at once gravely pronounced her homily and Eva became so frightened that it took forever to calm her down.

Another one of Grandma Brown's favourite exhortations was "Hard work is its own reward." At least that one made some sense.

Eva's seemingly tireless efforts on behalf of her clients to win the licence for *Vault!* finally paid off. Already the work involved had provided some serious and often effective sublimation of grief, but then, bonus of bonuses, *Vault!* was a winner in its bid for a licence, along with *Wars of the Twentieth Century* (which Eva privately called the Hitler channel) and *Fields of Wonders* – a nature documentary service targeted at those who find field mice endlessly fascinating. Asked if she would consider watching *Fields of Wonders*, a colleague of Eva's replied simply that she would probably rather put pins in her eyes.

The Fireplace Channel sadly did not win a licence, even though the applicants had promised to feature something for everyone: hours of log-burning fires interspersed with gas fires, coal fires, and even the occasional electric fireplace with shiny red wrapping paper flickering in the breeze of an off-screen fan. Eva had briefly enjoyed thinking up programme variations for that channel, such as *Savonarola Day*, or *The Pendle Witches versus Salem*.

The win party for *Vault!* was a lot of fun, with various speeches of praise for Eva and her team and digital camcorders as party favours. The next morning Felicity and Teddy found the camera in the party bag near the front door where Eva had left it as she arrived home, and immediately started making their own "feature" movies with Felicity as the director and Teddy as a combination camera operator and gofer. (Even at 11 the twins knew that "cameraman" was not the kind of word Eva liked to hear.)

Back at her desk at The Pearson Paradigm, Eva relished the prospect of a week or two spent filling out her expense reports and catching up with the office gossip. Most of the other consultants were off on assignment, so things were likely to be mercifully quiet.

On her third day back, as Eva was happily tidying the upper right quadrant of her desk, she got a phone call from Bill Arkwright, the CEO of FutureMedia and her client for the *Vault!* assignment.

"Hi, Eva," Bill began warmly. "How are you doing?"

"Just great, Bill," she replied with a smile in her voice. "I really enjoyed winning the licence for your team, and now I'm really enjoying doing brainless things like filling in my timesheets."

"Right off I wanted to tell you again what a great job you did for us and how much we appreciate your efforts. Old Frank nearly burst a gut laughing when he told us about how you found The Duke of Edinburgh's Awards budget tucked away under 'Travel and Sundries'."

"Well, Bill, you know better than most how silly accountants can be."

"Yes, I certainly do. But I'm not just calling to praise your accounting acumen. It seems I need your help again. As you're already aware, we now have several specialty channels and a television production company in one subsidiary, and our cable and satellite transmission business in another, and we're seriously wondering if we ought to put the two together under one management and then take that company public."

He drew a deep breath. "Before starting down that path, though, I really need someone to help me think through our corporate strategy. All my executives are flat out right now so I also need someone who can help me and my board to work out how to maximize the value we might achieve by looking at ways to spin off another public company. Assuming that the idea is sound, I think the person to do that job for me should have the potential someday to be the CEO of that new company."

Eva was accustomed to helping her clients think about how to staff key positions in their organizations. "So you're looking for a strategist with a flair for execution. Is that right?"

"Yes, that sounds like just what I'm looking for."

"Hum. Leave it with me and I'll see if I can come up with a couple of ideas. You maybe should have a talk with Anne Faulkner over at Faulkner Executives too and see what she thinks."

"Leaving it with you is just what I want to do Eva – but not the task of thinking up other candidates. I want to leave a job offer with you. I already asked Anne her opinion, and she told me that you're definitely a good candidate, even though she won't get any commission if I succeed in hiring you."

"Me?" Eva stuttered, taken totally by surprise. "But I'm a consultant, not an operator."

"Now, here is an extremely rare occasion where I think you're wrong. While you define yourself as a consultant who loves to do projects, I see you as an extremely skilled operator who knows how to get the job done. I really would like you to come and work for me as Senior Vice President, Strategic Projects.

"Please give my idea some thought and come and have lunch with me at the top of the TD Centre next Monday. At the very least you can have a great lunch and a chance to look out the window at the lake."

"Okay," agreed Eva. "I can at least do that."

"I'll see you there."

And, as suddenly as that, Eva was on her way to the next level: a senior job in corporate management.

Chapter 37: A New Field to Conquer

The transition from being a consultant to working as an executive in a big corporation was a welcome challenge for Eva. While she had never minded the uncertainty and pressure to perform that characterise the life of a consultant, she revelled in the prospect of a job where the good things she had achieved last week might still matter to those with whom she was still dealing this week or even the week after.

While her partners at Paradigm were sorry to see her go, both she and they knew that consulting alumni can be great future customers, so the goodbyes were warm on both sides. Eva's position as head of strategic planning in a company listed in the Toronto Stock Exchange Composite Index reflected very favourably on them.

There were those at FutureMedia who wondered how it had come about that Eva was suddenly announced one day as Senior Vice President, Strategic Projects, but when one of them had the nerve to ask she simply replied, "Oh, I slept with Bill Arkwright." Since Bill was widely known to be gay, that answer immediately shut the questioner, and those hiding behind the cubicle wall who had encouraged him to ask this presumptuous question, right up.

It took some months to properly plan and organise a new company that produced both niche programming and mainstream commercials, programmed several specialty channels and had a sideline in satellite distribution services. But slowly it began to take shape. Eva loved the challenge of trying to figure out how to make the pieces work together, and the legal discipline of preparing the prospectus provided her with further valuable education.

In parallel, Eva worked with Bill and Andy Frith, Bill's Chief Financial Officer, to identify a partner for the project – a minority shareholder who could bring both money and markets to the party.

It was all a lot of hard work and quite a bit of fun. At the board meeting where Eva presented the detailed business plan and Bill asked his board for approval to start the processes that would end up with FutureMedia having a 51 per cent position in a new public company, Eva felt slightly giddy with fatigue. She had been up all night working with her team to make sure that her presentation anticipated every imaginable question from a board member. Her enormous relief at the board's unanimous motion to approve the whole plan only served to remind her that she had been holding her breath while awaiting their decision.

Afterward, Eva and Bill tossed on their overcoats and headed out onto the snowy street to share a celebratory mid-afternoon cappuccino at their favourite trendy coffee bar.

"Well, that's one hurdle cleared," said Bill. "Are you ready for the next one?"

"I feel almost certain that I *will* be able to recover the use of my hands and feet," sighed Eva, "though maybe just not this week."

"Well, it is only Wednesday, but I do need you to gear up again quickly. Now we have to choose the right partner and to do that we have to get some key details tied down."

"Which ones are you thinking about? The prospectus is on the shelf, the names are down to a shortlist of three, and your comptroller has put his hand up to come and be the finance chief for the new company. I think he would be a good choice, incidentally."

"There remains the little matter of the CEO for the new venture," Bill explained. "During our *in-camera* session the board quizzed me pretty aggressively on who I thought was the 'best man' for the job, and I told them I think the very best man is you. Some of the less confident members were nervous about the idea, but our chair was strong in his support of you. I believe his exact words were, 'I think we should give Eva the job.' That certainly quieted down the temporizers and the nay-sayers."

"Wow! Is that how it happens, just as simple as that?"

"Sometimes," said Bill. "But not often. I think you can count yourself lucky. And us, too," he added with a smile.

Chapter 38: Halfway Down the Table is the Place Where I Sit...

After considerable angst, the new company was finally named Futurity.

"Not a great name," said Eva, "but it'll do." Secretly she'd fancied the name FutureSchlock, but she feared, correctly, that others might not see the humour in such a choice.

The start-up had its moments. During her first presentation to the investment community, Eva was well into her outline of corporate prospects before she noticed that she was missing the last several pages of her carefully rehearsed speech. As she continued to deliver the pages in hand, she tried simultaneously to assess whether or not she could remember enough of the remainder of the piece to deliver it without notes. Concluding that there were too many detailed financial points to be made, she quickly made a decision to stop when her script ran out and confess. "I seem to be out of notes, although I'm not yet out of prospects," she explained to the interested audience, smiling courageously.

Glancing back from the podium in the direction of her seat at the presenters' table, with great relief she spotted the abandoned pages just as the CFO also saw them. Immediately, he stood up and passed the pages over to Eva with a little flourish.

"Ah," she quipped, "A modern-day Sir Walter Raleigh has saved me from stepping into something nasty."

One Saturday, Eva, needing to go and pick up some work at the office, thought she would try to turn it into a fun expedition for the twins. They saw right through her ploy, but were interested in seeing her new workplace and went along happily.

While Eva was looking through the papers that had been left on her desk, Felicity and Teddy went next door to check out the boardroom. Felicity soon gravitated toward the executive washroom and the cloakroom next door.

"Wow, Mom," she exclaimed as Eva came in through the door. "Look at all the cool soaps! Each one is shaped and painted like a real flower. They look too pretty to use to wash your hands."

"Yes," admitted Eva, ruefully. "My assistant thought it would be nice to have some feminine touches in there. I find it a little embarrassing, but her intentions were so good I didn't want to say anything. Still don't really. I wouldn't want to hurt her feelings."

"Would it be okay if I took one of these soaps home?"

"Certainly, take several. Take some of those pink paper towels with you too. I fear there are plenty more where they came from."

Joining Teddy in the boardroom, Felicity and Eva found him walking round and round the rectangular table, looking at it carefully.

"Where do you sit, Mom? Do you sit at the end near the wall screen or near the cloakroom door?"

"I sit in the middle, facing the big double doors," replied Eva.

"But you're the boss. Why don't you sit at the head of the table? That's where bosses are supposed to sit."

"Remember when you were little, and you didn't want to do what you were told, you used to cross your arms and say, 'You're not the boss of me.' Well, you were right. I'm not really the boss of anybody; people just let me pretend to be the boss sometimes for a little while."

"So why do you sit in the middle?"

"Well it may sound silly, but I like to sit in the middle of the table facing the door so that when a disgruntled customer with a sub-machine gun comes to wipe us all out, I'll at least see him before he starts shooting."

"That is really silly. Let's go and get a hotdog," concluded Felicity. And off they went, with Teddy looking back a little fearfully as Eva shut the big double doors with a quick slam.

Chapter 39: Down There on the Floor

Sitting in her own tasteful and comparatively sumptuous office, largely bereft of feminine touches and overlooking the park, Eva was relaxing at the end of a long day and talking with her new programme director, who was out in Los Angeles trying to buy large amounts of inexpensive programmes to fill the shoulder periods of the broadcast schedule on *Vault!*. The phone line's quality was poor and Eva unclipped her earring – a large clump of gold-coloured metal – so that she could hold the phone closer. Absent-mindedly, she twiddled with the earring until it suddenly went flying through the air.

As soon as she had hung up the phone, Eva began to hunt for the earring. Felicity and Teddy had given her this pair of earrings for her birthday and she really liked them.

Under the desk, on the desk, inside the desk, under the sofa, in the corner, under the credenza... she looked everywhere.

"Where, oh, where could my earring have gone?" she sang to herself, crawling around the floor on her hands and knees, combing the carpet with her fingers.

At that moment Richard Olsen, head of corporate communications, put his head around the door. "Are you regressing?" he asked mildly, "or is this some hot new exercise for executives that's being promoted by one of our incredibly focused channels?"

"You know how I just love to contribute content ideas. I thought you would have figured out by now that innovative new exercise ideas don't just come from sitting and thinking. Sometimes you need to give them a test run. Actually, this position reminds me of a line from that old Helen Reddy song, *I am Woman.*"

"You mean the bit that goes, *'Cause I've heard it all before and I've been down there on the floor. No one's ever gonna keep me down again?'"*

152

"My goodness, Richard. I am impressed. Where did you learn that?"

"You aren't the only one who grew up with women's lib, you know. My first girlfriend was a real bra-burner."

"Sounds like she was hot stuff. Do you want to join me down here and help me find my earring?"

"You've met her; draw your own conclusions. Anyway, I'm on my way to dinner and you should be too. I just stopped by to see if you'd be willing to lunch with the Premier's new special advisor. He wants to test some policy ideas with you."

"Oh sure, I love to hear what the political types are thinking. It amazes me sometimes to realise that we even share the same planet. Remember when the Premier came up to me at the event for The Duke of Edinburgh's Awards, took my right hand between his two hands, looked deeply into my eyes, and said 'Thank you for doing all that you're doing'? Now that I think about it, that was a pretty good all-purpose comment. Maybe I should find some occasions to use it myself."

"Whatever," offered Richard as he turned to leave.

"I didn't have you down as the kind of guy that married his first girlfriend," Eva called after him, still on her hands and knees, checking behind the potted plant.

Chapter 40: Free To Be... You and Me...

Held at an out-of-the-way crêperie, the lunch with the newly promoted political advisor was a lot of fun. Sam and Eva traded gossip and shared insights over spinach crêpes with béchamel sauce.

According to Sam, the Premier was interested in attracting more women to run as candidates at the next election. Eva didn't have many ideas on that topic – the intricacies of politics didn't especially interest her – but she did have some strong views on equal pay for work of equal value and better representation of women in senior positions in the civil service.

It was just another one of those lunches, lively and pleasant but with no real outcome. As they emerged from the restaurant they were greeted by a typical sunny Indian summer afternoon and together they walked slowly back towards the business end of town. Sam talked with just a faint touch of pride about how his son was trying out for his high school football team and that, if he succeeded in making the squad, he would be the first male in his family to ever have had any success in sport.

Sam's self-effacing comment made Eva laugh.

"I know what you mean," she chortled. "My kids are really determined to win the mixed relay race at the interschool games next week, but their chances are slim. Apart from a tenuous connection to an illustrious fighter pilot, whose exploits probably required some hand/eye coordination, we don't have many athletic achievements to point to in our family either."

"Your kids?" queried Sam, "I didn't know that you have children."

"Yes, twins – a boy and a girl."

"Really? Wow. So are they identical?"

"No, they're fraternal. One's a boy and one's a girl."

"What a stupid question," offered Sam. "Of course they couldn't be identical."
"Don't feel bad. People ask me that all the time."
"I must admit you really took me by surprise. I never imagined that you could be running a company and have children too. What do your kids do every day while you're out working in the corporate jungle?"
It was Eva's turn to be taken aback. Without thinking she replied, "They get older. They get up in the morning and eat breakfast and go to school. They play with their friends. They do their homework. What did you think they would do?"
Realizing how sexist his question had been – not to mention how extensively he'd managed to undermine his carefully constructed liberal persona in a moment of thoughtlessness – Sam had the grace to look embarrassed.
"I was so focused on your business accomplishments that I just hadn't realised you might also be a parent," he explained, trying to dig himself out the hole.
"Well, better briefing next time," Eva laughed gently as she left him at the door to her office.

That evening, over dinner with Felicity and Teddy, Eva reminisced about the Marlo Thomas album *Free to be You and Me* that they all used to listen to.
"I really liked the song *Parents are People*," said Teddy.
"Ya, me too," said Felicity.
"I have an idea. Do you want us to sing your part to you, Mommy?"
"Yes, please."

> *Mommies are people, people with children*
> *When mommies were little, they used to be girls*
> *Like some of you, but then they grew*
> *And now mommies are women, women with children*
> *Busy with children, and things that they do*

155

There are a lot of things a lot of mommies can do...

Chapter 41: Glasnost and Perestroika

Not only were the twins getting older while Eva was off working, but the geopolitical makeup of the world was rapidly changing too. In Ronald Reagan the Americans had elected an actor who at least knew how to act like a president and, perhaps partly from long experience in movies about the military, also knew how to rattle his sabre rather convincingly. In fact, he managed to alarm the USSR leadership enough that they diverted still more of their already limited national output into missile defence. The Soviet people, already demoralised by failure in Afghanistan and now faced with further economic hardship, were soon expressing their criticisms more openly and Moscow's grip on its Warsaw Pact allies was beginning to weaken.

Despite his remarkably rapid climb up the Soviet political apparatus, Gorbachev, at least notionally a reformer, was surprised that fortune had delivered to him the impetus for dramatic change, and it was so powerful that it was almost frightening.

Meanwhile, much to her surprise, no sooner had Eva learned that the Russian word *glasnost* meant "openness" and that *perestroika* meant "change from within" than she was presented with the chance to do some business with what she thought of as "actual Russians."

Futurity's satellite and cable distribution business was looking to expand, and the USSR's space programme was suddenly open to the possibility of making some hard currency by sharing the most impressive of their technological achievements. The company was first approached through a Russian intermediary charged by his government with the task of trying to make deals with capitalist companies, and the potential of such a partnership immediately caught the interest of Eva's investment team. The fact that the dealmaker had previously been, and still probably was, a member of the GRU – the Russian foreign military intelligence – only added cachet and a little spice for the naïve Canadians.

Both sides were feeling their way. Futurity certainly didn't yet know how to do a deal with the USSR, and no one they were dealing with in Moscow actually knew what kind of constraints or benefits would be endorsed by the rapidly changing government departments involved. They didn't even know whom to ask.

Jim O'Donnell, the "facilitator" who had brought the parties together, was bright and energetic, but the truth was that no one in the world had actually succeeded in doing a deal quite like this before. All the same, both sides were willing to give it a try.

The first small wave of Futurity executives sent over to assess the transmission standards and manufacturing capability for satellites launched from the USSR returned both excited and intimidated.

"It's like the Wild West over there," confided Gregory Isaacs, Futurity's lead transmission engineer, to Eva. "They kept showing me things and then getting afraid that I shouldn't have been allowed to see them and then suddenly remembering glasnost and, after all, showing me even more things. Once, after I'd just been to the toilet, I came out to find a little group of Soviet executives standing at a distance, looking at me and laughing. When I asked my guide what was happening he told me they all wanted the chance to look at a man whose 'big boss' is a pretty young woman."

"I hope you immediately took out your wallet and showed them the picture of me which I know you always keep close to your heart," suggested Eva, drily.

"Oh no, I didn't need to. They were passing around a copy of our annual report with your photo beside the President's message and the group photo with you standing in the middle, right beside me, I might add. That was enough for them. Besides, I keep my wallet in the back pocket of my trousers."

Eva could hardly wait for her turn to go to Moscow. News that the Cancosmos team, as they impressively styled themselves, had secured the passage of an act in the USSR parliament endorsing their nascent joint venture seemed almost unbelievable. Of course, she had no choice but to take their claim on faith since the official copy of the act itself, which she had received, frame and all, was written in elegant Cyrillic characters.

From the moment, on a shockingly hot August day, when she landed at Moscow's Sheremetyevo Airport, Eva was surprised at every turn by the country and its people. While she had visited Cuba in the 70s and Venezuela in the 80s, they were countries where the rigidities and deprivations of socialism seemed to be ameliorated by geography, climate and a cheerful congenial attitude. In the capital of the Soviet Union, the heartland of communism, with its ancient history of serfdom, famine and sacrifice, both the system and the place itself seemed somehow more bereft of humanity.

Gregory and Jim O'Donnell had both warned Eva to pack some tinned liver paste, smoked oysters, crackers and dried fruit for her stay, and Juliet and the twins had carefully made up a special travel care package for her, including love notes and 'hurry home' requests tucked amongst the goodies. Nevertheless, she hadn't actually expected to have to rely on those provisions. Her second day in Moscow was filled with meetings and briefings, and she approached the hotel restaurant eager for a quiet meal and an even quieter evening. As she neared the restaurant she noticed a couple of staff sitting on the stairs in front of the French doors, which surprisingly, were not open.

"Closed. No food. Go away," the larger and more humourless of the attendants told her, shaking his head. Despite some confused, awkward pantomiming on Eva's part, involving pointing at her mouth and rubbing her stomach, the waiter repeated his five words of English and moved closer to his companion on the stairs as if concerned that Eva might take a surprise run at the restaurant door. In the total absence of any alternative suggestions, she retreated to her room for a dinner of liver paste and oily oysters on crackers and a cup of boiled water dispensed by the baba in charge of the samovar at the end of the hall, greatly relieved that she'd remembered to pack a can opener.

The next morning at breakfast, when the staff indicated that there were no more eggs or cheese, she accepted the toast on offer with alacrity and then proceeded without hesitation to eat the bits of cheese left on the abandoned plate of a previous diner. "How quickly the thin veneer of civilization falls away," she thought, silently vowing to be one of the first people at breakfast the next morning.

Eva's official role in Moscow was to participate in the formal signing of an agreement between Futurity and the Ministry of Communications of the USSR to work together on satellite and cable ventures. The actual signing involved special gold-plated pens and several cork blocks with maple leaf and hammer-and-sickle flags sticking out of them, and a great deal of reassurance from the legal staff of the Canadian embassy that what she was signing was just a commitment to "best efforts" on both sides.

A celebratory dinner (with actual food) was scheduled for the end of the day and Eva went back to the hotel to freshen up, only to discover that while she was out at the signing ceremony her room had been so thoroughly tidied that a couple of her prettier lacy undergarments had disappeared. Realizing what a temptation they must have been to the drably dressed female staff that she had passed in the halls, she hoped that the new owner would enjoy wearing them.

Dinner was provided by her hosts in a busy restaurant and the food was plentiful. The Russian dignitaries and the translator sat on one side of the table while Eva and her intermediary and some helpers from the Embassy were arrayed, roughly matched by status, down the other. Conversation was stilted – both due to pauses for translation and because it turned out that certain aspects of business and finance which Eva had simply assumed to be more or less universal simply were not.

Her learning process began in earnest when she suggested that it would be useful to get started on a business plan to help nail down how a jointly run Cancosmos business might work. Reaching into her old consulting bag of tricks, she began to ask questions about wages and fees and the cost of business accommodation and services, only to receive some decidedly strange answers. Undeterred, she asked her hosts about interest rates and the cost of capital in the USSR.

"There is no interest rate," appeared to be the answer she was getting.

Bewildered, Eva persisted. "Well, what rate do you pay if you borrow money?"

"We don't."

"Don't what? Don't earn interest? Or don't borrow?"

"Both," said one.

"Neither," chimed in another.

"Do you get paid extra for lending your money to the bank?" asked Eva, doggedly trying to come at the same issue from a different angle.

"We don't do that. We keep our money in a leather bag or under the mattress."

"How do you get a mortgage if you buy a house?"

This question prompted a great deal of conversation on the other side of the table, until finally someone who had previously only spoken in Russian volunteered in quite acceptable English that the apartments in his building were soon to be made available for the tenants to purchase, and that it appeared as if a rate of 3 or 4 per cent interest would be charged.

"Okay, 4 per cent it is," said Eva with a confidence that belied her dawning realization that doing business with the Russians was going to be quite challenging and full of surprises.

The evening continued to limp along until one of the more junior and ebullient Russians asked Eva, through the interpreter, if she liked the Beatles' songs.
"Oh, yes. I grew up singing all of them."
After hearing the interpreter's version of Eva's response, the young Russian began to sing. First he sang *Love, love me do* in recognizable English, then he segued into *I want to hold your hand,* followed by *Michelle, ma belle* and so on, all parroted, but, except for the Russian accent, word perfect. Many in the host party on the opposite side of the table sang along enthusiastically, while Eva and her colleagues smiled as they listened with wonder – and in some cases also joined in. All the other diners in the restaurant behaved as if nothing even slightly unusual was happening.

Chapter 42: Arbat Street

Next morning, Eva, having breakfasted very early, went off with the guide provided by her hosts to see the collection of Fabergé eggs in the Kremlin Armory. Ever since she'd seen one of those extraordinary objects in the Russian antiquities shop just beside the Sherry Netherland on Fifth Avenue in New York, she'd wanted to see more of the amazing collection once owned by the Russian Imperial family. The display of dresses and furniture owned by Catherine the Great in the room where the guide led Eva next was a delightful addition to her visit.

"I can't believe how small Catherine the Great's waist was!" Eva exclaimed to her guide. "The waist on that ball gown looks like it's only 14 inches." The guide merely gave her a puzzled look and directed her attention to the three-horse sled called a *troika*, which was exhibited nearby.

As they were on their way out of the Kremlin, Eva was pleasantly surprised to find herself in the midst of an absolute sea of delegates to the Congress of the Communist Party of the Soviet Union – most of them resplendent in national costume. She was embarrassed to realise how little she knew about the extraordinary geographic and religious diversity of the country, and she was surprised to see so many political delegates from different ethnic groups milling around in the courtyard outside the hall where they were meeting. CBC's Moscow correspondent, there with his camera crew, was in turn surprised to find Eva in such exalted company and stopped to talk before hurrying along in pursuit of his story.

It was humid and grey in the late afternoon, but before leaving Moscow Eva was determined to make her planned journey to Arbat Street in search of souvenirs – in particular a matryoshka doll. Jim O'Donnell had advised her that Arbat Street, a pedestrian mall in the old city, was used by Russian artisans to sell their wares to tourists, and he had even agreed to go there with her.

Jim and Eva began a slow walk down the mall, pausing occasionally to look at the once elegant pre-revolutionary residences and restaurants that lined the street, as well as the small caches of handicrafts on offer. As they walked, they gradually attracted a horde of beggar children. The tattered children following them saddened and frightened Eva. She'd been warned by several people not to risk giving them money, but just the sight of them made her very unhappy and she told Jim, if he didn't mind, that she would like to turn back.

As Jim started to look for a route down which they could retreat, he was distracted by one particularly large-eyed, shoeless toddler in a worn sundress a size or two too large for her. Without thinking Jim reached into his pocket and handed the child a five-rouble note.

She immediately stood stock still on the street, holding the note up to the light to check its authenticity. Then she ran quickly across the mall and gave the money to an older child who looked towards Jim and bent down to make sure the tiny girl could hear whatever he was saying to her. Moments later she reappeared directly in front of Jim, placed both her filthy little bare feet on one of his manly oxfords, and wrapped her arms tightly around his calf. As he stood looking down in horror at his right leg and glancing fearfully at his left, other children began to encircle him.

Eva convulsed with laughter at the sight of the confused businessman with a beggar child attached to his leg. Hoping movement might make her let go, Jim tried to walk but, if anything, the child's hold only became tighter and Jim began to look about desperately for help.

Out of the corner of her eye Eva noticed a man holding a camera with professional ease, clicking photos of Jim's predicament and laughing too. As Jim tried prying the fingers of the little girl from his leg, while shouting powerlessly at the child to "please, for god's sake let go," the man with the camera called to him in English, "Have you any coins in your pocket? Take a handful and throw them as far as you can."

Jim did as he was told and the photographer joined him, tossing his own coins as far from Jim as he could. The beggar children, including Jim's little leg accessory, scattered to pick up the coins. Suddenly Jim was free, and he hurried to join Eva and the photographer in the safety of a restaurant doorway.

"Let's go inside and have a cup of tea," the Englishman suggested. "It'll give the kids a chance to find some other prey."

Inside the restaurant, Jim's saviour introduced himself as John Curran – a freelance photographer. Eva felt immediately comforted by his mellow voice and his deep smile. He even put Jim at ease, telling him that those who got into trouble through their generosity were at the very least a special brand of fool, and they spent a happy hour or so recovering from the excitement and drinking Russian tea as the afternoon turned into evening. By the time they left it was too late for Eva to get a matryoshka doll, but John insisted on giving her the consolation prize of a tin of caviar that he pulled magically out of his camera case.

"What a kind man," thought Eva as she and Jim set off for the airport.

Chapter 43: A Picture is Worth a Thousand Words

"Have you seen the latest issue of *Time* magazine?" asked Gregory as he passed Eva's office door. He'd caught her gazing vaguely about the room, still looking for the missing earring.

"No. Why?"

"Just wondering."

At lunchtime, remembering Greg's rather runic question, Eva went into the news agency across the street and checked the shelves. There it was. Right on the cover of *Time* under the headline "Changing Cold War Relationships."

The photograph featured a frantic-looking Jim O'Donnell staring down at the tiny Moscow ragamuffin. The neckline of the child's dress had slid off her shoulder a little and her arms were wrapped so tightly around his leg that her head appeared to be nestling just above Jim's knee while her bare feet were planted firmly on his shoelaces. Jim's golden maple leaf lapel pin was caught by the setting sun, as were some coins in his hand which he seemed about to offer the child – although Eva knew that he was actually about to throw the money as far away from her as he could. A street sign in Cyrillic in the background said *Arbat*.

The photo credit inside the front cover simply read *John Curran, Reuters*. Eva smiled wistfully.

Back at her desk, her secretary mimed that she had a persistent caller on the line, and when Eva took the call she heard John's warm voice ask, "Do you fancy a cup of Russian tea, or will it be something stronger this evening?"

"Oh, John, how good to hear from you. I'm sorry, I can't see you tonight. I have to look after the twins. But how about tomorrow?"

"I'm due in Boston tomorrow, but don't worry about a babysitter – I've spoken to Juliet and it's all arranged for this evening."

"What?"

"Yes, I did a little research, then phoned Juliet and explained to her that your one genuine chance for love and happiness forever is in town tonight and you must be free to have dinner with me. It turns out that not only is she extremely pleased by the prospect of the personally autographed photograph of Julie Andrews that I'm going to get for her, but also she earnestly wants you to seize this chance for love – even though she chose to describe it, rather inaccurately I thought, as a 'long shot.' She and the twins are meeting us at the restaurant for Shirley Temples and hors d'oeuvres so that they can check me out before leaving you alone with me, which seems reasonable enough."

"Don't I have any say in this?"

"Yes, of course. Do you prefer red or white wine? By the way, how was the caviar?"

"It was very good."

"Fine, then. See you at Fenton's at seven."

As she put down the phone, Eva looked up and saw a trace of something shiny caught on the underside of the venetian blinds. It was her missing earring.

Chapter 44: In the Alternative

A last-minute call from a member of her board made Eva a little late arriving at Fenton's, but no one at the Curran table seemed even to notice. The twins were busy peppering John with questions while Juliet sat smiling and reading the cover notes on the CD of Julie Andrew's greatest hits that John had brought for her.

"Hi, Mom, guess what?" asked Felicity, suddenly alerted to her mother's arrival by the fact that John had stood up from his place at the table in well-mannered greeting. "John has twins, too!"

"Yes," he smiled. "Yet another good omen. But my twins are girls and they're almost twenty years old."

"And they are *identical,*" added Teddy.

"Named Genevieve and Josephine," added Felicity, not to be outdone.

"We were going through a bit of a French phase," explained John with just the hint of a blush.

"And look what he brought us," added Teddy, holding up a large, glossy photograph book. "He brought us a copy of a book about twins!"

Eva looked carefully at the proffered book. "If I knew you better I'd accuse you of inventing the twins to make us seem more alike," she laughed.

"That's an idea," agreed John, thoughtfully.

"I like your book title – *In the Alternative* – said Evaline. "It's a legal usage, of course, but it covers such an interesting range of possible meanings. I'm surprised I haven't seen your book before. People are always giving me twin stuff, but if I'd seen this one I probably would have bought it for myself."

"Only published in the United Kingdom," John volunteered modestly. "And not a huge print run at that. Nice catch on the legal meaning."

"More than just a pretty face," Eva returned.

Eva sat quietly for a bit, just turning pages, while the server brought drinks for everyone, including a club soda for her. "Best to stay cold sober for a bit," she thought.

"It looks just fascinating. All these pictures of twins looking like negatives or shadows or multiplied in funny mirrors. I also particularly like the captions written by the subjects. Mostly they seem to be struggling to explain what it feels like to know that they have a kind of parallel existence."

"Are Genevieve and Josephine in the book?"

"Oh yes. That's how it all started. I used to play with them and the camera, letting them try to take pictures of themselves and each other. At first I was just trying to create a record of their lives, but then my project changed into something much more complex. As they grew older the three of us tried to figure out how elements of the twin experience could be portrayed in photographs. Doppelgangers, negatives, black and white, the meaning of colour... we had avid conversations over the years on all manner of variations."

Realizing they were monopolizing the conversation, Eva redirected herself to the kids and asked, "What have you ordered for your hors d'oeuvres?"

"I picked frog's legs," reported Teddy, "but Felicity wanted chicken fingers and they don't have any. John asked them to try to make some out of a chicken breast. And Juliet is having gravlax which she says is just a fancy word for smoked salmon."

"Now how about some champagne?" offered John. "Juliet and I have started the bottle in the ice bucket over there without you, but I'm sure there's still some left."

Once Juliet and the children had left the restaurant, armed with a cab fare for a quick journey home, the table seemed deliciously quiet.

"A toast to our first date," suggested John, holding up his champagne glass.

169

"Maybe a little more biographical information about you before we get to that," Eva demurred. "I don't know what we talked about back on Arbat Street, but clearly I'm still short of a few details about your life. You, on the other hand, seem to have done quite a thorough job on me. I'm not even certain I realised that you live in Toronto. You seemed more like a citizen of the world to me."

"So, what do you want to know?"

"Let's start with the current whereabouts of the mother of your twins."

"Ah yes, the indefatigable Marianne," John sighed. "Actually, indefatigable might not be the perfect adjective for her since she did manage to become fatigued with me. Marianne is an interior decorator and she's very dedicated to her clients and their projects. She just found over time that she didn't feel so dedicated to our marriage. She was happy enough to move to Toronto from Montreal with me when the twins were ready to start school, but I realise now that such a big change in culture and surroundings must have been harder for her than either of us had anticipated."

John continued, "I was away a lot, shooting photos at centenaries and panda weddings and trouble-spots, and it was a lonely life for her trying to work and raise the twins with only intermittent help and companionship. It certainly wasn't her fault that she found someone else to keep her company, though I probably would have preferred it not to have been our accountant."

"So what did you do?"

"It seemed best for the twins that I simply bow out gracefully. They were getting older and were free to see me whenever they wanted to. Privately, they told me it was great to see their mother happy and that they would like me to 'get happy' too."

"And what about the accountant?"

"Oh, I still use him, of course. A really good tax accountant is almost impossible to find. Besides, I figured that the scandalous amount of money I pay him for his tax work would be spent, at least in part, on the well-being of my daughters."

"That makes sense," mused Eva, finally accepting the proffered glass of champagne.

Chapter 45: A Private Affair

After a short period of time and a lot of serious thought, John and Eva eloped. John claimed that he'd asked Eva to marry him while they were sharing yet another glass of champagne after the awards ceremony where *Jim and the Gypsies*, as they called his *Time* shot, won the prize for best magazine cover photograph. But Eva insisted that John was suffering from 'recovered proposal memory syndrome.' There never was an actual proposal of marriage, she swore, simply a tacit understanding dating back almost to Arbat Street that they would marry and that the only questions ever entertained were exactly when and where.

Although private, the nuptials were carefully planned, with Eva a vision in silver taffeta carrying a rose bouquet copied from a photo that she had cut out of *Vogue* magazine, and John resplendent in a new Armani tuxedo. While they were attended at their wedding only by Eva's brother Dean and his wife Gibby, both of them sworn to deepest secrecy, Eva and John still wanted there to be a genuine sense of ritual, reflecting the traditions in which they had both grown up and the future they hoped to share.

Eva had been momentarily unsettled when the florist phoned on the day before the wedding to check on the details of the bouquet.

"Did you realise that the roses in the bouquet in the photograph you gave me are framed by stalks of wheat?" the florist asked.

"No, but why would I mind that?" she replied.

"Well, wheat is a fertility symbol, and I know you have children already, so I wasn't sure if you'd want to tempt fate."

"Of course I would!" Eva replied, laughing. "We're not finished with all that yet."

Later, during the rehearsal in the local cathedral, the dean mentioned in passing that he intended to substitute the 'be fruitful and multiply' part of the service with something more suitable for a mature couple.

"No way," was John's considered response.

"You'd think getting married in your forties automatically transfers you to Death's Waiting Room," he joked to Eva later.

"At least we were granted the 'life experience' credit," said Eva, "so we didn't have to attend the preparation for marriage classes."

It was a beautiful autumn day, briefly overcast just before they went into the cathedral and then sunny and warm when they came out. In fact, the whole wedding was as special as John and Eva had hoped. Dean and Gibby were perfect witnesses and, in the spirit of the event, John produced a bottle of Dom Perignon that he'd been saving for a special occasion.

"I guess this probably just about qualifies as 'special,'" he volunteered with a cheeky smile.

The "twins squared," as John liked to call them collectively, were not greatly pleased that they had only learned about the wedding at a special dinner at the Keg Mansion which Eva and John hosted for them a couple of days later. Still, one unanticipated benefit of their pained and widely aired disappointment was that it served to bond the four children more closely together, even though Felicity and Teddy were sometimes simply "teenagers" to the more worldly Curran girls.

While John was gently but determinedly unapologetic with their kids, Eva was a little more bolshie. "Where is it written that children should be allowed to attend their parents' wedding?" she asked rhetorically. "This wasn't about you – it was about us."

Despite what Eva believed was the reasonableness of her position, and despite John's unwavering support, Felicity and Genevieve found it impossible to forgive the couple their transgression, while Teddy and Josephine remained resolutely unimpressed with Eva and John's "childish" behaviour.

Chapter 46: Miss Congeniality

Eva was on a professional roll. The Russian venture was progressing, albeit slowly, Futurity's transmission business was steadily winning new customers, and *Vault!* had attracted an American network that was looking to co-produce an "out-of-the-box, no gimmick-resisted" health and fitness show.

Eva had also been approached by a specialist recruiter who wanted to know if she was ready to consider joining a corporate board. At least as important in an immediate sense, as far as Eva was concerned, was that she had finally found herself a really skilled dressmaker who was able to deliver the classic yet dramatic look Eva favoured.

Staff meetings at Futurity were spirited affairs where all of the vice-presidents felt comfortable suggesting new projects – some of which were decidedly off the wall, but Eva rather enjoyed listening to unusual ideas. She was in a particularly relaxed frame of mind when the *BarBelles* idea was suggested, and, as the famously rueful phrase goes, it seemed like a good idea at the time.

A pair of entrepreneurs with minor successes to their credit had approached Futurity's VP of development, Kevin Jones, with the idea of a specialty television service to be sold to bars and pubs using footage from hundreds, even thousands, of beauty contests and pageants. *BarBelles* would be pitched to potential customers as a way for bars to attract more female clientele while providing wholesome-yet-girlie entertainment for those males who might glance over at a screen filled with beauty contestants when their football game breaks for a commercial.

The concept seemed to make at least some sense to Eva. Like most women of her age, when she was a young girl she had quite enjoyed watching beauty pageants – imagining what it must be like to be a contestant and thinking about how she would walk and what she would say and do if ever she had the chance. She understood why American Beauty Queen Barbie was such a best seller: It was because from a very young age many girls love to daydream of being both beautiful... and a winner.

"What about your feminist principles?" asked John when Eva outlined the proposed venture. "It sounds to me like *BarBelles* will do everything to women that you say you're against. You're proposing to fill television screens in bars with pictures of women who are competing for attention solely on the basis of their looks."

"Oh, John, we don't have to take ourselves so seriously all the time. I like to think that a venture like this would show that even I have a sense of humour. More importantly, it looks like it could be a good money-maker. Besides, we do intend to have a section that focuses on the winners of the Miss Congeniality part of the contest. Many contestants claim that being seen as having a pleasant and accommodating personality is much more important than being recognised for something as shallow as looks alone."

"I'm truly amazed that you could utter all of that drivel while managing to maintain a straight face," said John, intentionally not smiling for emphasis. "Let me rephrase one of my favourite quotations to fit the situation. What I think you really just said to me is "If *I* don't like *my* principles, I have others.'"

"I'll match you quote for quote," replied Eva. "Oscar Wilde and I both believe that 'consistency is the last refuge of the unimaginative.' Besides, I prefer to describe *BarBelles* as a chance to give women an equal place on the television screens in the bars of the nation."

John snorted and slowly shook his head.

Later that evening, John suggested that *Totty on TV* would be a better name for the bar TV service.

"Too British," Eva replied dismissively.

As the plans gathered momentum, Kevin set up a lunch with the entrepreneurs, Dick Dee and Rick Blass, so that Eva could get a sense of the men who would be their partners in the venture. Dick and Rick's proposed contribution to the enterprise, apart from the original and rather clever-seeming idea for the service, was that they had a line on some surplus American satellite transmission capacity that could be used to help get *BarBelles* up and running at a very low cost. According to them, from their discussions to date, the supplier would be willing to enter into an agreement where the amount to be paid for transmission would only ramp up as the number of participating bars increased, and would top out at a pre-negotiated figure.

In his briefing the day before the meeting, Kevin explained to Eva that Dick and Rick were not the type of individuals she normally would choose to work with. He acknowledged that they were a little "rough around the edges" and might even seem a bit "sleazy" to her, but he assured her that he had checked them out and they did appear to be able to deliver the transmission deal they were promising.

Kevin was totally right. Eva did not like Dick and Rick much at all and she found their conversation full of bullshit stories and personal aggrandisement. They talked with their mouths full and Dick was wearing white socks with his shiny dark suit. She couldn't wait to get back to the office. But, whether Kevin had intended it or not, his preparatory talk with her had succeeded in inoculating Eva against trusting her own intuition and judgment.

Sadly, John was off on a shoot and did not hear the details about the lunch with Tweedle Dumb and Tweedle Dee, as Eva had named them, until a week or so later. She had considered referring to them jointly as Dreck, but feared that might be too close to the truth.

"Those guys don't sound like the kind of people you should be doing business with," said John, sounding genuinely worried.

"I know, I know," admitted Eva, almost wringing her hands. "But the deal is on the board agenda for next week, and my chair really likes it. He agrees that the idea seems pretty sound. Also, with the ramp-up transmission deal we aren't risking much as long as we can get a lot of bars to sign up with us. Our business plan says we need to sign 20 bars a week, but Kevin and the Tweedles assure me that they can sign up three times that number."

"Anyway, tell me more about your girlish dreams of being a beauty queen," asked John, deftly changing the direction of the conversation. "It seems to me that my youthful enthusiasm for the milkmaid competition at the county fair is a very far cry from the kind of network televised competitions for Miss Canada and Miss Universe that you've described to me."

Eager to explain herself, Eva began enthusiastically: "I guess I started watching beauty contests on television when I was about twelve. It seemed almost magical – as if the contestants were vying to be chosen as princesses. I used to try to put myself in the place of the judges while at the same time wondering how I would perform if I had the chance. I always knew I wasn't really pretty enough, but it was fun to dream."

"Pretty enough?" interjected John. "Strange that there's this one whole area where you always seem determined to sell yourself short. You sure seem pretty enough to me. As a matter of fact, when I first saw you, you were the prettiest woman on the entire street."

"Arbat Street. Humph. The only other women on the street that day were tired babushkas trying to sell some trinkets. Anyway, that just shows how little you know about the art of enhanced beauty. Even now I still don't know how to apply makeup properly or to walk gracefully down stairs in high heels, and I certainly don't have a demonstrable talent. You see, the format for these competitions has long been established. The competitors are judged in three major categories: swim suit, talent, and, lastly, personality and intelligence."

She continued, "Of course the swim suit phase is generally accepted as the real beauty focus of the pageants, but winners also have to put up a reasonable show of talent and then conclude by appearing in a beautiful dress and demonstrating an ability to answer questions in front of a large audience. That last bit is kind of an echo of the age of debutantes, when young women of gentility were introduced to society in a whirl of white dresses.

"I knew from the start that I didn't have the figure for a beauty contest, but I still paid a lot of attention to what kind of talent the winners displayed. Being able to play a musical instrument – especially the piano – is a real asset, as is a good singing voice and certain kinds of dancing. But my favourite talent demonstration of all time was by the contestant whose skill was in packing a suitcase."

"Are you being serious?"

"Yes. She walked onto a set where there was a large empty suitcase resting on the floor beside a table. She put the suitcase on the table, opened it, and then filled it, expertly, with clothes and shoes. I think there was a time limit, but I'm not sure."

"Amazing," yawned John.

"You sound bored just hearing about it all, but a lot of tension and drama is built into the competitions, with around ten winners surviving the swimsuit phase, and maybe five left after the talent. Then there's the live questioning of the finalists to see how well they can think on their feet. Points are given for avoiding controversy – in other words banality – and for personal charm, although they don't describe the judging that way. But it's clear that no one is looking for incisive or even thought-provoking answers.

"The correct answers to most of the questions, the highest scoring ones, are "world peace" or "finding a solution to world hunger," that sort of thing. I used to imagine that it would be refreshing and perhaps even clinch the title if one of the finalists gave a truly individual answer."

"Like what?" asked John.

"Oh, I don't know, like saying that she wanted to help eradicate malaria by supporting the charity that focuses on providing mosquito nets to protect against disease-causing bites."

"And you don't think that would win it now?"

"No, sadly, I don't. From what I've read about the beauty industry preparing for this channel, individualism is still not rewarded. There is, however, a consolation prize for being sweet and helpful and no real threat for the real crown. The women who fall into that category get to be Miss Congeniality. But if you really want to win a beauty title you need to seriously embrace world peace."

"Has that realization put you off the project, Eva?"

"No – I think I've long known that beauty contests are geared to reward conformity."

Eva thought for a moment and went on: "In essence, I'd argue that beauty contests are about art and the ideal of feminine beauty, and that they tell us something important about what our society values. And, over the years, for some women they have provided the ticket to wealth and celebrity that sports prowess has traditionally provided to some young men."

"Nice social commentary, Eva, but I still don't quite understand how you're going to explain all this to your feminist friends."

"I don't think I'll even try," admitted Eva reluctantly. "Let's just hope they don't hang out in bars with lots of TVs."

Chapter 47: Choppy Waters

BarBelles elicited the expected jokes when it was presented to Futurity's board, but most of the directors actually liked the idea. During the discussion Brian Wales, a comparatively new board member and no particular fan of Eva's, conspicuously circled the rather optimistic revenue forecasts on the page in front of him but made no vocal objection to the company proceeding to launch the service.

Kevin and the Dicks, as John privately called them, were unleashed to get bars signed up for the launch, and the programming procurement team was challenged to confirm those deals where they could get the most footage possible for the least amount of money.

Eva turned her attention back to Futurity's overall operations while at the same time trying to address her twins' back-to-school needs. Reasonably dispassionate about business, she found questions about organizational structure and capital investment much easier than those concerning most aspects of her children's education.

For years, first with some help from Leo, and later with more from John, Eva had tried to make intelligent decisions about the twins' education based on the pot pourri of liberal values that she had accumulated. As Eva described it, she was struggling "personfully" to ensure that her children were prepared to be useful, decent and honest citizens of the world. To her, this included having them grow up believing that while differences in race and religion could be interesting, they are not defining.

Some years back, when kindergarten student Felicity had reported over dinner that her friend Sinikka could speak two languages, "Finnish and human," Eva had realised how easy it is to grow up believing that *our way* is the only right way. As a result she had sought out schools where the twins shared a classroom with students from varied economic and cultural backgrounds. Believing that they were both now pretty much on track in the *one world* approach to life, she had shifted her focus towards actively encouraging them to express themselves as individuals, not each of them as half of a pair. For his part, John felt that her concern about ensuring the twins' separateness was misplaced, but Gen and Jo assured him that he still had a lot to learn about raising twins.

In an effort to foster individuality, Eva urged Felicity and Teddy to choose different high schools. During weekly family dinners, Genevieve and Josephine pitched in with plenty of advice and insight of their own. After much angst and talking on the telephone for hours – reliving the day in real time with her many friends and then exhaustively dissecting their respective options for the future – Felicity chose to go to a school for performing arts, while Teddy considered his alternatives carefully and then chose the school for science nerds.

"I have no experience with this stuff," confessed Eva to John as she sat doing the family mending. Despite Juliet's willingness to take it on, Eva found tasks like replacing missing buttons somehow soothing. "I just went to the high school in the district where I grew up. Its greatest selling feature was a curling rink, although I didn't even fully appreciate that benefit until I took up curling."

"I did too," agreed John, "Not the curling – I mean I also went to school where I grew up. But I don't think you should worry too much, love," he continued. "While I still haven't entirely worked out the ingredients of a happy life, I doubt that where you go to high school is hugely decisive, at least not in North America. Sadly, I think it still may matter quite a bit in the UK."

"Well I hope you're right," muttered Eva, sufficiently anxious and distracted that she accidentally sewed Felicity's nametag on Teddy's new gym shorts.

Spirits were high as the Futurity team crammed onto a Lake Ontario cruise ship for the autumn dinner party to kick off the new fiscal year. The company's growth and vibrancy was apparent in the number and style of those aboard. One of the "old-timers" got a little carried away and started regaling the newer staff with stories of how the crowd was small enough in the early years that there were enough life vests for everyone, but Kevin put a quick stop to that when he caught a glimpse of Eva's face.

The loftily titled "cruise" simply involved motoring a few miles out onto the lake, then cruising in gentle circles until it was time to make a leisurely trip back, but the relaxation and good food and drink meant that most people had quite a lot of fun.

"Eva, you look white as a ghost," remarked Richard Olsen as the ship began a lazy turn back towards shore.

"Yes, I'm feeling a bit seasick. I guess I shouldn't have eaten all those shrimp – or maybe it was the Margaritas. 'Scuse me while I find the Ladies."

Eva didn't resurface to lead the conga line around the main deck as she had done the year before, but a lot of the younger staff had been drinking Harvey Wallbangers and B52s and they had plenty of momentum of their own.

When John got home from assignment the next evening, Eva was still feeling rather ill. Juliet, Teddy and Felicity each took him aside and told him that he really ought to make her stay in bed and get properly better.

"I hear you have some kind of bug," he greeted, coming into their bedroom to find her tucked up under the cashmere blanket he'd given her for Christmas. "Anything I can do to help?"

"Oh I'm *so* glad you're home. Yes, there's much you can do to help. First, come and sit here beside me and tell me about your trip."

"Tiring. I spent all my time following presidents and prime ministers around trying to catch them in an unguarded moment. And they spent all their time trying to make sure that they didn't have even one. What about you? Can I get you something to eat or drink? Some ginger ale, maybe?"

"No thanks. There's really nothing wrong with me that a visit to a hospital in about eight months won't cure."

"Oh," said John after a second or two of startled reflection. "So the wheat worked. How wonderful!" His eyes teared up a little as he beamed at her.

"I know. This is just what we hoped for. But we have a really long way to go yet."

"Of course," whispered John. And then, with Eva's hand wrapped around a couple of his fingers, he sat on the bed for a while, just thinking and hoping she might get some more rest.

Eva and John confided in no one about their expected baby. Nevertheless, at times when they were alone together they shared a few hopes and dreams and tried out various names.

Chapter 48: Blows to All Our Hopes

Paula Fredrick, Eva's former colleague from her Cumberland days, with whom she had maintained contact over the years, had moved on to manage the administrative side of a Toronto law office. She loved the work, which was a perfect fit for her energy and initiative. Somewhat surprisingly, she had been a great source of comfort when Leo died, and since then Eva often called upon her for practical wisdom.

It was over a lunch of udon and edamame at a new Japanese restaurant that Eva confided to Paula that Kevin and his team had so far been unable to convince most of the important bar operators to sign up for *BarBelles*. It was due to go live in one month and all they had secured were 107 bars.

"Somehow," she sighed, looking bleakly at the pile of empty green bean pods in front of her, "rather than seeing failure as a spur to more effort, they seem to be spending most of their time these days coming up with excuses for their lack of success."

"I do have one idea," suggested Paula. "A friend of mine who works in real estate says that the best way to get an agent to focus on getting your house sold is to call the agent every day and ask how many showings they've had and how many showings they have lined up. He says that even though it's irritating, the relentless focus from the client on showing the house does make the agent give priority to that property, if for no other reason than to stop having to hear your voice on the phone every day."

"What a good approach! I think I'll ask Kevin to call me late every afternoon to let me know how many additional bars they've signed up."

"I must admit," added Paula, "I'm surprised that *BarBelles* is a tough sell. I would've thought bar keepers would be eager to get it."

"The main problem seems to be the level of investment in technology required," explained Eva. "It turns out our cheap US satellite transmission space is on a satellite that most of our potential customers don't currently receive, and the cost of additional receiving equipment just doesn't seem worth it to them. So they all want to wait and see if the service takes off before they make any investment."

"Have you thought about just providing the necessary equipment and amortizing it?" asked Paula, a natural businesswoman.

"I did, but the capital outlay is simply too great. I just have to rely on my team to keep selling the idea to the point where no respectable barkeep would want to be without *BarBelles*."

Elsewhere in Eva's geopolitical sphere of operations, power was rapidly shifting from Gorbachev to Yeltsin, who had proven to have more nerve – even if, as rumoured, it was partly fuelled by vodka – and the Soviet Union was becoming Russia while most of the European countries which had for decades been part of the Soviet bloc saw the exit lights and started to head for them. Meanwhile it was increasingly difficult, even for the Futurity connections situated in Moscow, to figure out with whom to negotiate over the future of Cancosmos.

"I can't figure out why tanks in front of buildings take precedence over my carefully translated missives about the need for a market penetration strategy," Eva observed dryly to John. "Maybe my adverbs are not compelling enough. Or could it be my adjectives?"

As the weeks passed, despite her explicit instructions, Kevin did not call Eva every day to report progress in signing up customers for *BarBelles*. At first it was every other day, and then he quit initiating calls altogether, although he did still answer the phone when Eva called. The service had started up in pilot mode, and it seemed as funny and fun as she had hoped, but expenses were adding up much more quickly than new customers. Sadly, it was increasingly evident that even though they'd spent quite a lot on start-up research they had either not asked all the right questions, or had not been given all the right answers, and they seemed to be up a creek with a teaspoon instead of a paddle.

After grilling the team once more about signing prospects and the steeply climbing run rate of the service's costs, Eva scheduled a meeting with Bill Arkwright to break the news that *BarBelles* looked like a failure. Despite all the cleverness employed by her CFO in minimizing the impact of the losses, Eva knew that announcing the abandonment of *BarBelles* at her quarterly results meeting was going to result in a small dent in her earnings and a much bigger dent in her reputation.

The twins were out at Bronze Medallion life-saving training and Juliet was away for the weekend when John came home to find Eva again in bed, this time right under the sheets and the duvet. That she was lying staring at a performance by the World Wrestling Federation on the bedroom TV right away signalled that the news was bad.

"Oh, sweetheart," he whispered, taking Eva into his arms. "What happened that has brought you this low? You hate wrestling."

"I lost it," she sobbed. "At first I had a bad pain but I thought that might be because I had to tell the board on a conference call that we were cancelling *BarBelles*. Then I had a bad feeling all over and the baby just went away. I feel so sad. I feel like a real failure. First I screwed up with *BarBelles*, then Cancosmos got caught up in politics and now I've lost the baby and really ruined everything."

John was quiet for a moment, and then he joined Eva under the duvet, still wearing his navy suit, pink silk tie and black brogues.

"Not quite everything," John cautioned her. "You're still stuck with me and the twins squared. And none of us is ruined yet. So, I have to tell you that your ruinous work here is not yet complete."

He lay quietly beside her for some time, holding her hand, and then he suggested, "Let's think of this baby as Baby Celeste, because she would undoubtedly have been heavenly. And I know the next one will be, too. But let's hope that it's also a little more down to earth and able to stay here with us for a really long time."

The room darkened, then the twins came clattering home and shouted a greeting as they dropped their swimming gear and headed out to a movie.

"I have a suggestion for your business problems," John at last volunteered. "I think you should think about how to get Gorbachev to help launch *BarBelles* in the Republic of Georgia. He seems to be without a job these days, and he might be a real help. I bet Raisa would enjoy watching the occasional beauty contest while Gorby sucks back a few vodkas..."

Eva laughed, wiping her eyes. "When I was in Russia I learned that they don't have very many TV channels. I don't know if you ever turned on the TV while you were there, but one evening, probably the night when there was no food at the restaurant, I worked out that they were running the same programming on both channel 2 and channel 7, and that channels 9 and 5 were identical. I also determined that channel 5 had the same programming as 2, and that all the rest of the channels were blank. In other words, there was only one actual channel."

"A perfect market for *BarBelles*, don't you think?"

"One thing that really bugs me is that the new board member, Brian Wales, with his not-so-subtle underlining of the board presentation, turns out to be right. I just hate proving my doubters right."

"Well, he taught you something."

"What's that?"

"Even your detractors aren't always wrong."

"You know, if I wasn't feeling so totally devastated I'd be upset that you got into bed with your shoes on."

"Yes, but you're too upset to be upset and my behaviour was entirely well-intentioned. The situation just seemed to call for a little heedless action. Now let's have a cuddle and a nap."

"I should look at the time. Ugh. I promised I'd order pizza for the kids and their friends to eat after the movie. No attenuated mourning for us, I guess."

"It may not be enough time, but it's all we get," smiled John, wisely.

Chapter 49: Boardom

As John had anticipated, events moved on quickly and Eva's various setbacks took their respective places in her personal history. Futurity was prospering overall, the twins liked high school, John had a number of assignments close to home, and Eva's health and good spirits fully returned.

Bill Arkwright greatly appreciated Eva's resilience. He agreed with the school of thought that a large measure of business success comes from being willing to keep trying new ideas with the expectation that a reasonable percentage will turn out right.

"We all make mistakes," he shrugged when one of Futurity's board members suggested to him that Eva's salary increase should be lower than originally planned. "If earnings suffer, or the stock price suffers, because she made a small error in judgment, her total income suffers too. But I don't think you should underestimate the punishment that she has already meted out to herself."

Political scandals, a pending federal election and the continuing rise of separatism in Quebec provided plenty of distraction for everyone. Eva was asked to make a comment for a newspaper article on the trials of modern female leaders and she instead suggested the reporter talk to the recently defeated Prime Minister, Kim Campbell.

"Just ask *her* what it's like," she advised.

One quiet afternoon Eva received two very disparate calls.

Around two-thirty her assistant told her there was a man on the line who said that he needed her help in a venture he was operating in North Carolina. Mildly curious, she agreed to take the call.

As she picked up the receiver, a booming masculine voice greeted her with "Hello, Eva, this is Mr. Wesley."

"Hello, Mr. Wesley," she answered a bit ironically, "what can I do for you?"

"I understand that your company originates a satellite service called *Vault!* and I happened to catch some of its programmes the other day. I really liked what I saw. You see, Eva, I run a chain of fitness clubs down here called Fit for All and I was hoping you'd let me beam your channel into my clubs. It would help make my premises a bit different from my competitors."

"Thank you so much for the compliment, Mr. Wesley. I'm glad you found our service entertaining. Unfortunately, my channels are not licenced to run in your area."

"Oh, that shouldn't be a problem. All I need is for you to send me down one of your decoding machines and I can put your channel on my closed circuit system here. I'm sure that free exposure for your advertisers to the high-end clientele who patronise my clubs would provide a big boost for you."

"Patronise, what a good word," Eva thought.

"I'm very sorry Mr. Wesley, but I don't think your plan will work. I can send you some tapes of one of our shows, though, if you want to run them on a video tape player in your lounge."

"You know, Eva, if the cost of shipping the decoder is a problem for you, I could help out with the postage."

"Thanks anyway, Mr. Wesley. If you don't mind leaving your address with my assistant she will arrange to mail those tapes. I have to go now – I'm late for a meeting. Good-bye."

"Did I hear right?" asked Sherri, Eva's assistant, putting her head around the door after taking down Mr. Wesley's address in laborious detail. "When I passed over the call, did he actually say 'Hello, Eva, this is Mr. Wesley'?"

"Yes, he sure did. I guess it was a helpful reminder of how far we still have to go. He said he runs a chain called Fit for All, but after talking to him I think it probably should be renamed Fit to be Tied."

The other call was rather more salutary. Sherri's interruption, "Call from Jean Montaigne," put a smile in Eva's voice. Jean had been a good and loyal client of Eva's at Paradigm and they enjoyed comparing impressions when they had the chance.

"Hi, Eva. How's your French?"

"*Affreux*, Jean, but I don't have to tell you. You heard that pitiful speech I gave the other day at the luncheon. And that was after quite a lot of practice."

"You're too hard on yourself. I think you speak the language well, albeit with a charming Western Canadian accent."

"What a nice way to put it. Are you in town and available for a lunch, or are you calling from your office with a lovely view of Mount Royal?"

"Sadly, I'm not near enough for lunch. The reason for my call is to find out how you might feel if someone approached you about joining the board of a company based here in Quebec. I was out to dinner the other night with some other CEOs and one of them asked me if I knew of a smart woman from Ontario who could handle board meetings in French, and I thought of you."

"What a kind thought, Jean, but I don't know if I have the time. I'd have to ask my board."

"I guessed that. So I took the opportunity to test the idea with Bill Arkwright and he thought it might be good for you. 'A real stretching exercise' I think he called it."

"Did he? Like the rack, you mean?"

"I imagine he was thinking more along the lines of something you'd do while watching one of your fitercise programs."

"Well, thanks, Jean. We'll see. I'll talk it over with Bill myself and get back to you within a week."

Two weeks later Sherri told Eva that Bill Arkwright's assistant had insisted that she make space in Eva's busy calendar for a meeting with a man called Andre Rivière, who was flying in from Montreal. He'd been described to her as chair of a pulp and paper company called Coureurs de Bois and he claimed it was urgent that they meet.

Andre was a real charmer. As Eva told Paula later, "It was as if Maurice Chevalier had flown in to give me a private performance of *I'm glad I'm not young anymore*, so of course I agreed to join his board."

"And how was the first board meeting?"

"Very French. I had to go out and find a special French glossary with words like "chain saw" and "lumberjack" in it. Unfortunately, *grève*, which means strike, seems to be quite an important word, too."

"Have fun," laughed Paula.

"*Mais oui!* As long as they don't find out that I thought I was voting for a motion with a show of hands when all they'd asked was who wanted more coffee..."

Chapter 50: Management is the Art of Getting Things Done Through People

One of the key "people" principles of Futurity, copied from the best practices of other companies, was that an employee was entitled to request a meeting with a senior executive if they felt they had been unfairly dealt with. Not many employees availed themselves of this opportunity since, regardless of how discreetly they were managed, such meetings drew a lot of attention, most of it unwanted.

So it was somewhat surprising to Eva when Sherri advised her that a young woman who had recently been released from the call centre had scheduled an interview with her. In preparation for the meeting, Eva learned that, simply put, the former employee had not been suited for the job and her supervisor's impression was that she did not particularly disagree with him when he suggested that she might be more comfortable working elsewhere.

In was late in the day when Sherri brought in a pleasant-looking and quite substantial young woman in her mid-twenties and introduced her as Consolation Jesperson.

"Hello Ms. Jesperson. I see you've already been given a coffee; can I get anything else for you?"

"No, thank you. I guess you've heard that I was let go from the call centre, and I just wanted to come by and tell you about my problems with working there."

"I'd be very interested to hear what you have to say. Do you mind if I call you Consolation, or do you prefer something else? You can call me Eva."

"My mother always tells me that she had me as a consolation in her old age, so that's what I got called. I don't like being called Connie because people think it's short for Constance, and that's not my name."

"So, Consolation, tell me about your experiences in the call centre."

"I came here to tell you that place is not a good place to be. For one thing, all they expect you to do there is work."

"What do you mean?"

"It's like this. When I go in to work in the morning, I have social needs. I can't just sit down right away and start working. I need to talk to my friends, find out if their boyfriend was good, get some coffee, look at the *Metro* paper I picked up in the subway, things like that. It just isn't healthy to expect people to sit down and start working right away." Gaining confidence, she continued, "My supervisor, Alan, mostly wanted me to just sit down and put on the headphones and get answering calls. Some days we started with a team meeting where we were supposed to talk about the customers. Well, I told him I can't think about customers until I know how my friends are feeling and I've had a chance to get my brain clear. It was when I said that to Alan last week that he told me he thought I'd be able to have a clearer brain in a different kind of work and we agreed that I should find another job."

"And how do you feel about it now?"

"Oh, I feel okay. I think I'm going to go work at my uncle's doughnut store. He got himself a Tim Horton's franchise and he's offering work to all us now."

"So, you just wanted to tell me that you thought the expectation that you sit down and answer the telephone at the call centre without some 'warm-up time' for socializing was too demanding?"

"Yes. I don't believe your managers at that centre think enough about how people want to be."

"How interesting. Well, thank you for taking the time to see me, Consolation," said Eva, standing to assist Miss Jesperson in realizing it was time for her to move towards the door. "You truly have opened my eyes to a different way of approaching work. And I wish you the very best of luck in your new job."

"Thanks, Ms. Sadlier – I mean Eva. They told me you'd be interested in what I had to say."

"I'm sure they did," murmured Eva, looking meaningfully at Sherri before shutting her door.

Chapter 51: Traces of History

Eva was more than overdue for a vacation, so she was delighted by John's suggestion that she accompany him on a shoot in Israel. He'd been commissioned to do a series of photographs for a book called *The Marks of Time* featuring aerial photography of ancient settlement patterns. In Israel, John was going to concentrate in particular on the patterns worn into the earth in AD73 by the besieging Roman soldiers and their encampments – patterns that can still be clearly seen from the heights of Masada.

"Stories about the siege are being revisited by scholars nowadays, but the wear patterns do seem to bear witness to a besieging army settling in to outwait the provisions of those who were trapped inside," explained John over Saturday Indian take-out with the twins squared.

Fascinated by John's task and interested in seeing all of the historical sites that she could, Eva was psychologically ready to leave the next day, although the actual arrangements to cover work and home took quite a while to put into place.

At Masada, the happy couple, dressed in white from head to toe to protect against the desert sun, experienced an interesting juxtaposition of past and future. As John took shots of the siege ramp and the ancient traces of Roman encampment at the base of the rock plateau, and Eva wandered around looking at mosaic tiles dating from Herod's use of Masada as a palace, two Israeli fighter jets flying very low sped past along the Jordanian border. "Menace still lingers in the air," thought Eva.

Afterwards Eva couldn't resist a dip in the Dead Sea, despite the warnings of harm that the minerals in the water would do to the shiny metal discs on her fancy new bathing suit. Heading back to Jerusalem, she was again fascinated by the bleakness and isolation of the caves where the Dead Sea scrolls had been discovered.

On their visit to the Sea of Galilee, Eva felt inspired to sing *I will make you fishers of men* – which John initially found cute but then, after more than enough repetitions, irritating. "It might be better if you could carry a tune," he suggested as they shared a pre-dinner drink, "although even then I'm not certain."

Overall, Eva found herself deeply impressed both with the still-vivid immediacy of the Bible and its stories, even after so many centuries, and by what she was able to learn about the significance to Muslims of the Dome of the Rock. The close jostling for position of the various Christian and Jewish sects also surprised her.

John was happy with his work. The clear dry days and his success in obtaining some fine shots looking down from Masada pleased him greatly. Dinner at a restaurant looking out on the flood-lit walls of Jerusalem after their visit to Moses Montefiore's windmill in Mishkenot Sha'ananim seemed to Eva almost unimaginably exotic.

"Sitting here looking at scars on the ancient wall, inflicted by generations of war, makes me feel very grateful for the life we're sharing," mused Eva. "From our privileged place in the New World we easily forget the centuries of misery and torment that bought our sometimes simplistic notions of 'peace and love.'"

"What I think I've learned from the hippies and the whole California scene is that it's a lot easier to set up a new culture than it is to change an old one. And, to touch on one of your favourite topics, I think that's why the advancement of women is gaining more traction in North America than it has anywhere else," added John.

"I'll drink to that," smiled Eva, holding up her glass of something local with a sparkle.

Chapter 52: A New Tack

Refreshed by her trip to Israel, Eva returned to Futurity determined to try a different approach. Since neither *BarBelles* nor her Russian satellite gambit had turned out to be new sources of revenue, she decided to focus on ways to reduce operating costs.

One large and growing expense item was the cost of transmitting video and data information by satellite. The company was faced with a government-controlled satellite service monopoly with the ridiculous name of StarTrans, and the Futurity organization had long felt that it was being run in a wasteful and inefficient manner.

Eva carefully selected a team whose job it would be to focus on reducing satellite transmission costs, consisting of an external consultant called Michelle Dumont, the new VP Development, Jane Saviour (who had replaced Kevin Jones), and Yves Tibeault, Futurity's head of Finance. At their first meeting the team gave the project the code name "Weed Killer".

The crux of the problem was the regulated rates for transmission that StarTrans was allowed – even required – to charge its customers. Full of cost-cutting zeal, the Weed Killer team, or the Weeders as they began to call themselves, determinedly set out to document exactly how the StarTrans rates came to be authorised by the government.

"I suppose it's better that they chose to call themselves Weeders rather than Killers," thought Eva.

The Futurity executives had believed that they had a pretty good idea of how transmission rates were set, but they were still quite shocked to discover just how straightforward the process really was. First, StarTrans created multiple year budgets for operations and for proposed capital investment, including major expenditures such as new satellites. Next, the StarTrans board, rather uncritically in the collective judgment of the Weeders, approved a rate structure for customers that would support the aspirations reflected by those budgets. Since the StarTrans board included government representatives, no further debate was deemed necessary. Finally, StarTrans management implemented the rates and proceeded to operate with no real motivation to reduce costs or improve efficiency, since such improvements might ultimately lead to a reduction in rates.

After their preliminary survey of the process, the Weeders' recommendation to Eva was that they assemble a fact-based argument as to why and how the rate setting process for StarTrans services would be greatly enhanced by more rigorous debate and challenge – especially from those companies who purchased StarTrans transmission services. True to her consulting roots, Michelle Dumont referred to those customers collectively as the "user community."

The Weeders recommended that since StarTrans was ultimately a tool of government and Futurity was a major user, they could simply obtain the budget details provided to the StarTrans board under Freedom of Information legislation, analyze the submissions, and make constructive recommendations to the parties involved.

Eva liked their ideas. She also suggested that the team look into the official creation of a StarTrans user group, which could manage the ongoing responsibility of making representations to the regulator about rates and practices and even question the ongoing relevance of a satellite transmission monopoly. The Weeders, in turn, liked Eva's idea and the team divvied up the various tasks and agreed to report back in a month.

Chapter 53: Honoris Causa

Eva was delighted by the letter from Banting University inviting her to address their Spring convocation and to receive an honorary doctorate of law. She couldn't wait to call John in New York and share the news.

"How wonderful, darling, and well deserved," applauded John. "And while I can think of many, many reasons, does the letter from Banting indicate why in particular they've chosen to single you out?"

"Let me look... oh, it says something here about 'contributions to the field of communications.' I guess that means they're honouring my propensity to talk a lot. Maybe they've heard of my lifelong tendency to tell family secrets to strangers I meet while sitting on the bus."

"Why else do you think we bought a second car?" asked John. "So, now you have to decide what you want to talk about in your address."

"Already? I was hoping to bask in the glory of my recognition for a little longer than two minutes. It's a tough assignment. One needs to be cogent and memorable, yet funny. I certainly don't want to talk about anything technical. Speeches about gizmos are so boring, and a young audience is guaranteed to be way ahead of you. What do you think a graduating class wants to hear about these days?"

"How to get a good job would be my guess. But I don't think that's what *you* should talk about. Let's ask the twins squared what they think when we get together on Friday."

They had all agreed to meet at their favourite Szechwan restaurant up a filthy flight of stairs in Chinatown, with Eva responsible for driving Teddy and Felicity over, John joining them from the airport, and Gen and Jo walking over together from the university library. John arrived first and was confronted by a crowded restaurant with only a smallish table for four available in the centre of the room. But, being John, by the time the others arrived the small table had been topped with a large circle of plywood which could seat six, hidden under a white tablecloth and several layers of clear plastic and embellished by a Lazy Susan in the centre.

Once seated, the happy party unfortunately did spill over into the personal space that normally would have been allotted to at least two tables nearby, but the pair on their right, who looked like a mother and her fortyish daughter out to catch up over a Chinese meal, smiled tolerantly, and the rumpled academic-looking British couple near the window were very accommodating – even to the point of letting John rest his umbrella on the adjacent window ledge.

After placing their usual order of sweet-and-sour soup, shrimp rolls, mu-shu pork with extra pancakes, curried shrimp without the potatoes, fried rice, steamed rice, crispy orange beef, and broccoli with button mushrooms, the family settled down to catch up and share their recent experiences.

Later, over a delicious dessert of deep-fried egg drop donuts, Eva took the opportunity to ask for advice about the commencement speech she needed to begin writing. "I need your help. I wouldn't want to talk about my personal accomplishments even if I had any that were relevant to the world of communications, and I certainly don't want to relive the failure of *BarBelles* – even for educational purposes. But I would like to be interesting and relevant and maybe even a bit funny."

"I liked the *BarBelles* idea," reassured Josephine, "but if you don't want to talk about your own accomplishments, how about talking about the essence of human communication, about how electronic devices are changing the ways that people interact, stripping away some of the niceties that were previously thought to be essential parts of civility?"

A fine writer herself, Jo was daily engaged in trying to figure out what kind of writing career she wanted to have, and she was preoccupied with media, the different expectations of style and emerging forms of expression.

Genevieve, who was leaning toward a career as a psychologist, expanded on Jo's suggestion. "You know, the psychological research being done on new methods of communication seems to reveal that we're isolating people, stripping away the support of the village or the community from their daily life, leaving them feeling alienated, and then expecting them to be considerate towards others. Keep in mind that people *need* to feel part of something real outside of themselves."

Teddy leaned forward and said; "Last week we had a whole hour in my *The Role of Society* course on the importance of empathy. And one of the things the teacher stressed is that if you can't see someone or hear from or about them, and you don't have to deal with them in your daily life, it's easy to dehumanise them."

"Just like in the Third Reich", added Felicity, and everyone moaned. Ever since she'd done an assignment on Primo Levi and his book *The Drowned and the Saved*, Felicity had exhibited a grim fascination with the Nazis, and she loved to share all the new horrors she learned.

"Let's get the bill," suggested John, "I'm beat."

Chapter 54: Redaction

"This is an outrage," announced Jane Saviour, dropping a large sheaf of black-streaked papers on Eva's desk. "It really upsets me that my taxes are going to pay the salaries of petty bureaucrats who make things difficult for people like us to learn about what they're doing in their expensively furnished offices with panoramic views of Parliament Hill."

"All that, eh?" responded Eva, laconically. Sometimes the fact that she actually said 'eh' embarrassed her, and sometimes she simply viewed this habit of speech as proof that she was *a bona fide* Canadian.

"Look at these documents. After weeks and weeks of waiting they finally send us six hundred pages covered in black whiteout. Or maybe it's supposed to be white blackout. Whatever it is, it sure seems negative. Take this one, for example. There's the title: *Proposed staffing for supervision of new satellite contract*, and the page numbers and two headings called *Proposer* and *Approver* and everything else is blacked out."

Her anger rising, she added, "This morning we all arrived early with high hopes to review the documents, only to realise after less than 15 minutes that there's nothing to analyze. The other Weeders talked about wanting to murder the officials who approved the mutilation of the documents. My response was much more professional; I just wanted to neuter those who had neutered our documents."

"So, what's the plan and can I watch?"

"We called Sam over at Neville & White's and he's going to get in touch with their departmental lawyer and threaten them with an application to the federal court. He doesn't know if it'll work but he thinks it's worth a try."

"Good luck. And how are you progressing with the formation of a StarTrans user group? It's beginning to look like we may really need it."

"That's going really well. It's no big surprise that we aren't their only dissatisfied customer, and most of the companies we've approached have said they'd be happy to contribute time and some money to help get things going and help to hire a director for the association. It turns out that there are management companies that offer shared staff and offices for a start-up like ours, so we're already interviewing a couple of them next week."

"Interesting, that."

"What?"

"The law of unintended consequences. If StarTrans and its executives had been helpful to us and showered us with assistance in our efforts to understand their rates, we might never have had the focus or the energy to work at setting up a user group. Now, if we succeed in getting this user group going, it may turn out to be a thorn in their side forever."

"I personally would like to be a thorn in the side of the person in charge of wielding the black felt pen on all these documents."

Chapter 55: Beyond Words

This time they didn't even hope. Whether it was the exotic mixture of minerals and salts that had seeped into her pores as she floated in the Dead Sea, or the relaxation she'd enjoyed while quietly accompanying John as he practised his photographic art, Eva found herself pregnant again.

They tippy-toed around it, waiting anxiously until it seemed that seven or eight weeks had passed, then going hand in hand to see their favourite general practitioner. One of the many good omens that John and Eva had identified when they really got to know each other was that for many years their families had shared the same GP. "I knew you before you knew you," he sometimes reminded them.

The GP referred them to a clinic for an ultrasound with the comforting advice that 95 per cent of babies who appear viable on the ultrasound at the stage they had reached in the pregnancy go on to be live births. He also gave them instructions on how to make an appointment for genetic counselling.

"I'm sure you both know that Down's is a real risk at your age," he told them, "so you have to think about what kind of testing you'll want and the decisions you might have to make."

John took careful notes about the timing and types of foetus testing available. Well-matched optimists, John and Eva agreed tacitly that they would worry about any difficult decisions that might arise from the tests when they had to, and not before.

Afterward, they would always remember the ultrasound as their own little miracle. It took place in a stripped-down treatment room in an inauspicious clinic; Eva lay on the narrow hospital-style bed while the technician ran a gel-cooled amplifier over her still lean stomach. John sat holding her hand on the far side of the bed so that they could both see the ultrasound monitor, where, to their ever-abiding amazement and joy, a small pulsing light, like a flashing star, was revealed to them, surrounded by abstract amoeba-like shapes of light and dark.

"That pulsing light is the baby's heart," explained the technician.

And so it was.

Chapter 56: Voices in the Wilderness

John and Eva agreed to keep the pregnancy secret until after the foetal abnormality test results were in, and until Eva's embarrassment about looking like she was putting on a lot of weight had reached a threshold that was too hard for her to bear – or to stomach, as she joked to John.

After a rather perfunctory visit to the genetic counsellors, who found John and Eva's collective family medical backgrounds pretty unimaginative, they decided to have amniocentesis – a process designed to detect genetic or developmental problems with the by-product of revealing the baby's gender.

"This is a long way from surprise twins," Eva remarked. John, whose twins had not been a surprise but an anxiously anticipated and rather complicated birth, said nothing.

Back at the office, the Weeders had finally succeeded in wrenching detailed budget documents from the unwilling clutches of the government department responsible for StarTrans, and they were hard at work analyzing them. Their team had turned the little conference room near Eva's office into a workroom, and every day someone stopped by to describe some new outrage that the documents had revealed.

With Yves's agreement, Jane Saviour had appropriated several members of Futurity's smart and energetic finance staff to help with the analysis. Her particular outrage was the discovery that when StarTrans had built a new head office, with a very airy and spacious atrium, the cost of heating and cooling that large empty space in the extremes of the Ottawa climate had been accepted without challenge by the board and incorporated into the rate base.

"As if they didn't already have enough empty space at their disposal. They're a satellite company for heaven's sake!" fumed Jane. "Or should I say 'for stratosphere's sake'?"

Now that they had the information they needed, the task was proceeding quickly, and the Weeders estimate was that a careful and fair vetting of StarTrans' rate base could save the users as much as 15 per cent. For Futurity that would mean millions of dollars a year.

With their analysis almost complete, the team asked Eva to meet with them to discuss how best to approach StarTrans and the government with what they believed to be very reasonable and constructive cost-saving initiatives that would benefit the whole community. Also in attendance was Sam Spencer from Neville & White – Futurity's regulatory legal advisors – who had already warned Eva that any cost-cutting suggestions for StarTrans originating from Futurity were likely to be dismissed as naïve and self-serving. Nevertheless, he stressed, that didn't mean he felt they shouldn't try to be heard. His personal belief was that forming a user's association was their best long-term option.

At the meeting, after considering various alternatives, the Weeders and Eva agreed that their initial approach concerning reduction of the satellite transmission rates, or at least slowing the rate of increase, should be made to the assistant deputy minister, George Barnard, who served as the senior government representative on the StarTrans board. He had only been on the board for a couple of years, and the feeling was that he might be less defensive about the history of the rate-setting process and the array of corporate perks and "glaring inefficiencies" that Futurity had discovered through their analysis.

Were they ever wrong!

The meeting with Barnard started off rather well. Eva, Jane and Michelle caught a midday plane to Ottawa and arrived ten minutes early for their late-afternoon meeting where they were ushered right in to the ADM's office. Somewhat surprisingly, he was unaccompanied, which Eva optimistically construed as an indication of openness and efficiency.

Encouraged by George's relaxed manner, and sensitive to the darkness falling outside the office's enormous windows, the team spent only a little time chatting informally before they launched into their pitch. Convinced that any serious analytical thinker, as Barnard was reputed to be, would immediately see that the users were being overcharged – maybe even exploited – by their supplier, the team were probably too direct and confident in their presentation.

Still, it was a real shock when a red-faced ADM suddenly slammed his briefing binder shut, picked it up off the table, made a noise of disgust directed at the delegation, and stalked out of his office, leaving Eva in mid-sentence. The three women, speechless, sat staring wide-eyed at each other.

After a few extremely confusing minutes, the ADM came back in and sat down again, with no apology. Nodding for Eva to continue, he then used every pose of body language that his unconscious could supply to underscore that he did not like the points they were making. He sat with his hands over his ears, he pushed his chair well back from the table, he looked at the ceiling, he looked at his watch, he sighed and he harrumphed. And then he showed them the door.

Back out on the pavement among the smokers who clustered around the entry way, Eva, Michelle and Jane looked at each other in bewilderment.

"So that didn't go too well," sighed Michelle, speaking for them all.

"Looks like he feels he didn't make himself clear enough," remarked Jane, looking up.

"Why do you say that?"

"I can see him mooning us in the window of his office up there on the 10th floor."

"Are you kidding me?" asked Eva, craning for a look. "How can you see that high up?" Then she burst into laughter.

"You really had me going. That meeting was so weird I came out willing to believe almost anything."

The three women stood there on the street under the streetlights, laughing and laughing. If George had chosen to look down on them from the heights of his office at that point he would've seen that they'd taken him personally no more seriously than he'd taken their presentation. Once they'd dissipated their stress and disappointment by ridiculing his reaction to their ideas, they headed over to Henri Burger in Hull for a debrief with an equally mystified Sam Spencer and a delicious compensatory dinner.

Undaunted, Eva and Jane took their careful analysis of the StarTrans monopoly rate setting to the deputy director at the Competition Bureau. While their audience with the deputy also included staffers, and there were more questions, they didn't leave the multi-story building in Hull with a sense that their message had been any better received.

Over time, the absence of any follow-up or changes in the StarTrans rate-setting regime confirmed their impressions. Ultimately the user group was successfully established and some years later StarTrans was privatised.

Chapter 57: Testing…

The baby continued to develop, unperturbed by its mother's unsuccessful attempts to control satellite costs. Much more importantly, from its perspective, the designated date for the amniocentesis had arrived.

Eva had to take her assistant into her confidence, sharing the excitement of the pregnancy and asking Sherri to cover for her absence on amnio testing day by telling anyone who enquired that she had an appointment with the doctor to discuss some test results.

The test itself, which was in the morning, was straightforward and not at all uncomfortable, but Eva quite fancied idling in bed all afternoon with a solicitous John plying her with cups of tea and cinnamon toast. The house was otherwise empty and they simply enjoyed the peace and quiet. The results were due in two weeks, but Eva and John had been made aware that these test results often arrive later than promised.

The next morning, as Eva walked into the office, frothy hot milk in hand (her only dietary concession to pregnancy thus far), she was waylaid by Sherri, who warned her, "Mr. Arkwright phoned looking for you yesterday, and he was really persistent. When I told him you had an appointment with the doctor that would take all day he really quizzed me about what might be wrong with you. I didn't tell a lie, just said you needed to have a special test. You may hear from him this morning." As Sherri finished speaking, the phone began to ring.

"I bet that's him," she warned.

"Thanks for the warning Sherri, I'll go sit down at my desk and you can put him through."

"Good morning, Bill, how are you today? Sherri just told me you were looking for me yesterday – nothing urgent I hope?"

"No, I was just calling to hear how results for the quarter are looking, but Sherri got me a little worried. She said you were off having a medical test. Are you okay?"

Eva laughed. "Hummm. You know, Bill, I've always been glad that we're friends as well as business colleagues, especially now," she started, a little slowly. "It turns out that this is a bit of an unusual conversation for a CEO to have with the Chair of the Board; nevertheless, I'm really pleased to tell you that I'm better than okay – I'm pregnant."

Bill sighed. "Oh thank goodness. When I heard you were off on a mysterious trip to the doctor I feared the worst. I thought you had cancer, for heaven's sake! What a relief to hear that you're only pregnant. My best to John, by the way."

"I'll pass that along. And I sure hope you speak for the board, Bill. But can we keep it secret for a while? We had an amniocentesis yesterday and we want to make sure that the baby will be healthy before we announce anything."

"You can count on me. Discussing the pregnancy of the CEO of one of my subsidiaries is not the kind of thing I usually do with the press – although now I think about it, that might be fun…"

"Save your fun, Bill. I'll keep you posted. Now, about the quarterly results: we're up 8 per cent year over year, but we did have some 'one-off' expenses that indicate we could be doing even better. We've got future generations to provide for, you know."

"Great. The numbers, at least, are about what I expected. See you at the Chamber of Commerce dinner next week. I promise I won't even glance at your stomach."

"And I promise I won't look at yours."

Chapter 58: Wonderful to Relate

Eva got the call from the hospital on the twelfth day. Sherri put it right through.

"Mrs. Sadlier?" the caller asked.

"Close enough," replied Eva, nervously.

"I'm Dr. Merlin's nurse and I'm calling to tell you the results of your amniocentesis. The specialist has had a careful look at the scans and everything appears to be just fine."

Eva exhaled. "What a relief! And the gender?"

"Oh yes, I see here on your registration form that you indicated you want to know the gender. Not all parents do, you know?"

"Yes, I've heard that, but my husband and I agreed that we've already had enough big surprises concerning the children in our lives."

"Okay. Well... it's a boy."

"How wonderful! Thank you so very much. I can't wait to tell my husband. Lately he and our son have been feeling outnumbered by all the women in our family."

"You know, Mrs. Sadlier," the nurse continued, almost conspiratorially, "I always volunteer to make the calls with the normal test results. It really gives me a lift to hear a mother receive such happy news."

"Yes, I can imagine calls like this must be tremendously satisfying. But who has to make the calls when things aren't all right?"

"Oh, the doctors make those calls because the mothers need to know their treatment options. I suppose that's one of the benefits of my not being so important."

"Well you've certainly been very important to me," said Eva warmly, "and it was lovely to hear from you."

John was in town for the week, between assignments, and that morning he'd suggested to Eva that they have lunch together at their favourite Italian meatball sandwich joint. At exactly 12:30 he pulled up by the side of the road near her office and she hopped in his car and cheerily asked him about his morning.

"The photos from Israel have come out beautifully. I'll need your help choosing which ones to use in the book. But I'm spoiled for choice, which is a real luxury."

"*Everything* about that trip has come out extremely well," replied Eva, portentously.

"What do you mean?" John asked.

"The hospital phoned me this morning with the results from the amnio. All the baby's little chromosomes are properly in line, and his fingers and toes are in the right places."

"His?"

"Yes, his."

"My goodness, I am surprised... a boy... Teddy will be especially pleased to have another boy around the house. Oh, my! How amazing and wonderful! We're going to have a healthy baby!"

Carina had left *Il Globo* and was now working for Booz, Allen's entertainment division in Rio. "Critical paths for *Carnivales* a specialty" was how she described her work.

Since Carina had long since been assigned the role as test market for family news, a few days later Eva called her to tell her about the baby.

"*Mirable dictu*," was her response this time, "which means 'wonderful to relate' for persons such as yourself who have not had the benefit of a strict Roman Catholic education."

"Hard to make that one into a name," replied Eva. "We're thinking Christine or Christopher, as in Christos."

"I know Christine and Christopher both derive from Christos, you silly Protestant, but I thought you said you had amniocentesis. Don't they tell you the gender when they do that?"

"Well *they* do, but *we* aren't."

"Then how will I know if I should knit something in blue or pink?"

"Have you taken up knitting?"

"No, but I will if you tell me the colour of wool to buy."

"Not tempting enough."

"I'll be there for the christening – or should I say the 'Christification'?"

"Just come."

Chapter 59: Innocents Abroad

The twins squared greeted the baby news with hoots of derision and a few dry comments about birth control. Nevertheless, the entire family was pleased and excited at the prospect of a new sibling.

The favourite family game became "name that baby," with Jo, who thought of herself as rather intellectual, leading off with De Trop, and Teddy suggesting Trop Tard. Teddy also expressed a mysterious liking for the name Lucifer ("although only if it's a boy", he specified).

Using her own name as a point of departure, Felicity contributed suggestions such as Utility or Diligent – nice transgender names. Genevieve tried to be serious and wrote "Tara" on the growing list that had been placed under a pink *Barbelles* magnet on the fridge. "Tara can be a boy's name or a girl's name," she defended when Jo argued that Tara was the name of a house on a southern plantation, not a person.

John and Eva added suggestions like Marmaduke ("an old family name", explained Eva) and Justice to the list to keep the ideas flowing.

Although she tired easily, Eva was able to keep up with all her work, but when Bill Arkwright suggested she attend the World Communications Congress in Dallas on both of their behalves she happily acquiesced.

There was no confusion on either part about what such a trip entailed. Bill and Eva often joked that being a member of the WCC was like participating in a global travel and dining club with a thin veneer of substance. The membership was primarily made up of old friends from far-flung English-speaking countries who got together periodically to exchange "scholarly" papers about communications, compare notes about regulation, and generally have fun.

Eva felt certain that John would be happy to attend with her, and she was not wrong.

"I'd really quite like to see the famous 'grassy knoll'," admitted John. "And I believe they have a Kennedy assassination photo exhibit in the museum."

The legendary shopping malls of Dallas were almost as important to Eva as the opportunity to visit the historic site of the assassination of an American president, but she didn't see any reason to emphasise that to Bill or John – although Gen, Jo and Felicity certainly guessed.

The weather in Dallas was perfect: very sunny but not too hot. The malls were as big and glittering as Eva had hoped, with a hockey arena-sized skating rink in the centre of one where you could look down and watch young people taking lessons while sitting in a balcony restaurant eating delicious Chinese sweetcorn soup and Emperor spicy shrimp.

It was a lot of fun to see friends and colleagues from elsewhere, and Dallas really put on a show for the Congress, with an opening dinner at the Southfork Ranch where the television programme *Dallas* was filmed, followed the next night by an excursion to Arlington to watch the Texas Rangers play baseball. Scheduled to fly home on Monday, it was Sunday morning by the time Eva and John had a chance to make their pilgrimage to the Texas Book Depository Museum.

The museum was really quite absorbing, with its audio exhibits and detailed photographs. Having wandered slowly around trying to take in all the evidence and background information, John and Eva agreed that they each felt more confused than ever about what really happened that day in November 1963.

Emerging from the Museum building into the bright midday sun, the couple blinked and crossed to the shady side of the quiet street to get their bearings and decide which way to go to find some lunch. Neither really noticed a slim, young black man approaching them until he sought their attention by speaking to them.

Not having heard what he said, Eva reflexively turned and said, "Pardon me?" – a relic of her grandma Brown's misplaced notion of gentility.

Now directing her gaze towards the speaker, Eva saw a pleasant-looking man of about twenty wearing a grey sweatshirt with kangaroo pockets at the front. Attuned to the size of people's stomachs on account of her own protruding middle, she noticed that his stomach seemed to be protruding a bit as well.

As the stranger repeated what Eva understood this time to be "Mumph, mumph, mumph, mumph, mumph," she noticed out of the corner of her eye that John was moving away, at an angle which was increasing the distance between the two of them.

Still confused, Eva automatically said, "Pardon me?" again while trying to look more closely at what might be causing the stranger's sweatshirt pocket to stick out in a pointy way.

This time, enunciating clearly enough that Eva could see the stranger's shining orthodontia – both top and bottom – he said, "This is a stick-up. Give me your money."

To which John, now almost on the opposite side of the man, replied, "No. Just fuck off."

Eva, totally bewildered, stood frozen to the spot. For another moment the three of them just remained still, with the stranger looking, somewhat confused himself by now, first at Eva and then at John.

Then the erstwhile robber sighed with exasperation, pulled his pointing finger from underneath his sweatshirt, cocked his thumb, made a shooting gesture, and said, "Bang. You're dead." And then he ran away.

Over a calming lunch of crab cakes and copious amounts of real iced tea, an exasperated John tried to explain to Eva that he had been trying to draw the attention of the would-be mugger away from her so that she could move away and run if there was an opportunity.

"In future, darling, when someone accosts us on the street, will you please spend less time trying to understand his dialect and more time trying to preserve your life and that of our unborn child?"

"I thought he wanted directions," argued Eva, innocently.

John sighed. And then he smiled fondly at his wife.

Back at the hotel to mingle before the closing banquet, Eva regaled their friends with the stick-up story. Among those listening, the American attendees in particular marvelled at their lucky escape.

"When we're out for the evening in New York, my husband always carries two wallets," confided a friendly woman from Comcast. "One to surrender to muggers right away with enough cash in it that they won't get angry and try to hurt him. If it had been me at the Depository Museum this afternoon I would just have handed over my purse and felt lucky to be left alone."

"God protects fools and babies," muttered John.

"And which one am I?" whispered Eva.

"Right now, I think it would be fair say that you are both."

Chapter 60: Brief Interlude

Despite the near-mugging, Eva returned from Dallas rested and cheerful, and she remained healthy for the rest of her pregnancy. She found trying to come up with appropriate executive maternity outfits increasingly challenging, but John helped by lending her some of his older, wide ties and showing her how to tie them so that, as he explained it, the bulge underneath the bottom of the tie was slightly disguised. "Certainly, no one would think you're secreting a gun under that blouse," he reassured her.

At Futurity, preparation for a regulatory review hearing kept everyone very busy and focused. Suddenly it was spring, with the baby due in two weeks and the hearing scheduled for two months later.

Christopher's actual arrival was rather faster and more frightening than anyone had expected, but it turned out all right in the end and the announcement of his birth was greeted with a container-load of irises and lilies and daffodils and roses from friends, business associates, customers and suppliers.

As Eva commented wryly, she wished she could give all the flowers back to the florists and ask them to send her one arrangement a week for the next several months. As it was, after giving many away she still had twelve or thirteen beautiful bouquets all crammed into the living room giving everyone in the family hay fever.

As predicted, Teddy was extremely pleased to welcome another boy into the family, and all the girls were just delighted to have a real live baby to cuddle and dress and bathe.

Eva was perfectly content to loll around the house watching television in the silky peignoir sets that John had purchased for her. When she was feeling like a serious person, she and Christopher watched the parliamentary channel, which provided them with endless hours of federal budget debate and the findings of an inquiry into the cod fishing industry.

Otherwise they lounged on the sofa, feeding and watching "evil but true" made-for-television movies and *Law and Order*. Christopher revealed a particular preference for *Law and Order*, twisting his head around, even when feeding, whenever the programme made the distinctive "plink" sound used to introduce a new scene.

When Eva had to participate in a conference call, or talk on the phone about business, she advised the baby in advance that he had to be really quiet, and usually he was, but when he was unable to contain himself, Juliet slipped into the room and scooped him up and took him away to bathe or burp.

When Chris was a couple of weeks old, John and Eva packed up their car and set off for a few days in Washington with Juliet and the baby safe in the back seat. While John was at work at the Smithsonian, Eva pushed Chris in his elaborate baby buggy, which doubled as a baby crib.

"Never too early to acquire the museum habit," she told a bemused guard.

After Washington, the pressures of business meant Eva had to make occasional forays into the office. On those days Juliet and Chris set up shop in Eva's little conference room and Eva held meetings in her office. Sherri proved excellent at directing traffic around the baby and helping Eva get all her work done without undue distraction.

Fortunately for Eva and John, Juliet had made it clear early in the pregnancy that she was up for the task of taking on a newborn, even though it had been some time since she looked after such a young child.

"There are some things you just don't forget," she stressed to Eva.

"Yes, like the exhaustion of night-time feedings, and the unpleasant surprise of a poorly fastened diaper," agreed Eva.

With the regulatory review hearing looming, a still plumpish Eva returned to work. As she pointed out to John, "Luckily, the parliamentary channel is in such low demand at present that they're going to cover our hearing gavel to gavel. Juliet can set Christopher up in front of the TV and he'll think I'm right there in the room with him, watching the same old boring stuff as usual."

"Maybe we could invest in a hologram or a cardboard mock-up of you and we wouldn't need you around at all. Matter of fact, I think I already have a photo that would be perfect to blow up."

"Yeah, right. You'd miss me when you wanted some of my delicious Bananas Foster to eat. Or my scintillating conversation."

"I suppose. But I bet I could get my favourite ice cream specialist at Dairy Queen to learn how to make a passable Bananas Foster."

"I wouldn't bet against you on that one. Last time we were there she almost licked you while she was admiring Chris in your arms."

"You know, a sensitive-looking man with a baby in his arms really is something of a chick magnet."

"In my experience you don't actually need the baby."

Chapter 61: Making Choices

"You seem to have a new admirer," announced Sherri as Eva hurried into the office, simultaneously checking her suit for Pablum and her hair for dampness as she unloaded her briefcase. The demands of Futurity's regulatory hearing had doubled as a weight loss programme and she felt as close to fighting trim as she figured an older mother was likely to feel. Since the regulators had been very positive about Futurity's management in granting their licence renewal, Eva felt that the combined process could be described as 'win-win'.

"Oh?" enquired Eva, only mildly curious. She had five meetings and a difficult negotiation scheduled and her mind was on the day ahead.

"Yes. Mr. Akabas has phoned twice already today to see if he can meet with you."

"That's unusual. I certainly know him but I don't know if we've ever had an actual meeting. Anyway, as you know, my day is packed. What does tomorrow look like?"

"It's packed too, but he was so insistent that you should see him that I've wedged him in at lunchtime. I'll get catering from the kosher deli downstairs and you can eat in your conference room."

"Great," called Eva over her shoulder as she hurried down the hall towards the big meeting room.

Eva had known Solly Akabas for several years, first by reputation and then through contact at various industry events. She liked his forthright style, his energy and his sense of humour. Solly was known for his philanthropic zeal, and Eva suspected that not only was she going to have to provide lunch for their meeting, but she would also be pressured into committing time or money or both to one of his laudable causes.

Solly had a high profile in the business community due to his astute – although sometimes very risky – acquisitions. He had ratcheted up his early investments in radio and cable on the Canadian prairies into an international conglomerate called Centrepoint, with UK cable holdings, a Scandinavian broadcasting venture and a share of a venture called Euronet. Most recently he'd been reported to be lobbying for the licence to start a private radio station in Israel.

The lunch began on a relaxed note. Despite her crammed day, Eva found she was enjoying Solly's company and his running commentary on events in the worlds of business and politics. But before she could even fit her mouth around the enormous pastrami sandwich Sherri had served, Solly launched into his pitch.

"I want you to come and work for me," he began abruptly.

"Doesn't everyone?" Eva joked, taking a large bite out of her dill pickle.

"No, I'm serious. I want you to come and be in charge of Centrepoint's future business development. I really need someone to help me find new investment opportunities, and I've been watching you for some time now. I think you have the business instincts and the energy that it takes to identify and negotiate new business deals."

"Well, I'm surprised and flattered. But I'm also very happy working as CEO of Futurity, and there's plenty of room left here to grow."

"That may well be true, but for all its public float, Futurity is still a subsidiary and Bill will always get the big kudos. And I don't see him going anywhere soon."

"Maybe not. But I am not restless." Eva was quiet for a moment. "Still, I've never left a job because I was unhappy… Tell me, what exactly do you have in mind?"

"I'm thinking about new ventures like satellite radio – areas where Centrepoint can build on what we already know how to do. I'm also thinking about the business of outdoor advertising; you know, billboards, bus and taxi ads, things like that. That's a business that could really stand some updating and I was thinking we might be the ones to find a way to do that. There's a lot of potential to export some of the techniques we've learned about deploying satellite and broadcasting into small markets, and how to match 'eyeballs with advertising' in parts of the world that aren't ready for the full-on sophistication of the American media but are still very interested in new ways of communicating."

Somewhat regretfully, Eva looked at her watch. "I'm really sorry but I did sandwich you in, no pun intended, and I've got to meet with my negotiation team right now. I still don't think I'm right for your job, but I will give it some more thought before I say 'no.'"

"That's all I can ask," smiled Solly. "It would be great to work with you – if not now, maybe someday on something else."

"Yes, maybe," called Eva, as she shook Solly's hand and hurried out the door, where Sherri was standing with Solly's coat in hand.

As was her habit, after dinner that night, with Chris tucked safely into bed, Eva told John all about the events of her day, including Solly's offer.

"You were right about the 'compliment' part," John told her, "From what I hear, Solly is bit of a risk taker – although most entrepreneurs are – but if he's interested in hiring you he must think you're very capable."

"I really like him, and I like the business he's built. But I'm not sure I want to go back to being a 'recommender' instead of a 'doer.' When I worked as a consultant I took real pride in my ability to advise customers on a strategic direction for their businesses, but now that I've had some experience being the person who gives the directions, rather than just identifying where to go, I think I'd find an advisory role too frustrating."

"Well I don't want a frustrated wife, regardless of the reason she might feel that way. Maybe you should thank

Solly and tell him you've had a chance to think things over and it turns out that particular job just isn't for you."

"I agree," said Eva.

Chapter 62: The Occasional Merits of Cul-de-Sac Technology

From the early days, Futurity had used its satellite distribution capabilities and its bundle of specialty channels as the core of a direct-to-home satellite business. DTH, as they called it, only made a small contribution to Futurity's profitability, but it offered viewers in remote areas the opportunity to watch an array of TV channels by installing their own backyard dish. Eva felt that the service, named Skyviewer, helped round out Futurity's product offerings, and it operated fairly cheaply on the margin.

The cash register for Skyviewer was a decoder box which was rented to dish owners as part of their service contract. Once a subscriber hooked the box up to a dish system, Futurity could turn on or off the Skyviewer channels and keep a record of services for which the subscriber would be charged.

The notion was simple, but not foolproof. Skyviewer's competition – a much more sophisticated and substantial service called Realview, with a much broader range of channels and a much larger subscriber base – had begun to experience problems with hackers modifying or cloning their decoders and stealing their signals.

At the meeting called by Eva to discuss the hacking threat, she was amused to learn from her engineering team that the reason Skyviewer was not experiencing the same level of signal theft, even proportionately, as Realview was because the Skyviewer decoder was based on old analogue technology which was not being used by services elsewhere in North America and their product offering and subscriber base were not what one might call "mainstream." As a result, hackers had neither the incentive nor, often, the skills to steal their signals.

Having explored their security options, which were few, Eva and the team made the practical decision to keep a low profile on the topic and to try to keep existing customers as happy as possible. Since Realview hackers were charging dish owners some kind of fee for the hacked decoders, there was still space in the marketplace for Futurity's low-cost offering – although it was uncertain for how long.

A few weeks later the head of engineering, David Wingrove, arrived at Eva's office doorway with a long face. He had just been informed that the supplier of Skyviewer's decoders, a small niche technology manufacturer in California called NewT, had decided, without even talking to him, much less consulting him in advance, to stop manufacturing the analogue equipment.

"That is bad news," agreed Eva. "How many decoders do you have in inventory right now?"

"About 453."

"About 453?" mused Eva. "Vague and yet precise..."

"Well, we have 437 that are new and 16 that have been returned by subscribers which may or may not work."

"And how many new sales are we making a week?"

"About 193."

"Another vaguely precise number. Where did you get that one?"

"Well, Joe from Accounting told me that's how many new subscriptions we sold three weeks ago, which is the most recent data that he has."

"David, I need you to get in touch with the production manager at NewT and find out how many decoders he has still in inventory, and how fast he can ship them up here. Also, I want to know who at NewT made the decision to quit building the decoders and what I can do about it."

"Yes, boss," said David, somewhat irreverently, as he went off to phone.

Three days later David returned to report that, following his call to NewT, and a hunt by the NewT production team throughout their warehouse and along the production line, they had located 853 decoders in shippable condition, and another 39 which had been rejected for one reason or another but which could be cleaned and reconditioned. And that was it.

As Eva explained to Bill Arkwright, "I have to go to California and beg the president of NewT – who believe it or not is called Skippy Hopper, which I can hardly say with a straight face – to continue manufacturing our decoders, or the growth of our Skyviewer business is finished."

"And what can you offer him in return?"

"I'm working on it. Do you think John would mind if I offered him Chris as collateral against us paying for everything he continues to manufacture for Skyviewer?"

"Hmmm…"

"How do I end up in these ridiculous situations?" asked Eva without any expectation of an answer. And off she went to ask Sherri to make her reservations to fly to San Diego to visit Skippy at NewT.

Leaving a rainy autumn day in Toronto and arriving in the warmth and beauty of Southern California made Eva question her life choices. "I could be living in the sunshine, looking at the ocean, and earning lots of money," she whispered to herself, although she had to admit that no one had offered her the opportunity to do so. Still, she did know people who had found a way to make that kind of choice, and as far as she knew they were happy. "Too bad Solly wasn't offering me a chance to develop new business here…"

In preparation for her visit, Skippy and his team, all newly appointed by the venture capital company who had recently purchased NewT, had looked at Futurity's request for continued analogue decoder production with fresh eyes. Instead of seeing the dying business that the previous management had recommended they exit, they now saw an opportunity to design and sell a new digital decoder that would be much more difficult to hack than those already on the market.

Over a generous serving of grilled shrimp with a hot chilli sauce in an elegant restaurant facing the ocean in La Jolla, Skippy made Eva an offer. "If we continue to supply you with the old decoders while we work to develop our digital offering, will you commit to letting Skyviewer be our reference site for the NewT digital decoders once we have them ready for commercial distribution?"

"Your sales lead suggested to David Wingrove that you might be asking me that, so I've already given the idea some thought. I'll need your commitment to a significant initial discount on the price and a favoured-nation clause for the long term," responded Eva, "but your offer does seem feasible. I can talk to my team in the morning and let you know tomorrow. I think we're scheduled to take a tour of your plant in the afternoon, so we can discuss this further then."

"Sounds good to me," replied Skippy. "Now, let's have some more of this fabulous Californian Chardonnay."

Eva, impaired already by jet lag, was happy to have another glass or two of wine and return comparatively early to her hotel for her nightly call with John.

"Funny, isn't it?" she mused to John. "Here we are, the dish service with the dragging edge technology, and we're probably going to be able not only to keep our humble band of subscribers, but to migrate them over time to what will be, however briefly, the most advanced digital decoder technology of all."

"Yes," agreed John. "Personally, I don't think it's bad that you'll be stuck on analogue for a while. Everyone in my business is all excited about digital, but I can foresee a time when my exquisite Leica camera will be recognised for what I already know it is: the apogee of the photographer's artistic experience. Now go to sleep or you'll be useless tomorrow."

Chapter 63: Tidings of Comfort and Joy

The Christmas season was invariably stress-filled for Eva. Work parties, children's parties, buying presents, too much food and drink... She knew herself to be a typical working mother and she had no idea how to approach the situation any differently.

Sharing a delicious dinner of Kentucky Fried Chicken (with extra coleslaw) with the twins squared, Chris and John in early December, she was surprised and pleased when Jo suggested that this year they try to compose a family message that they could send to all their friends and relatives.

"Great idea," agreed John. "Who wants to take the first crack at the missive?"

"I'll do a draft," volunteered Jo, "and then the rest of you can add anything you want."

<u>Our First Annual Christmas Letter</u>
And so it came to pass, in a town called Toronto, in the province of Ontario, that a message was written and argued over and rewritten and finally disseminated with a lot of trepidation, and it said:

This has been a busy and happy year in the Curran-Sadlier-von Richthofen household.

John's latest book, Traces of History, *was shortlisted for the illustrated photography (or coffee table) book category for the North American Photographic Association's awards. John claims the awards for his category are given out on the basis of poundage and, if so, his book, which weighs in at a hefty 3.75 lbs – or 1700 grams for you metric types – is in with a real chance. The awards ceremony will be in New York in March and the entire family already has plans to attend and cheer for our man. (Some of us also want to go to see* A Chorus Line, but that is entirely secondary to our desire to cheer John on at the awards' banquet.)

Eva has almost completed what she wishes to have described as a "busy and productive" year. The editorial board of this letter met with her and pointed out that "busy" doesn't even come close to describing her frenetic pace, and "productive" is a weasel word. As a result of lengthy negotiations, it has been agreed that we will say that Eva worked hard all year, failed to exercise enough, was often irritable or sleepy when at home, but all in all continued to laugh heartily, sometimes even at herself, and found time to attend enough family milestone events that she can still be called a mother in good standing. And the value of her company's shares went up 17 percent.

Josephine, whose patience has been sorely tried in her role as author of this bulletin, is excited to announce that she has landed her dream job as assistant to the editor of Women on the Go and, consistent with the title of that publication, rented what she plans to transform into a chic bachelor(ette?) pad just steps away from the GO train.

Christopher's response to hearing this news was to chant: "Jo to GO, Jo to GO," and then, echoing his Dr. Seuss book, he interspersed his chant with "Hop on Pop" and began bouncing on his father, who was trying to rest on the couch.

Genevieve has now waded halfway through what she describes as the exhausting mire of statistics and theory of human psychology which will enable her to one day be a person who will earn money by listening to the challenges that other people are encountering in life. John says that people could save a lot of money by just riding around on buses or planes telling their life story to strangers as Eva does, but that fortunately Gen will always have a lot of work because there simply are not enough conveyances to go around.

Both Teddy and Felicity graduated from high school this year and went off to universities at opposite ends of the country. Teddy's graduating class was a serious-looking lot and Felicity claims that she counted seven nerd packs in the white shirt pockets of the graduands. Teddy won the Wilfred Beatty medal for the best heuristic approach to debugging an examination scheduling problem. We all congratulated him and pretended we knew what the medal was about. Felicity was asked to perform a rendition of "I sing the body electric" at her graduation and we all proclaimed "I'm going to live forever" at intervals for the rest of the evening.

When asked what he would like to say about his year, Christopher thought for a bit and then replied, with some dismay, that he is still "too little to have a year." After some gentle leading by the author, Chris agreed that it was noteworthy that he does not like broccoli but really likes Chinese food.

Everybody but Christopher happily has a "significant other," unless Elmo qualifies, in which case everyone in the family has a significant other. Only John and Eva were willing to let the name of their significant other appear in this bulletin, since the remainder of the mature members of the family are either afraid of spooking the horses, or simply jinxing the relationship. Fortunately for family stability, John and Eva mentioned each other when asked to provide a name.

Juliet continues to be the cake in our fruitcake.

Happy Holidays,
John, Eva, Jo, Gen, Teddy, Felicity and Chris (and Elmo)

Chapter 64: I've Got a Gal in Kalamazoo

After a couple of years of enthusiastic service on the board of Coureurs de Bois, during which Eva was certain she had occasionally made pronouncements in French during meetings that were either incoherent or tantamount to declaring "I am a challenge" when what she actually meant was "the task looks daunting," an attractive merger opportunity arose for the company.

Serving on a special committee of independent directors to advise the shareholders on the true merits of the offer had greatly enhanced Eva's knowledge of the fiduciary responsibilities of a director. After listening to lot of advice from lawyers and investment bankers, the committee decided that the merger was in the interest of the shareholders, following which a fine and long established company simply disappeared into an entity called Renewable Forest Products Ltd. – a name Eva privately found a bit unctuous.

She was sorry to say *adieu* to both the executives of Coureurs de Bois and her fellow directors, all of whom seemed to her to be hardworking and likeable. Also, she was a little saddened that she no longer had an outside board on her résumé. However, only a month or so after Eva had finally proffered her shares in Coureurs de Bois, her brother Dean called with a surprising request.

"There's this guy I palled around with in Sea Scouts back on the prairies. We went to the World Scouting Jamboree in Ottawa together and after that we hung out in high school and then in university. We've kind of kept in touch and now he's some big executive with a major pharmaceutical company in the US. Anyway, he phoned me the other day and asked if I'd help him get in touch with you because he has a business proposition to discuss."

"Is this your geeky friend Norm, with the Buddy Holly glasses and the duck tail?"

"That's the one. His last name is Bradlake and he's changed his hairstyle. Matter of fact, he went prematurely bald so these days he doesn't have much hair at all."
"Well in that case you can give him my number. It'll be interesting to talk to him."
"Okay, but I'd better warn you, he always had a bit of a crush on you."
"Really Dean, did you think I didn't already know that? Prepubescent sisters of male pals seem to have some kind of magical attraction for geeky adolescent guys. I hope he's over it."
"He certainly is keen to reach you. See you for dinner on Sunday?"
"Yah, it's your turn to bring dessert. How about Gibby's excellent apple crumble?"

Ten days later Norm Bradlake called, and Sherri, who had been warned and so had placed him on what she privately termed the "approved caller list," put him straight through to Eva.
"Hi, Eva, Dean told me he'd let you know I might call," began Norm.
"Yes, he did, but he was vague about why you might be calling. He told me you work for a pharmaceutical company in the US these days. Is that a Michigan number I see on my call display?"
"Good spotting. Yes – I work for Uppsala Pharmaceuticals in a company town in Michigan. The town's called Kalamazoo."
"Kalamazoo? I always thought that was a made-up name for a town in a musical production number."
"So did I, but here I am living and working in the heart of Norman Rockwell country."
"Really? I didn't know that either, but I always liked Norman Rockwell paintings. I can't think of *The Saturday Evening Post* without picturing one of his works on the cover."

"Well we have plenty Rockwell originals here at Uppsala Pharmaceuticals. I must admit that sometimes I yearn for something a little more abstract on my wall."

"I can see why you might feel that way. Anyway, Dean said something about a business proposition?"

"More a request for guidance than a business proposition, actually. The reason I'm calling you is that I was recently appointed head of the animal health pharmaceuticals business here at Uppsala, and we're setting up a small international board to advise us and to be in position when we're ready to make our case to go for an initial public offering as a spin-off from the main company. The Chair of the Veterinary School at Cornell, Jim Flowers, has agreed to join us, as has Carlos Cimet, the lead partner of Booz Allen in Mexico. If you would do me the great favour of joining our board, it would round out our North American team and, I must admit, help with gender balance, too."

"Animal pharmaceuticals, huh. I've never given a moment's thought to the market for drugs for animals. What kinds of drugs do animals take? Nothing recreational, I'm guessing."

"We supply a lot of drugs that have been used on humans for a long time," Norm laughed, "but we haven't set our sights on recreational drugs for pets quite yet. Vet schools, like Cornell, help us do research into the efficacy and dosages appropriate for animals of various species and sizes. When some doctor comes forward with a proposal for teaching dogs to inhale, however, we might begin to question the intent of that research."

"Another whole world I know absolutely nothing about," muttered Eva, almost to herself.

To Norm she responded, "Thanks for thinking of me Norm, but I doubt I can commit the time or make the travel. I suspect there are no direct flights from Toronto to Kalamazoo. And despite some contradictory indications from my dating days, I know very little about animals."

"Don't worry, I anticipated those problems – although I do still remember when Dean made a trail of hot dogs on the porch in an attempt to lure that howling cocker spaniel that your family indulged back into the house in the middle of the night. He had some silly name; was it Eeyore? You must have been somewhere around the house in those days. Certainly no one could have slept through that howling."

"I was there," Eva sighed, "either cowering under the covers in my bed or hoping the neighbours wouldn't call to complain, again, or hiding behind the door in my nightie waiting to grab his collar if he got near enough for me to pull him inside. You were close: the spaniel's name was Roo, and yes, he was a dreadfully spoiled dog."

"I'm not surprised. Anyway, I can arrange for the Uppsala corporate jet to pick you up and bring you to meetings, with a quick stop at Ithaca to pick up Dr. Flowers. Also, I anticipate there will be only four in-person meetings a year. Any other business we can do by conference call. And, in case you're interested, I plan to set the board stipend at $10,000 per meeting."

"Your offer is certainly novel. However, it's not one I'm free to accept without talking to my chair."

"So can I leave it with you?"

"Yes, I'll get back to you inside a week with my answer."

After researching Uppsala Pharmaceuticals, animal health, animal drugs, Norm Bradlake, Dr. Jim Flowers, Carlos Cimet and even Kalamazoo, Eva approached Bill Arkwright to ask for his guidance on whether she should accept the appointment.

Bill found the notion of flying in a corporate jet to Kalamazoo for board meetings where marketing drugs for pets and domestic livestock would be the focus of discussion so compelling that he offered to be Eva's designate in case she ever fell ill.

"Does that mean you think I should take the appointment?" Eva asked, somewhat incredulously.

"Oh, yes. What a great opportunity. And international too. Our company will be the better for the broadening of your perspective."

"Are you sure the directors of Futurity won't think I've gone to the dogs?"

"I'll just tell them to take a hamster valium..."

When Eva told John about Bill's reaction to her new board, he chuckled and said, "Just what I always wanted: A gal in Kalamazoo."

It was on the way home from Kalamazoo on the corporate jet after her second Uppsala board meeting, while enjoying a scotch-on-the-rocks served by the co-pilot, that Eva accidentally swallowed one of her contact lenses.

One of her eyes had been irritating her mildly all day – probably because the jet's early departure from Toronto that morning had meant she'd inserted her contact lenses into partially closed eyes. The distraction of drug marketing presentations and a tour of the manufacturing plant had enabled Eva to ignore her sore eye, but after takeoff, as she relaxed into her comfy leather aircraft seat, she discreetly slipped the lens from the irritated eye into the little paper napkin she used for wiping cashew salt off her fingers. When her scotch was delivered she distractedly wiped her fingers again and stirred the ice around in the tumbler with her finger to speed the cooling of her drink.

It was only a few sips later that she noticed that the contact lens was no longer on the napkin, nor anywhere else in her immediate area. "Oh well," she sighed, already feeling the effects of the alcohol. "Maybe I'll acquire a taste for scotch with a contact lens chaser."

Chapter 65: Just When You Thought Everything Was Under Control...

Bill Arkwright loved sports; he loved to play and he loved to watch. According to Eva's sources, he was an aggressive and proficient squash player and he enjoyed taking part in organised 10K runs, especially if he could raise money for charity at the same time.

On Sunday mornings Eva would sometimes see Bill and his close friend Ben in their flashy running shoes jogging along the lakeside down near the old Woodbine race track. She admired their energy. Her idea of a good Sunday morning activity was to corral as many twins as she could awaken to go out with her and John and Chris to the Sundown Grill for eggs Florentine.

One particular Sunday, Teddy and Felicity were both home from their respective universities for reading week, and the five of them were well into the hashed brown potatoes when Eva's phone rang.

"Hello, is this Evaline Sadlier?"

"Yes, who's calling?"

"This is the Toronto General Hospital emergency ward nurses' station calling. I've been asked by a man called Ben Powell to call you to let you know that your friend Bill Arkwright has had a stroke. Ben asked me to say that he can't leave Bill's side, but that he knew you'd know who to notify."

"Oh my goodness! Can you tell me anything about Bill's condition?"

"All I can tell you is that Mr. Arkwright has had a stroke and the doctors are attending to him."

"Thank you for calling. Please tell Ben I'll do what I can. Is there a number I can call later to find out how Bill is doing?"

"Mr. Powell said to tell you he'll call you when he has some information."

Later that afternoon Eva finally managed to reach Henry Peterson, FutureMedia's chair, at his cottage in the Muskokas. It was immediately obvious he was as floored as she had been by the news of Bill's stroke and equally unsure about what to do next.

"Do you have any sense of how long it'll be before Bill can be back in the office?"

"Not a clue," said Eva bluntly. "But we should probably be thinking months at least."

"Oh dear. Months. I'll have to call a special board meeting to appoint an interim CEO."

"I've asked Communications to prepare a press release for your approval, and yes, a special board meeting will have to be convened. I've also called Andy Frith and told him you'll probably want to be in touch."

"Oh yes, Finance. I'd better call him right away."

"Please let me know if there's anything else you want me to do."

"Thanks, Eva. I'm sure you'll be hearing from me again soon."

The board of FutureMedia met by teleconference the next day and appointed Andy Frith, who was the chief financial officer, acting CEO. Andy and Eva had what she described as an "adequate" working relationship, but there was little genuine warmth or camaraderie between them. That was no real problem since they each had plenty of work to do that didn't require the involvement of the other, and that's what they focused on in the weeks following Bill's stroke.

Eva tried to visit Bill at least twice a week with messages of cheer from his colleagues and funny stories about their customers and competitors. He especially seemed to enjoy Eva's special delivery of the Christmas wishes video prepared for him by the slightly inebriated attendees of the FutureMedia office party.

In an effort to provide some unique and memorable entertainment at Futurity's own family holiday party, held in the event room at the fancy new downtown Y, Eva's communications team spent weeks attending various Mighty Mites hockey games and gymnastics practices and school concerts so that they could videotape a wide range of employee's children giving answers to a series of prepared questions. The edited answers offered a revealing and amusing array of comments about what the children perceived their parents did every day at work, and Eva couldn't resist playing that video for Bill as well.

"He plays computer games at the office all day," was one telling response – although when the video was shown at the party the father in question shouted out "Untrue!" in a loud, alcohol-assisted voice.

Another child said, "One day my dad had to do a phone call with work, and he didn't want to tell his boss that Mom was starting to have a baby. By the time he got off the call, she was really distressed, but they made it to the hospital okay. Mom swore she wouldn't name the baby Dave, after his boss, no matter how much he begged, but luckily it was a girl."

One child reported that after her parents had returned from what the audience immediately recognised as a special celebration held at the Jasper Park Lodge for top performers and their spouses, her father told her mother, "I don't care if you have to travel a lot or work nights and weekends; that was an amazing event and I want you to qualify for it every year. The kids and I can manage everything on the home front just fine while you focus on your work. Just make sure you win again."

Ever since he'd learned about Eva's "secret" amniocentesis, Bill had felt proprietary towards Christopher, and he laughed and laughed when Chris, deliberately positioned as the last child interviewed on the video, used hand gestures to reinforce his comments. "My mom worries about the money going up (*gesture up*) and the money going down (*gesture down*). And that's about it." (*open hands presented palm upward accompanied by a rather Pierre Trudeau-like shrug.*)

The lingering physical impact of the stroke on Bill gradually became clear. The nerves in the right side of his body had been damaged, making it hard for him to pick up a pen or a fork, and his speech was difficult to understand. While Ben claimed that Bill's mind was perfectly clear, he seemed to be having some problems with his short-term memory and his vision was severely blurred.

Always a fighter, Bill went at his rehabilitation with a will, and the doctors were impressed with the speed of his recovery. Nevertheless, as they privately explained to Ben, while it was entirely possible that he would be able to return to work someday as an advisor or a consultant, it was extremely unlikely that he would ever return to a full-time executive role.

Chapter 66: The Not-so-New Broom

Very reluctantly, the FutureMedia board accepted Bill's elegantly worded resignation and began a search for a new CEO. Eva tried to remain positive during the search as what she described as a "seriatim of world-class egomaniacs" put themselves forward for the job, and she was disheartened when the board chose to fill the position with someone they described as a "senior statesman" from the telecommunications industry.

As she confided to John when she learned of their choice, "They've chosen someone who's been around a long time to lead a brand new kind of business. A man with his entire future behind him. Pretty clever, eh?"

"Ah, my little Canadian. That 'yesterday's man' is not only FutureMedia's new CEO, he's going to be the chair of Futurity's board, so you'd better just suck it up."

"'Suck it up'? What kind of husbandly solace is that? Besides, he's not even 'yesterday's man' – he's more 'yesterday's wannabe.' But you're right. I try to help the kids avoid career-limiting mistakes by reminding them that you can't always work for people that you like. Now it's time to follow my own advice."

"So you should. Everyone on your team is going to be watching you. This requires some of what you refer to as your Leadership in Mild Adversity skills."

"Trust me; I'm already working on them. As Teddy used to say: I've modified my attitude. All I'm hoping for at this point is that the new CEO doesn't undo any of the good initiatives Bill put in place."

"Like your appointment?" suggested John.

"That would be a good example of what I fear," agreed Eva.

Guy Heller, newly appointed chief executive officer of FutureMedia, arrived at the office carrying an old-style, rigid triangular brown leather briefcase that closed with a clasp. There was some speculation that inside the briefcase was a copy of the daily newspaper and a snack for his afternoon tea packed in a brown paper bag by his wife Gloria.

As he disclosed in his first media interview, in his first 100 days Guy intended to conduct a detailed review of the five-year plan for FutureMedia and its subsidiaries, and then he was going to announce his "new" plan of action.

On the face of it, that sounded like a reasonable approach. Eva arrived for the first review meeting with Guy's top executives and the presidents of the other divisions prepared to be open-minded and to take a fresh look at her plans for Futurity.

To start off the meeting, Guy suggested that those present take a moment or two to introduce themselves to him and to give a synopsis of what they thought were the most important issues facing the company at present.

"You can talk about issues that relate to your particular responsibilities, or broader corporate challenges," he encouraged.

Introductions and discussions were going along smoothly, if blandly, until it came Eva's turn to speak. For the first time that day, Guy interrupted the flow in order to introduce Eva to the others, although she already knew them all rather well. But what Guy said was "For those of you who don't know her, this is Eva Sadlier, president of our Futurity operation. And I'm not entirely certain why she's here with us today."

The room went silent. Gregarious Tony, head of marketing, was heard to take a sharp intake of breath. Eva looked stunned.

"Why don't you try to tell us all how you make yourself useful, Eva?" added Guy.

"Every day in every way I keep getting better and better," Eva thought to herself. Then she addressed the room: "Thank you, Guy. And thank you also for this opportunity to share my perspective on the challenges we're facing in the exploding digital entertainment universe."

"Yes, yes, Eva. There's a lot of what I call 'happy talk' out there about the potential of digital entertainment – most of it clearly exaggerated. Why don't you just focus now on telling us about the potential of that little direct-to-home business you have. It's called Skyline, isn't it?"

"It's called Skyviewer, Guy. And you're right; it is a little operation, but a serendipitous one. With Skyviewer we're in an unusual situation where being analogue in a digital world has enabled us to find a niche for a while. But the Skyviewer service is not the future; it's just a clever application of a dead-end technology. Our new satellite-based truck tracking and messaging service has a lot more potential. Being able to do things like remote monitoring for refrigerator trucks and downloading bills of lading into a computer in the cab of a transport truck will take us into some really exciting new markets."

"As I like to say, I think you should stick to your knitting," Guy interrupted. "Pay attention to tried and true businesses and let someone else worry about the new. Tony, you're next. How are the new corporate social responsibility messages coming along?"

"Stick to your knitting," Eva fumed to John later. "I don't think he even had a clue that he might be being sexist – much less unoriginal. The only reassuring thing that happened is that I think he treated the CFO, Andy, even more dismissively than he treated me."

The press release announcing Andy Firth's resignation in order to pursue other interests came out the following Monday.

Chapter 67: A Turn out of the Sun

In private, with John, Eva began to refer to Guy as "Mr. Could-you give-me-a-memo-on-that," shortened with usage into Mr. Memo. She tended to pronounce the word "memo" to sound like "nemo" – a word both she and John knew to mean "nobody" in Latin.

"He's such a squelch," she complained on the phone to John, who was off in the Amazon rain forest documenting the discovery of yet another new tribe for the *National Geographic*.

"I don't know where I'd be without the support of that magazine over the years," he'd confided to Eva before he left.

"Here with me during my season in purgatory," had been her quick response.

Eva's technique for dealing with Guy was to be positive and upbeat, regardless of how dismissive or rude he became, and to avoid gossiping about him to anyone. With John so far away she found that difficult, and a bewildered Chris was often the recipient of a diatribe on what that "silly man" had done today. Luckily, Chris thought the silly man was a character from a book, not a real person.

With Guy in the chair, the tone of board meetings at Futurity became less supportive. Previously, Bill's obvious enthusiasm for the business and general support for Eva meant that new initiatives were given a positive hearing. In addition, their comfortable relationship had enabled Eva to pre-sell new ideas to Bill before the meetings so that they could approach the rest of the board with a united front.

Despite the awkwardness between her and Guy, Eva was determined to continue to act as professionally and competently as she could. In her career she had seen otherwise capable executives become halting and anxious when confronted with a senior executive who they believed disapproved of them or their work, and she didn't want to fall into that kind of behaviour.

Eva had been encouraged by Bill to use some of the tools learned in her consulting days to analyze trends and opportunities when presenting to the board, so she was surprised when her business review incorporating the widely referenced Boston Consulting Group four-box matrix analyses was very poorly received at the next board meeting.

Employing the matrix as an analytical tool, Eva used it to describe the major component of Futurity's business – speciality channels such as *Vault!* – as a "cash cow" – a synonym in consulting terms for business with low potential for further growth but sufficient market share to almost guarantee sustained profit performance.

Skyviewer, which had been discussed in a lot of detail with the board during the decoder fiasco, was tagged a "dog," with low growth potential and low market share. By the same rubric, Sat-Track, as Eva had named her nascent truck tracking business, had the potential to be a "star:" It could grow and it could command the market. "To complete the matrix," she explained, "the team is assessing our advertising commercial production business and niche programme production to see what long-term potential they offer. In the terminology of the matrix, at present those Futurity businesses could be deemed 'question marks.'"

"What in heaven's name are you talking about Eva?" interjected Guy. "All this silly stuff about 'stars' and 'cows' and 'question marks'?" Personally, I really don't think it's appropriate for a leader to identify a business as a dog.

"Think of how that might affect the employees in that division," piled on Brian Wales – a board member who turned out to be an old friend of Guy's. When Bill Arkwright had originally selected him for the board he'd hoped Brian's conservatism would provide useful ballast, but it sure didn't seem to be working out that way.

"Did I hear you say that strategic consultants talk about 'milking the cows to provide nourishment for the stars'?"

asked Mimi Ross, a recent appointee that Bill had been reconsidering before his stroke. "That doesn't make any sense. Stars don't drink milk."

Raymond Lambert, by far the most venerable and experienced board member of the Futurity board, quietly intervened to stop the discussion from becoming even more unhelpful.

"Very interesting, Eva. I find your matrix a useful aid to discussion and analysis. I've read quite a bit about it over the years in the business press, but this is the first time I've had the chance to see it applied to an actual business. You've given us real food for thought. Guy, I don't want to rush anyone, but I do need to leave at four-thirty, so could we move on now to the insurance review?"

"Why, yes, Raymond. Eva, do you want to call in the Mitchell Insurers team?"

The meeting wound up in the usual shuffle of papers and coats and instructions on where to find the waiting limos.

That evening, after letting her rant for a while, John, now safely home again, reminded Eva that generally she enjoyed her work, that she was well remunerated, that she had a good reputation in the industry and that this, too, would pass.

"Well it can't pass fast enough for me," muttered Eva.

But it didn't pass – at least not quickly.

Chapter 68: Chilled to the Bone

Four days after the board meeting, as Eva arrived back into the office, rain-soaked, after lunch with a customer, Sherri greeted her with a summons.

"You're wanted up at The Big House."

The Big House was Sherri's pet name for the FutureMedia headquarters building, and Eva had to admit that the description seemed apt.

"Did they say when?" asked Eva, shaking out her umbrella and looking at the continuing storm outside.

"Oh, Monica kindly indicated that you could take your time, as long as it's right away." Recognizing their respective bosses' adversarial positions, Sherri and Guy's assistant liked to make gentle fun at each other's expense.

Sensing Eva's apprehension and correctly assuming that her involuntary shiver came from the notion of facing Guy, not the storm, Sherri bravely added, "Don't worry. He's got nothing on you. You're doing a really good job."

But they both knew that these things are never that simple.

On Eva's arrival at FutureMedia, Monica ushered her right into Guy's recently redecorated mahogany-panelled office. Eva declined the offer of coffee, brushing away an errant thought about hemlock, and seated herself in the chair indicated, across the large dark wood desk from Guy's imposing wing chair.

Clearly Guy had prepared himself psychologically for the meeting, and he got right to the point. "You know, Eva, I've always liked to work with my own team. I find it makes dealing with matters so much easier when you've all trained using the same play book. And you, of course, are a bit of a holdover from past seasons. There are some – Bill Arkwright, for example – who've argued that you're a franchise player, but I must admit that I have yet to see that kind of value in your performance."

He continued, "God knows, I've been trying to work with you as best I can, but you're making it very difficult for me, what with your crazy consulting gimmicks and your inappropriately casual manner with your subordinates. And did I hear that you've declared Easter Monday a statutory holiday for all Futurity staff? I hate to have to say it, but unless you shape up and run the plays as I call them, I'm afraid we'll have to think about going our separate ways."

Guy paused and looked gravely across the desk at Eva, trying to gauge her reaction to his delivery so far. Eva looked back blankly. "So, here's what I suggest we do. I've decided to put you on probation for six months to see if you can come around to my way of doing things. Of course, it's an informal kind of thing, but I've already talked to a couple of members of the board and made it clear that, as chair, I have a set of expectations and values that I need them to share. And I feel confident they'll come to see things my way. In the meantime, I expect you to consult me before you make any major operating decisions over at Futurity."

"What's 'major'?" Eva managed to gasp during Guy's second pause for emphasis.

"Oh, you know, the usual. New contract terms with customers, pricing, any purchases, staff appointments, parking spot allocations."

Eva gulped, struggling not to let him see her cry.

"Any questions?" Guy asked, standing to signify the end of the meeting.

Determined to maintain her composure, Eva simply shook her head and walked carefully out the door.

In an act of solidarity, Monica quietly phoned Sherri and told her that Eva had left their office "as white as a sheet," and that it was unlikely she'd be returning to her own office that day.

This time, not only was Eva tucked up under the duvet when John got home for dinner, but it was clear that she'd been crying. There was a pile of crumpled Kleenex on the bedside table, and her face, framed by the pillow, was red and blotchy.

On his way through the living room, Juliet and Chris had warned John that Eva had come home early from work that afternoon and gone straight to the bedroom. They agreed that they had heard the word "asshole" as she went down the hall. She had not responded to any knocks on the door.

"She didn't even stop to hug me or ask me about my day," Chris complained.

John had been increasingly anxious about Guy's obvious distaste for Eva's style, and he was certain that this retreat under the duvet was in response to some act of perceived persecution on Guy's part.

"I think this situation calls for strong liquor," he muttered to himself, and after giving the recumbent Eva a nuzzle and a big hug, he told her he'd be right back. He returned with two steaming mugs of hot rum and lemon with cinnamon sticks and some Walkers shortbread.

"My mum always said that rum and shortbread are the best cure for a crisis. Now tell me, what has happened to you?"

"Guy wants me gone, that's what's happened to me," Eva whimpered, blowing her nose.

"That's hardly news," consoled John, taking her hand and speaking in a mild and reassuring tone. "What is it that he's done now that has succeeded in piercing your armour of self-confidence?"

"He's put me on probation, for heaven's sake! He's given me six months to 'come around' to his way of doing things. And in the meantime I'm supposed to let him make all the decisions at Futurity. In addition, he intimated that he'd use the six months to get the board to align with his way of thinking. I'm sure Brian Wales is already there – in fact I think he'd like my job – and Raymond Lambert is due for retirement soon."

"Wow. He's playing for keeps, isn't he?"

"He sure is. In his jumble of sports metaphors and clichés I sensed a real determination to get rid of me."

"So let's think about how we can protect you – at least until you can find something else to do."

"I'll show him defense," muttered Eva.

"That's my girl. Now tell me what you're going to do."

"First, I'm going to do whatever he tells me to do. Now is not the time to screw up and get fired. And I'm going to hold my head up high. I'm nobody's whipped dog."

"A visit to that hot-shot employment lawyer you were talking about the other day also sounds like a good idea," encouraged John.

"Yes. A meeting with Elaine Phelps. Then I'm going to have a long gossipy dinner with Anne Faulkner at Faulkner Executives. That should keep me busy for a while."

"Good. Now, I hear Chris and Juliette getting restless. Let's go eat some shepherd's pie with some of that vintage Chateauneuf de Pape that Guy sent over for your work anniversary. Who knows when we'll get another bottle of wine like that?"

Chapter 69: An Unexpected Honour

The twins squared were engaged in various iterations of what Eva thought of as the "trying mates on for size" stage of life, although Gen seemed increasingly serious about an intelligent and handsome young man with bright green plastic-framed glasses whom she had met at a yoga class. It turned out that, despite the eyeglass frames, he was a rising young star in a major accounting firm.

"Not the abstract thinker we expected her to be interested in," Eva explained to Paula, "but the green frames give us hope that he might be a bit of a non-conformist and that's good sign. And we all like him. Gen has even hinted that maybe I'll get to be stepmother of the bride before too long."

At work, the tense atmosphere generated by Guy's probation gambit didn't disperse, but it didn't get worse either, and life proceeded in a largely uneventful way.

Eva developed a detailed approval form for Guy to use in signing off on operational decisions for Futurity, and Sherri and Monica kept track of the steady stream of papers going back and forth between the offices.

Eva kept her personal contact with Guy and FutureMedia to a minimum, while her own business marketplace delivered no particular surprises. She tried not to dwell on how much she missed her regular lunches with Bill and his unique business insights.

It was on a quiet, business-as-usual day that Sherri buzzed her to ask, "Would you like to take a call from someone at *Confederation* magazine?"

"Why not? I feel like I have sufficient wits about me this afternoon to avoid being tricked by a reporter into saying anything stupid. No guarantee, though. What do you guess they're writing about this time?"

"Sounds like it may be about you."

Eva laughed. "I certainly am an expert on that topic. Put that call right through."

Eva still had a smile in her voice when she received the transfer.

"Hello, Eva Sadlier here."

"Hello, Ms. Sadlier. This is Paul Welch of *Confederation* magazine. Do you mind if I call you Eva?"

"Fine with me Paul. How can I help you?"

"My editor asked me to call to see if you would mind if we included your name in our annual list of *Canadians of Renown*. I don't know if you're a regular reader of *Confederation*, but we've been publishing this list of four or five nominees for over forty years, and our editorial board agreed unanimously that we should include you this year as our first-ever female nominee in the category of *Accomplishments in Business*. In addition to a write-up in the magazine, we'll have an awards dinner later in the year where we would present you with a medal that we've specially cast for our honorees."

"Gee," responded Eva, taken aback. "Honour is the right word. I certainly would be honoured to be included in such a list. I've seen your lists in other years and found your previous selections very impressive. What do you need me to do?"

"Right off, we needed you to say 'yes.' I'm especially pleased that you've done so, since you're the first suggestion that I've ever made for the list, so I'll take a personal pride in your inclusion. Next, we need to arrange an interview and a photo shoot with you. I'll have the photographer get in touch. And could I come around and interview you in the next week or so? These assignments always seem to be on a bit of a tight deadline."

"Of course you can. My assistant, Sherri, can help work that out since she keeps track of my commitments, but I'm sure we'll be able to get together sometime in the next few days. Is there anything in particular you want me to think about for our interview?"

"Oh no, it's going to be the usual 'modern woman makes good' kind of thing. I'm sure you're already well-rehearsed on that subject."

"I suppose I am," said Eva. "But I would like to shy away from a 'Superwoman' kind of story. For one thing, I have neither the figure nor the snazzy belt and tiara. I'd really prefer to focus on how important it is for women to recognise that a satisfying life involves making personal choices – the kind of choices that are open to many of us."

"Well, you're hardly an everywoman, but I agree with you," said Paul reassuringly. "It's certainly not our plan to present you as an anomaly. Let's see what we can do."

John had strong opinions about what Eva should wear for the photo shoot. "The image I believe you want to project," he advised her, "is someone who is comfortable in her own skin. No work uniform of navy wool suit and bow-necked blouse, or silly recreational clothes, or skirts that look like big neckerchiefs with a hole cut in the middle to your waist and the points hanging down all around you. Something simple and classic should do."

When the *Confederation* photographer indicated that he wanted to take an outdoor shot in addition to some photos around the apartment, John was delighted since he really wanted the spread to include a photo of Eva in her deep purple wool winter coat with the fur trim around the hood.

"In that coat you look like my little Evaline of the North," he told her lovingly. "It's a great way to have you immortalised."

"These are hardly photos for posterity – they're just *Confederation's* end-of-year issue," reminded Eva. "How about my baggy pink chenille bathrobe for the photos at home? It's definitely a classic. And it has the added benefit of being what I usually wear."

"How many times do I have to tell you? This is about your image, not reality. Reality would be you lying on the bed reading a book while Chris rests against your haunches watching *Scooby-Doo*. And all the readers would think: 'She's not so special. I can do that'."

"So they could," Eva conceded readily. "And that's what I want them to think."

The interview, which was held at her home, to provide context, was a lot more fun for Eva than the photography session. Paul Welch had a relaxing style that encouraged her to tell him anecdotes from her business life and to confess to various shortcomings.

The interview was made much more congenial by the fact that Eva understood that the magazine was interested in making her sound as worthy as possible of the honour they were bestowing on her. And – "bonus!" as the kids would say – Paul made it clear that he did not intend to interview any of her colleagues, including Guy.

Towards the end of their discussion, which was being recorded to assist him in getting his quotes right, Paul asked, "I've listened to you talk about your work, your family and your wide-ranging interests. And I know from what I've read about you and heard you say that you're a strong believer in equality of opportunity for women, but I don't know exactly how to describe your approach. You aren't what most people think of as an 'aggressive woman' or a 'bra-burner' or a 'feminist.' So what are you?"

"Please let me correct you right away. I *am* a feminist. I think I've been a feminist ever since I understood what that term means – and maybe even before. I strongly believe in equal political, social and economic rights for women. When I was younger I paid a lot of attention to the people who were trying to create, for want of another term, a feminist manifesto. And every woman that I listened to enriched my understanding of what it is I personally want to try to achieve."

She went on, "One of the most telling arguments came from Adrienne Clarkson – a genuinely interesting woman of whom I'm sure you've heard. When asked what she thought a woman should do to advance our cause, she said something like this:

> *The Quakers have a special notion called 'bearing witness,' an expression which means to them that you can exemplify the values that you hold by living in accordance with your understanding of those beliefs. So what I would say to a young woman is this: Bear witness to the life that you believe you are entitled to live.*

"That message really struck a chord with me. It was as clear and direct as if she was speaking straight to me. And that's what I'm in the process of doing. I'm living the life to which I feel entitled."

The silence following Eva's pronouncement was interrupted by a commotion in the hall, and a call of "Mommy, Mommy, guess what?"

"That's my son Christopher home from school," Eva explained. "And that reminds me, in winding up with you I'd like to steal a quote Chris used one day to sum up his own comments for public consumption. So here goes: 'And that's about it.'"

The issue of *Confederation* came out early in the new year and John went out and bought several copies. He was especially pleased by the photo of Eva on the street near the office in her winter coat – although he privately thought he could have done even better.

While Eva was thrilled by the photos and the interview, almost none of her friends or relatives said anything much about it. She didn't know what that meant, and John didn't either.

Guy Heller sent her a 4x6" card that said *Congratulations* on the front in silver letters with sparkles and *You really did it this time* inside, and was signed 'Guy.' Eva chose to take the card as a genuine expression of approval from Guy, especially since she doubted he was capable of either subtlety or irony. FutureMedia's Chair, Henry Peterson, sent her a bottle of Dom Perignon, and she also received a large box of her favourite rum-filled Belgian chocolates and a card with no signature inscribed with the message "Way to go, girl." Once she was certain the chocolates had not been sent by John, she liked to think they might have come from Adrienne.

Chapter 70: No Particular Impediments

Eva's comfort in her job had been partially restored. Guy had quickly tired of the piles of approvals that kept appearing on his desk and had modified his directive to include only decisions involving $50,000 or more. Then, to keep her "on her toes," he called her into his office to tell her he was thinking about extending her probationary period to a year.

Secretly buoyed by the advice from her lawyer, Elaine, that letting her go would cost the company "plenty," and resigned to Guy's thinly disguised antipathy, Eva simply sighed in response to the new threat.

Throughout, Eva made a concerted effort to do nothing that appeared to undermine Guy's authority, confining any contact with Henry Peterson to chance encounters and making sure that Guy's *Message from the Chair* in Futurity's annual report gave him full credit and the chance to seem to be gracious in his comments about the operations.

Guy's sense of self was greatly assisted by his nomination for CEO of the Year by the Business Round Table. Now that he felt he was getting the recognition he deserved from the business world he seemed to have less need to disparage others.

Eva couldn't help wondering who had made the nominations.

FutureMedia's new CFO, a very capable and likeable woman called Krys Hunter, went a long way towards making Eva's life easier. Krys, a tall blond with short cropped hair, was smart and funny and a pleasure to work with, as well as being an accountant who was at the top of her game. Having personally chosen her, Guy was perfectly comfortable to have Krys take over most of his dealings with Eva.

The carefully planned marriage of Genevieve Curran and Simon Glass (or Greenglass as Eva and John secretly dubbed him) was a bit like a three-ring circus. Eva deferred to Gen's mother Marianne whenever she remembered, but her innate managerial style made her seem unfortunately decisive at times.

As Jo pointed out, just having two sets of twins in the wedding party – one identical to the bride – made the execution of a simple elegant wedding virtually unachievable. Add to that three sets of parents, a seven-year-old ring bearer with a yo-yo in his tuxedo pocket and a ceremony that ultimately satisfied neither the Anglican attendees, nor the Jewish relatives, nor the atheists, and you have all the ingredients of farce.

John decided he wanted to take photographs during the various lead-up events to use in a follow-on to his earlier twins book *In the Alternative*. "I'm thinking about calling it *Separated by Marriage*, but I may call it *Twins Undone*. It depends what kind of pictures result from it all," he informed anyone who asked. He hired a trusted colleague to take shots during the ceremony, but he also gave Chris and all the twins (even the bride) digital cameras and encouraged them to look for interesting perspectives that could enrich the book.

One of Futurity's specialty channels, aptly named *The Wedding Channel*, had asked to be allowed to make an episode using the wedding, but Eva had firmly said no. "It would seem dreadfully self-regarding," she confided to Felicity.

The invitees from Gen's mother and stepfather's list looked like upright citizens who always filed their taxes on time. Guy Heller and his wife, who had given Gen a beautiful flower vase, were subdued and dignified during the reception, and stayed just long enough to be polite. After much debate, Eva had also invited Henry Peterson and his wife, but she was secretly relieved when he informed her, with real regret, that he would be travelling in Europe at the time. Entertaining both Henry and Guy at such an important family event would definitely have sent her stress levels rocketing.

The bride was exquisite in a creamy long bias-cut satin dress with flowers in her hair. Jo managed to make herself look as different as an identical twin could look, with long straight hair in contrast to Gen's updo, make-up even more subdued than Gen's own, and a street-length dress of soft lime green with a fiftyish crinoline and cap sleeves. Felicity opted to deliver one of the readings, rather than stand beside Gen and Jo, and, at Simon's request, Teddy stood up as best man.

The toast to the newly married couple, delivered by Genevieve's favourite psychology professor and thesis advisor, was hilarious. She took the opportunity to use the differing backgrounds of the bride and groom, and their chosen professions, to imagine the kind of conversations they might have on sensitive issues such as household finances or educating their children. Eva smiled over at John as he muttered, "Too true," under his breath.

Chapter 71: With Apologies to Tom Wolfe

Management always has its challenges, and some mornings Evaline woke up with her adrenalin running high, her chest tight and her stomach host to a rampage of butterflies. Through trial and error, when that horrible combination of feelings arrived she had learned the deliberate steps that she needed to take to calm herself.

She would get up and shower, beginning while washing her hair to identify of all the things that she needed to do to address the source of anxiety. She would avoid drinking too much coffee with breakfast, because coffee in that particular physical situation just made her feel nauseated, which, when added to the butterflies, left her profoundly uncomfortable.

Once at work, she would immediately write down from memory, in rough order of priority, the list she had carefully been compiling of all the things she could do to ameliorate the problem, and then she would begin systematically working to cross off items from her list. Some of the tasks involved telephoning or calling a meeting to devise a strategy to address the problem and diffuse her tension, while others involved consulting with legal counsel or the communications team.

It was on those stressful days that Eva particularly missed Bill Arkwright. They had been well-attuned and his experience had broadened her perspective. In addition, he had been acquainted with many of her key customers for many years and knew how best to meet their particular needs.

One spring morning, by way of explaining to John why she was resisting his attempt to pour her another cup of breakfast coffee, Eva admitted that she was worried about what one of her suppliers, Eddy Walters, was up to.

While she sometimes enjoyed reports of Eddy's notoriously diabolical sense of humour – especially when it was directed at someone she didn't particularly like – she also knew he took pride in outsmarting his customers as well as his competitors. Now it looked like he was out to take advantage of some careless contracting by Futurity for his own profit.

The previous afternoon, the head of programme procurement, Ian Clark, had come to see Eva with a sheepish look on his face. It turned out that 18 months earlier he'd approved a deal to buy ten episodes per year for five years of a one-hour calisthenics show that would feature locations in some of the smaller towns in Western Canada, "cleverly" combining niche tourism with exercise.

The production company was owned by Eddy Walters, and during negotiations Eddy had made the argument that he needed to have a payment structure that skewed revenue towards the early episodes in order to get the series up and running. What he suggested, and what Ian thought he had agreed to, was $40,000 for each episode for the first two years, tapering to $20,000 each for a minimum of three more years.

As Ian had explained to Eva, "It was a long commitment, and a really big one for us, but I thought we could use it at our licence renewal as a demonstration of our corporate commitment to independent production and to nation building. And we figured we could tap into one of the independent production funds to help out."

"I remember our discussions at the time," Eva reassured him. "And I remember agreeing to the front-end loading. I also remember thinking that Eddy's plan to wrap a little personal intro into each episode suggested political aspirations. Either that or he thinks he's the reincarnation of Alfred Hitchcock. Having watched several of the finished programmes," Eva went on, "they come across as a bit rustic, but they're a lot of fun. And they offer the exercising public a bit of a change of scene. There's even a rumour that a broadcaster from India has approached Eddy to see if it would work if they did a voiceover in Hindi. So what's happened now?"

Ian elaborated, "These negotiations always seem to end in a big rush. I'm not certain how it happened, but in the push to finalise this negotiation I sent Eddy a confirming note that can be construed as saying we'll pay $40,000 an episode. The contract is clear that the rate is only for the first two years, but now, in addition to using my note to say our agreement was different, Eddy's claiming that he actually produced thirty episodes in the first two years and that all of those would automatically have been for $40,000, regardless of any other dispute we might have."

"How like Eddy! On the one hand he's claiming that your note supersedes the contract, and on the other hand he's saying that if his first claim doesn't hold, he's entitled to his second claim concerning timing. If it makes you feel any better Ian, I suspect Eddy planned to try to paint you into some kind of corner all along. So we just have to figure out how to help you clamber out."

Futurity's legal team advised Eva that the case was not at all clear-cut and that Eddy had a reputation for enjoying litigation. In her briefing to Guy, Eva reminded him of the obvious – that litigating with a supplier never looks good unless the behaviour involved was really egregious or your legal position is ironclad. Neither of those descriptions fit this situation.

Distancing himself from a potentially sticky situation, Guy admonished Eva to get the problem sorted out before he had to warn the board that she'd exposed them to litigation from a supplier. "Thanks for the insight and guidance," Eva groused under her breath as she left his office.

Later, reviewing her Action List, Eva found that she had reached Item 8 – *Go see Eddy on his home turf and see if we can reach a compromise* – so she set up a meeting.

Over coffee in his spacious and comfortable office in Regina, Eddy showed very little inclination to compromise. Gazing around the room as she struggled to keep from telling Eddy what she thought of his shenanigans, Eva noticed a photo of former Conservative Prime Minister, John

Diefenbaker, on the wall adjacent to his desk. As she stood to leave, Eva smiled and remarked, "You know, Eddy, I never noticed before, but you look a lot like John Diefenbaker."

"Do you really think so? That's interesting; you aren't the first person to comment on that. I certainly admire the man and what he accomplished. He was sort of an Abe Lincoln character. I'd kind of like to follow in his footsteps."

"Hum. Well, we'll talk again."

"Sure thing. Sorry the town's hotels are all booked up tonight, Eva. I hope you don't mind the Triple 7 motel. I've heard varying reports."

"I'm sure it'll be fine."

Back in her clean and perhaps formerly comfortable motel room that evening, Eva tried to think about what she'd learned from Eddy and how she might find the basis for some kind of compromise. The next day, after getting up early to consult with her team back at the office, she went to see him again with a number of items to discuss. As soon as she had the inevitable coffee in hand, she launched right into their discussion.

"Eddy, since we met yesterday I've been trying to figure out some way that we can resolve our differences, and I think I may have come up with a solution. Now, you told me that you've just wound up the work for the first 30 episodes of *Highway to Fitness*, although there are those who might argue that you needed our permission to change the production schedule. But, say we let you continue on with the schedule that you unilaterally revised, but we taper your payments. We'll allow $30,000 per episode for ten you already produced that, under the schedule, would have been made next year, and then go to the $20,000 level for the last two years."

She went on, "And I have a suggestion for a slight shift in content as well. How about in the last couple of years you feature small towns that were the hometowns of famous prairie politicians like John Diefenbaker in your programs?

Then you could perhaps use your introductions to provide a little history of how those towns might have shaped those politicians."

"I'll have to think about that," responded Eddy in a neutral tone.

"Of course you do. But I will need to hear soon. My planning team tells me that we have the right in your contract to step in after two years and specify the towns that you use for your settings, and I'd hate them to come up with a plan that requires you to travel great distances at great expense to your production budget for what could amount to very little additional audience value. Now, my cab is waiting to take me to the airport. No, don't get up. Finish your coffee. I'm certain I can find my own way out. By the way, I told the owner of the Triple 7 Motel that you would love to provide uniforms for the little league baseball team he coaches. It's for girl players under 11. Isn't that fun? He'll be in touch later this morning."

"Did you ever read Tom Wolfe's book *The Right Stuff?*" Eva asked John over a late dinner of Kraft pasta at home that night.

"Yes, I sure did. It made a good movie, too."

"It had a big impact on me," continued Eva. "I remember being fascinated by the fearless flyboys with their big fancy wrist watches and how they responded to danger. What I've always thought since reading that book is that having the right stuff means resolutely trying in a cool-headed and clear-minded manner to solve whatever challenge is before you – even if you're plummeting towards earth in a tube of metal likely to become your coffin – until you succeed in pulling out of the crisis or you die."

"Don't be so melodramatic. You weren't about to die, Eva, you were just at risk of being outsmarted by an unscrupulous operator. And then, maybe, being fired by another."

"Believe me John, Eddy wanted to kill me today. He just couldn't figure out how to get away with it. We aren't really as civilised as we like to think we are – especially out on the prairies."

John stood up and came over to Eva, wrapping her up in his arms.

"I'll protect you, whatever happens. And I do think you have the right stuff."

Within a week Eddy capitulated and agreed to Eva's proposals, but later that year he exacted a little revenge. At a retirement party thrown by the broadcast industry for one of their popular pioneers, Eddy had been selected to make some remarks. An excellent speaker with a good sense of timing, he began by complimenting the evening's organisers for assembling a stellar crowd.

"It's like being in Hollywood here tonight, surrounded by movie stars. Take Zack over there," he said, gesturing towards the head of an independent TV network. "Is it just me, or does he remind you all of Marlon Brando playing the Godfather?

"And, let me see... who else... who else?"

He scanned the room as if just casually looking around for another target for his wit.

"Ah, do I see Eva, our lady of small ventures, right here down at the front?

Now you all definitely have to agree with me on this one. There is absolutely no question that she is a *reeaal* Babe."

Sensing some confusion in the audience, he added, "You know, like the one in that cute Australian movie."

After a brief pause, the audience laughed a little uncomfortably, a few people surreptitiously glancing sideways, trying to gauge the reactions of both Zack and Eva.

Eva, shocked at Eddy's audacity, sat up straight in her chair, looked straight ahead and smiled as if being compared to a pig was somehow funny.

Zack Grossman, a quick-witted man who was also nimble despite his solid appearance, suddenly appeared at the podium beside Eddy. Unlike Eva, he'd had a minute or two to react. "While I haven't had a chance to check with her, I'm sure Eva would agree with me that you too, Eddy, have a kind of movieland aura. In fact, I believe it really was *you* who had a small but highly dramatic role in *The Godfather*."

Zack turned full on to face the increasingly tense audience. "I'm sure you all remember? The bedroom scene? Of course, when they turned back the blood-stained sheets all the audience saw was the head. We never did see the other end of you, the part that seems to do most of the talking."

There was another long moment of silence and then the room exploded into alcohol-fuelled hilarity.

"I told you he was a real horse's..." whispered Henry Peterson, with obvious satisfaction, to a shocked Guy Heller. Reluctantly, Guy was forced to pretend to agree.

Consolidation of Experience

Chapter 72: A Change of Scene

"I hear Eddy compared you to Miss Piggy at the big do last night," said Sherri as Eva arrived at work the next morning.

"Absolutely not true. It was Babe he compared me to, not Miss Piggy – although it appears he doesn't know that the Babe in the movie is actually a boy pig. Or he may just be an equal opportunities kind of slanderer. Anyway, Babe is a sensitive and refined kind of pig while Miss Piggy is all porcine sex appeal and big gestures…"

"Anyway," interrupted Sherri, "I heard that Zack Grossman put him in his place? Made some comment about Eddy being a horse's rear end? Solly was still laughing about it when he called to ask if you might be free today for a "delicious Shopsey's lunch". He told me to make it clear that the rules say it's still kosher if you only eat *with* a pig. And as it turns out, you are free. The customer in town from Lethbridge that you were scheduled to eat lunch with just called to say he's ill."

"That's no surprise – I saw him at the do last night; I'd say he overdid the B52s. Or maybe it was the Black Russians. Sure, I would enjoy a lunch with Solly."

As anticipated, lunch with Solly was a lot of fun, filled with lively industry gossip. Eva was delighted to relax in one of Shopsey's comfortable booths and enjoy one of her favourite meals of matzo ball soup and potato latkes while speculating with Solly about the future of the industry and the various key players.

As she was finishing up her enormous serving of lemonade, Solly announced, "In the spirit of last night's speeches, I think I have for you an offer you can't refuse."

"Really? Does it involve any horse parts – fore or aft?"

"If it does, they're in another country, which means a change of scenery at least."

"So, what do you have in mind?"

"I don't know if you've been watching our recent business developments, but Centrepoint's holdings in the UK and Scandinavia have been growing and we've been diversifying into specialty TV and outdoor advertising, to the point where my board and I agree that we need to hire a president for Centrepoint Europe."

"Centrepoint Europe… Hum, that's interesting. What about your investments in the rest of the world?"

"Good question. I want to stay 'hands-on' with our other far-flung investments, but to be certain that you understand what I'm suggesting here, my board has already empowered me to ask you if you'd take over the management of all of Centrepoint Europe's operations – including Ireland and Africa."

"Most people don't include Africa in Europe," smiled Eva, "but then what do they know. Where would the position be based?"

"Your choice, but I think London is probably best."

After a few moments of silence, Eva said thoughtfully: "You may be right. This may be an offer I can't refuse. But I want to make sure that you really know what kind of executive you'd be getting if you hire me. I think it would be fair to say that while I'm indisputably hardworking, energetic and full of ideas, I do have my detractors."

"Don't we all?" laughed Solly. "And while I appreciate your desire to warn me of your possible shortcomings, you'd be doing me a disservice to imagine that I didn't do my homework on your ability to do the job I'm offering before I took your name to my board. I assure you, not everyone is as threatened by originality as your friend Guy is rumoured to be."

"Thank you, Solly. Enough said. Let me think about your offer and talk it over with John. By the way, am I right in assuming that the financial package would be competitive?"

"I think you'll find it fair enough. I realise it's a lot to digest and you'll probably have many other questions. Should we meet here again in a few days to talk further?"

"Why not? Next time I think I'd like to try the blinis again – with the sour cream though, not the apple sauce."

John's reaction to Solly's offer was enthusiastic. "A move to London would be great for us. The twins are pretty much on their own, Chris is young enough to adapt quickly to a new school system, and you could definitely use a new challenge. What a relief it would be for all of us for you to be able to kiss Guy good-bye! As it happens, I've been thinking about a book on satanic imagery and the early church, and London is a very good place to begin. And Juliet has been muttering for a while about retiring. I say: Go for it, Babe.'"

Chapter 73: "That Will Do, Pig"

The blinis with sour cream were good – although not as good as the latkes when the cooking oil is at its freshest – and the compensation and relocation packages were satisfactory. Solly and Eva agreed to make the announcement about her move in a month's time so that she'd have a chance to properly inform Guy, who would need to brief the board in turn. She and John would then fly to London so that she could begin to take hold of the new operation while John found a place for them to live.

Everyone in the family was excited by the move. The twins collectively welcomed the chance to have a base in London that they could use to explore the city and take trips to the continent. Fortunately for John and Eva, Chris had inherited their enthusiastic attitude towards trying new things, and an endearing willingness to watch from the fringes in new situations until he could find a chance to join in.

One of Eva's greatest regrets was leaving Sherri behind. They had been a very successful team and Eva really valued Sherri's insights and enjoyed her dry sense of humour. But Sherri promised to come to London for a visit as soon as Eva was well settled.

Guy received Eva's resignation with a surprising hint of regret. "We didn't always see eye to eye," he conceded to Eva, as always the master of understatement, "but I was beginning to get used to your unfettered style. And you may be hard to replace."

"Unfettered style," grumbled Eva to John at dinner that evening. "What do you think he meant by that?"

"Don't look too deeply for meaning, Eva," advised John wisely. "Just take it as a tribute to your irrepressible nature. Besides, Guy is not your problem anymore; now you have Solly and his board to worry about."

"Speaking of new worlds to conquer, what do you think about a name change to Evaline as I fly over the North Atlantic Ocean? I've always thought of Evaline as the name of a mature woman, and perhaps now I am one. Besides, I like the notion of having a slightly new identity."
John sighed. "You wouldn't change your name to Curran when we married, but now you want to leave Eva behind?"
"Not exactly behind. Let's think in terms of metamorphosis. Besides, you already had a Mrs. Curran and look at the silly choices she made."
"So, less of a pig and more of a butterfly?"
"Sounds good to me."

Centrepoint Europe's administrative officer, Mary Richardson, and the CFO, Martin Crick, had already taken a lease on a well located set of offices on Tavistock Square in central London, and Evaline and John flew over to find somewhere to live and a school for Christopher – although John had knowledgeably been advised by his London agent, Ethan Jones, to find the school first, then look for accommodation nearby.

A well-regarded church school near the British Museum had an unexpected vacancy, and the headmaster made reassuring noises about making Christopher feel at home, although, as he pointed out, he would soon have to move on to a school of the next level. Susie, a bright and cheerful Australian au pair, was engaged to shepherd Chris about, to keep him company when his parents travelled and to make sure that he had at least one clean school uniform on reserve.

Finding a place to live for the Curran-Sadlier family – now including Susie – was more complicated. Centrepoint offered a generous housing allowance, but a dwelling in London with at least three bedrooms proved hard to come by. Evaline was both charmed and relieved when they found a good-sized comfortable flat on Bedford Square in Bloomsbury.

"Evaline has always wanted to be thought of as a bluestocking," confided John to Ethan Jones. "I think she believes that Bloomsbury will bring out her inner Virginia Woolf."

"So will you be her Leonard?"

"Heaven forfend," replied John, in character. "Besides, she has already had a Leo – although come to think of it, that was in another country."

"A good joke in bad taste," remarked Evaline as she joined them, overhearing the last bit of the conversation.

International travel had become steadily more complicated in the years since 9/11, but both Evaline and John favoured quick exits and, before most of their friends had become accustomed to the notion that they were leaving, they were gone.

Chapter 74: A Whole New world...

Disney's *Aladdin* was one of Christopher's many favourites. Evaline reckoned that she'd watched it at least ten times, maybe more. In spite of that overexposure, she still felt gently stirred by the theme song "A Whole New World" and the notion of flying off on a carpet to *"a new fantastic point of view."* It certainly did not surprise John to come home from a meeting with his London publisher to find her unpacking boxes of clothes in the bedroom and singing: *"A whole new world, A dazzling place I never knew, But when I'm way up here it's crystal clear that now I'm in a whole new world with you..."*

John laughed and sat down on the only clear space left on the bed. "So, my cheerful nut bucket, how were things in your part of the business world today?"

"Oh, good. Today we learned that we've been granted the opportunity to bid for the contract to manage all the advertising billboards in Transport for London's buses and tubes, including the stations, and tomorrow we'll start putting together the bidding team and working on a win strategy."

"Goodness, that would be a really big contract. Does Centrepoint Outdoors really have a chance – or will you just be making up the weight so that the competition will look fair?"

"We think we really have a chance, but it'll take a lot of effort. That's why I'm unpacking our clothes right now; I don't know when I'll have the time once the competition process gets going.

"So, how was *your* meeting?" asked Evaline, in turn.

"I'm about to descend into the satanic world of Hawksmoor and the Masons," replied John, looking quite relaxed about it.

"Sounds diabolical to me. How about a field trip this weekend? I read that Nicholas Hawksmoor designed the

Orangery in Kensington Gardens. I also read that the Orangery has an espresso machine and an array of mouth-watering pastries. Chris and I can eat... as you know, one of our best things... while you eyeball the building and its decoration."

"How like you, cleverly combining your commitment to my work with a chance to keep Chris adequately nourished while the au pair has some time off."

"I know, I know – I really do think of everything," agreed Evaline, smiling.

As John had immediately understood, the competition for the Transport for London advertising contract was very important. Not only was it a large contract, but it would help put both Evaline and Centrepoint Europe's newly acquired outdoor advertising assets on the business map in England.

Solly and his board had rightly divined that outdoor advertising was about to change dramatically with the use of electronic media. For those who got there first, the economies inherent in being able to change illustrations from a central computer instead of physically changing paper billboards were enormous, and the chance to animate the posters to hold spectators' interest was a further bonus.

The Centrepoint business development team had carefully put together a mosaic of advertising assets throughout Europe, but England looked most likely to provide the proof for their conviction that shifting from paper to electronic billboards could dramatically change the nature of the business.

During lengthy sessions where they mapped out their strategy to win the contract – "Truffle," as they referred to it in a half-hearted attempt at a code name based on Transport for London's short form TfL – everyone in the fledgling Centrepoint operation was assigned a role.

Evaline's job was to get to know Glenn Turner, TfL's Deputy Director in charge of operations and the individual that the team had identified as having the final say on the contract. Her prime responsibility, apart from assuring Solly and the board that the contract would be both doable and profitable, was to convince Glenn that Centrepoint Outdoors, while seemingly a new entity in the UK, was in fact both established and reliable.

Solly and Evaline agreed that people like to do business with people that they like and trust, and Evaline's job was to make Glenn Turner like and trust her and, by extension, her company.

"Relationships a specialty," she professed to John, who rolled his eyes and softly whispered "Don't I know it" under his breath.

Chapter 75: A Handbag?

Another benefit of their move to the United Kingdom was the chance it gave them to be nearer to Auntie Grace. John's father had died serving in Italy in World War II and his mother, a feisty woman by all accounts, had died suddenly from a particularly virulent pneumonia while John was off at university. His mother's sister, Grace, a resilient spinster whose Intended had also died in the war, had lived with John and his mother throughout his childhood and he was extremely fond of her.

Auntie Grace lived in a little cottage in Tunbridge Wells, where she worked for many years as a companion for young ladies. That job had required her to be resourceful, energetic and reassuring to the families she worked for, but not subservient. In her role as a latter-day chaperone, she established her personal out-of-doors style by always wearing a navy blue beret, cashmere in winter with navy gloves, and silky cotton in summer with white gloves.

John had taken Eva to visit Grace soon after they'd fallen in love, and their mutual appreciation was just as he'd hoped. On that first visit Grace had served them a light lunch of ham, sliced very fine, and potato salad followed by just-picked tiny strawberries with clotted cream. Then she took the lovebirds in her little red Morris Minor over to visit Hever Castle where Anne Boleyn, Henry VIII's second wife, had lived as a child and where Henry had stayed during their courtship.

"Take heed of how that relationship turned out," Grace had warned Eva.

"Come on, Auntie, I have no current plans to have her head cut off," protested John, while Grace just smiled wisely and whispered something in Eva's ear. Later, when John asked Eva what Auntie had whispered, Eva demurred. Grace's comment, which was that the restless Henry soon tired of Anne when she was no longer a mystery to him, had actually given Eva some food for thought.

While privately surprised at the occasional jarring gaps in Eva's knowledge of British history, John was touched by her enthusiasm and desire to know everything about the history of the stately homes that Grace had them tour when they came for visits, and Grace invariably enjoyed having someone sympathetic to whom she could from time to time complain about John and his eccentricities.

Grace was long beloved by Gen and Jo, and Felicity and Teddy cheerfully embraced her as an elderly auntie. But it was Grace's introduction to Chris that provoked the most mirth.

When Eva first discovered that she was pregnant with Chris, one of her few attendant disappointments had been that the baby was due within weeks of the dates she and John had already booked to go on her inaugural trip to Greece. At first their choice seemed obvious; they would have to cancel the trip. After all, who climbs up the Acropolis to see the Caryatids of the Erechtheion with a five-week-old baby? But once they'd adjusted to the prospect of the baby, they decided there was no reason for them not to go, baby in tow, after all.

So, at around the thirty-day mark in Chris' life, ridiculous passport with a photo of "anybaby" tucked in John's breast pocket, he was bundled into a travel seat and off they went. It turned out that Chris was a perfect modular baby. The bassinette component of his baby buggy, stuffed with onesies with matching tiny undershirts, and many, many size one disposable diapers, all fit neatly into Teddy's old hockey equipment bag with only a little pre-packing fumigation required.

As John observed, it was a quintessentially Canadian solution, and it certainly was an efficient way to travel with a tiny baby.

"Don't get absent-minded and zip the baby into the bag and check him with the other luggage," warned Felicity, only half joking. "You are older parents, you know."

"Not yet completely gaga," remarked John, neutrally.

"Speak for yourself," yawned a packing-weary Eva.

The travel to Athens connected through London with a several-hour stopover, so John and Eva decided to surprise Auntie Grace by driving quickly down to Tunbridge Wells to show her the new baby. They'd landed in the early morning and it was only eight o'clock when they got to Grace's cottage.

The couple, slightly giddy with fatigue, had agreed upon how they would introduce Christopher to his great aunt on the drive down. John parked quickly and took the drowsy Christopher, wrapped up in fluffy yellow blankets in his car seat, put him on the front porch of Grace's home facing the door, rang the doorbell twice, and hurried to crouch beside Eva who had already hidden herself behind some bushes.

Still dressed in her blue wool housecoat and bedroom slippers, Grace slowly opened her front door and peered out. She looked, in turn, surprised, shocked, confused and then, after John and Eva had stepped out of hiding, delighted to see her new great nephew. When the baby opened his eyes, looked at her curiously and then smiled, she was totally won over.

Over breakfast tea, having fully recovered her wits, Grace looked over at John and said, "Really, John, my sister and I seem to have raised you rather poorly. Didn't you know that an occasion such as this calls for a handbag?"

Chapter 76: A Phantasmagoric Good-bye

As Chris grew up, the three of them made a point of visiting Grace as often as they could. The drive to "Auntie's house" through the countryside was beautiful, and Auntie always had something unusual for Chris to look at or play with, and a picnic or a special outing planned for them all. Grace's tales of the lifestyles and escapades of her young lady companions were fascinating to Evaline, and she would sit quietly listening and drinking tea while John and Chris tossed a ball around over near the duck pond. From her unique perspective as companion, Grace had the opportunity to observe the rich and famous behaving in naughty and sometimes outrageous ways, and to Evaline it was all at least as much fun as reading a really early edition of *People* magazine.

In her day, as Grace referred to her past, she especially enjoyed trips to the theatre followed by a light meal in The Fountain Room at Fortnum and Masons, where her charges would often try to flirt with inappropriate men while relishing the decadent ice cream sundaes.

"It was a lovely, innocent time, when a smile and a wink could lift one's spirits for days," she reminisced, "although one did occasionally find oneself in slightly deeper water than one had anticipated."

"Who was the 'one' to which you're referring here?" asked Evaline, curiously. "Was it you that got your ankles wet, Auntie?"

"Heaven's no," Grace protested unconvincingly.

Shortly after their move to London, John rented a car and drove Evaline and an increasingly lanky Chris to visit Auntie. On this occasion Grace organised a walk in the bluebell woods, capped off by afternoon tea at Sissinghurst Castle. The woods shimmered a periwinkle blue, which left them feeling as though magic was afoot, then the castle maze almost stumped them all, leading to a lot of laughter as they ate their scones and jam.

After kisses all around, as they drove away Chris said happily, "I love visiting Auntie Grace. She's just exactly like an auntie should be."

"Remember Chris, she's actually your great auntie and that makes her even more special."

A couple of months later, Evaline, lunch sandwich in hand, was just emerging from the Burlington Arcade on her way to buy a book at Hatchards for John's birthday when she saw a dignified woman with excellent posture wearing white gloves and a dark blue beret heading along Piccadilly towards Fortnum's.

"There's Auntie Grace," she thought. "I didn't know she was coming into town? I'll hurry and catch up with her."

Evaline watched as Grace started down Duke Street towards Jermyn Street and the door of The Fountain. Caught half way across Piccadilly on a pedestrian island, she lost sight of Grace while three large buses lumbered by. Just as she was about to hurry over to Duke Street, Evaline's mobile phone rang.

It was Centrepoint's CFO, Martin Crick, telling her that the Truffle Team had found a serious mistake in their bid numbers and they desperately needed her direction. She had to return to the office right away.

It was almost seven when Evaline, finally freed from the morass of bid financing and on her way home from work, got a call from John.

"Are you standing somewhere safe, Evaline? I have dreadful news. Auntie Grace died today."

"No, she didn't," replied Evaline, crumpling onto the nearby chair outside of Café Nero.

"She couldn't have. I saw her at lunchtime today across the street over near Fortnum's."

"That wasn't Grace, dear," John replied softly. "Her daily cleaner found her around midday, sitting in her reading chair. Quite dead."

"Oh no, oh no," Evaline sobbed. "If only I'd run after her. I got distracted and she got away."

"Maybe she just wanted you to see her go," John comforted Evaline later as she sat beside him on their loveseat. "Maybe it was her essence that wanted to catch your attention as she left. I'm so happy that she had such a special connection with you. I haven't had much family to offer you and your love for Grace warms my heart."

"I'll really miss Auntie Grace too," said Christopher, who had abandoned his homework while they were talking and was now sitting at their feet on the floor. "She's the first person that I ever knew who died and it makes me feel very sad." Chris moved over to hug John's legs.

John was the main beneficiary of Grace's will, which included small bequests to each of the twins and to Chris. To Evaline, Grace left a first edition of *The Spy Who Loved Me* by Ian Fleming, which bore the flyleaf inscription: *To the eponymous Grace, from a friend who is also an avid ornithologist. Ian.*

"Did you know that the name James Bond was chosen by Ian Fleming from the name of an ornithologist called James Bond who wrote *Birds of the West Indies*?" asked Evaline, looking up from her computer where she was trying to unravel the mystery of the inscription on the book she'd inherited.

"Can't say as I did," answered John. "But then I didn't know Grace was a birdwatcher either."

"Hum... actually I don't think she was. I think she might have been the *watchee* in the relationship in question – not the watcher."

"Oh," smiled John. "Interesting. Come to think of it, she was a very fine old bird."

Chapter 77: Sometimes it's Better to be the Underdog

The competition for the Truffle contract steadily heated up. Consistent with her particular assignment from the win team, Evaline had a very agreeable lunch of grilled Dover sole with TfL's Glenn Turner at J Sheekey, where they talked about the state of the economy, the virtues of horse racing – including Glenn's expert handicapping of some of the favourites at Ascot – and life as an expat in London. Anything but the competition for the signage contract.

Surprisingly, given his name and the absence of any accent, Glenn had been born and raised in Paris.

"I have an American father," he explained, obviously not for the first time. "Father tongue 'English' is how a census statistician would describe me."

As Evaline subsequently explained to Martin Crick, who had taken on the task of directly supervising the financial side of the bid following the numbers debacle, the purpose of the lunch had been to make friends with Glenn by showing him the kind of person who worked at Centrepoint, and making him comfortable with the notion of doing business with the firm. The easy friendliness of her parting with Glenn made Evaline feel confident in reporting to the team that that she had taken a first step toward their goal of levelling the relationship part of the playing field for the bid.

The Truffle team had come up with an innovative plan. They decided to use a large room in their suite of offices to build a realistic replica bus shelter, littered with abandoned Starbucks cups, *Evening Standards* and all, and to wire it up to demonstrate how advertising and notices could be displayed at bus shelters right now, as well as the kind of changes that could be introduced in the future.

It was a lot of fun to build. The team used all their ingenuity to create a series of displays that morphed from the current, rather ordinary bus shelter billboards into something that actually interacted with passengers while they were waiting.

By the time Evaline invited Glenn over to "experience" their bus shelter, a whiz kid working for her had prepared a sub-programme for the shelter wall that not only gave the numbers and estimated time of arrival of the nearest six buses, but also displayed a table that handicapped the buses so that you could see the odds of your bus, say the Number 30, actually arriving before the Number 28 even though the 28 was currently closer.

That feature really made Glenn laugh. "It looks here like I could subcontract with a betting shop to help pay for these fancy shelters."

"Someday we'll be able to provide job vacancy information and help people call 911 by simply touching the shelter screen," added Evaline. "If we create the right infrastructure it's amazing what services we might be able to offer."

The Truffle team, constantly trawling the prospective client's organization for feedback, gleaned two important pieces of information in the weeks approaching the final contract decision. One, a report from a reliable source that Glenn had directed his team to go with the Centrepoint bid if all other competitive criteria were equal, gave Evaline a real lift.

The other, likely more important, piece of intelligence that they'd ferreted out was that their competition, Network Outdoors, had assured their bosses in New York that the Transport for London contract was in the bag and that they would not need to do any price cutting or call in high-level relationship assistance. TfL had been a good customer of Network Outdoors for many years and Glenn Turner, while comparatively new in his job, had never complained about any of their services.

"We won! We won!" crowed a euphoric Evaline, dancing about the living room swinging her Liberty print silk scarf in circles in the air like a rally towel.

"Way to go, Mum!" encouraged Christopher, looking up from his computer.

"Of course you did, dear," added John. "I always believed you would."

"I can hardly wait to call Solly," said Evaline, breathless. "He's going to be so pleased! Also, he'll be happy that the competition is over so that I can pay more attention to our Scandinavian house-and-home channel and our Irish outdoor advertising. And I should probably try to get down to Johannesburg…"

"This calls for a big celebration. Do you guys want to have dinner at Pizza Express tomorrow?" asked John.

"Yes!" Chris beamed. "How about the one at the square named for me?"

"What better venue to celebrate winning a multi-million pound contract? We may even splurge and have sparkling water," added Evaline.

"Speaking of sparkling, I happen to know there's some vintage Dom Perignon in the fridge. Any takers?" asked John.

"Me! Me! But give me time to call Solly first."

Chapter 78: A Different Kind of God

It was a pleasant summer's day and Evaline and the team had just begun a meeting in their smallish, windowless boardroom when they heard an enormous explosion from the direction of the street. Unschooled in the proper response to the sound of devastation, they ran towards the windows at the front of the office building, overlooking Tavistock Square.

Out on the square they could see a large red double-decker London bus with its top blown off and people running across the square towards it. Martin, who had been working at Canary Wharf when the IRA set off a truck bomb there, took decisive action.

"Everyone away from the windows," he shouted. "Evaline, gather up all the staff, no exceptions, and get them to the back of the building. Probably the boardroom is safest as it has no exterior glass. Turn the television on in there and see if you can find out what's happening. Lew, make sure that our backups are all in order. I'll go outside and see what I can do to help. Keep your mobile phone close. I'll call or text if you need to bring anything out. Flora, quick, find the first aid box and then gather up all the cushions from reception, bag them if you can, and pass them to me as I go out the door. Hurry everyone!"

The TV in the boardroom was carrying confusing reports of many explosions in London Underground stations. At first it was thought that the tube explosions had been caused by power surges, but as more information poured in it became unmistakably clear that bombs had gone off in at least four locations: in the tube between King's Cross and Russell Square, at Edgware Road, at Liverpool Street, and on a number 30 bus in Tavistock Square.

John was just leaving home when Evaline reached him with the news and assurances that she and her team were all right so far. Busy preparing for a day in a quiet corner in the British Library researching Masonic symbols, he had not tuned into any news and was surprised and upset. They agreed that he would get in touch with Chris' school and then call Evaline back.

"Don't worry, Sweetie, he's likely just fine. I'll call you soon."

Fifteen minutes later John called to tell Evaline that he'd managed to reach the headmaster at Chris's school, who'd told him that while some of the parents had been by to pick up their children, he personally thought it was best to leave Chris at school until the end of day.

A dishevelled and exhausted-looking Martin returned after a time to report that emergency services had now taken charge of the scene. Initially, he'd been able to help by following instructions from a group of doctors who were immediately on the spot. By a stroke of luck, the doctors had been attending a meeting at the British Medical Association offices when they heard the blast, almost right outside their door, and they'd raced outside to provide medical care to the injured passengers and passers-by. Martin's grim face foretold the rest of the story.

In the final count, thirteen victims and the bomber died from the explosion in the bus on Tavistock Square.

Like many others, Evaline opted to make the long walk home that evening rather than take the bus or tube. Over dinner it was clear that the whole family was shaken.

When 9/11 had occurred Evaline had been with Teddy in Boston, settling him into his student apartment near MIT, and Chris and John had been in Toronto, watching the television with increasing horror as events unfolded across the border. Even then they'd felt scorched by the proximity of the terror; this time it had happened literally right outside their door.

As they prepared for bed that night, Evaline, still feeling the shock of the day's events, shared with John her conclusion that terrorism must be the last refuge of the hopeless.

"Why else would you set out to harm innocent people?" she asked.

"Are fanatics really hopeless?" John responded. "I'm not so sure. I'd like to think they're crazy, but I think the truth is something much more complex. I certainly think it's safe to say they believe in a different kind of god."

"Imponderables are frightening," Evaline agreed. "I hope I'll be able to go in tomorrow and 'keep calm and carry on'. But that bus with the ripped-off roof on our square will certainly be a grim reminder of this day."

The tarpaulin-covered bus continued to haunt Tavistock Square until at last it was hauled away for further forensic examination.

Chapter 79: Authenticity Rules!

"Mom, do you remember when we made a list of *Mommy's Rules* when I was little?" asked Felicity during their regular weekly Toronto/London catch-up phone call.
"Of course I do, Liss. I often think of them. Especially rule number four: *Be nice, it's good.* That rule is as important today for all of us as it ever was. I do my best to follow it, but sometimes I'm afraid I don't do such a good job."
"Yeah, me too."
"Why are you asking about the list of rules?"
"I was just wondering. I've been invited to perform at a congress of women artists in New York called "Living on Our Own Terms" and I was thinking I'd do a slam poem of an updated version of your rules… sort of contemporary advice for women trying to make their way in the working world."

Felicity's ability to make a living as a performance artist specialising in women's issues was both amazing and gratifying to Evaline and she loved to hear about her 'gigs'. "Gee, that's really interesting," she said, "but do you really think you could come up with something that would be compelling enough to hold their attention?"

"I dunno. Let's try. What rule comes first to mind?"

"Uh… *Live near where you work.* A few years ago I was lucky enough to spend a weekend with a bunch of amazingly impressive women from many countries, and we all agreed that life is way too short to spend a lot of time travelling back and forth to work in a conveyance, even if you're proficient at working while you travel."

"Conveyance. What a great word! I love your little Briticisms. 'Bunch' as a collective noun for high-powered women is good too. So when you weren't admiring each other, you decided that if I want to make my mark I shouldn't allow 'conveyance time' to take up my precious allotment, especially on work days?"

"I guess so."

"What else did you *belles dames sans merci* talk about?"

"We talked a lot about guilt – especially the kind that seems to afflict working women who think they ought to be at home with their children. We were pretty ruthless. Our collective wisdom was that young mothers who need to work should resist adding guilt to their already overburdened psyches. Put a little more sensitively, I think our prescription for that problem was something like: *Try to resolve any guilt you feel about the life you need to live. Guilt works like an anchor; it drags you down and won't let you free yourself from where you are.*"

"But don't you think most women find it tough to let guilt go?"

"Maybe, but perhaps it's just a way of not owning your own desires."

"That's heavy, Mom. I'll have to think hard about how to make that rule into poetry – even slam poetry!"

"I totally agree. Dealing with guilt involves understanding your own motives, and often we don't want to do that. Some motives are really selfish or embarrassing, but you don't have to reveal them to others to deal with your guilt; you just have to know yourself."

"I guess so... what else?"

"Hum... the next rule could address the fact that we all need help. Help is essential. Life becomes too hard if you don't ask for help, accept help, pay for help, beg for help, offer help. No woman is self-sufficient – even though I do like the image of that Indian goddess Kali with many, many arms."

"I get that one, Mom. No need for me to paraphrase there. What about spouses, where do they fit in?"

"Spouses... let me think... I guess I believe that you should let your spouse participate fully in all the joys and all the burdens of a shared existence. It can be as selfish to withhold the frustration and satisfaction of struggle as it is to withhold the euphoria of accomplishment."

"I really like that one, Mom, and it will speak to *all* of my audience, regardless of what the politically correct like to refer to as their 'sexual orientation'."

"Is that enough? It may be just after lunch where you are, but it's dinnertime for me."

"Okay, Mom. I'll call you again in a couple of hours to see if you've come up with any other rules. I think I need one or two more. I know, what about something about the big picture?"

"The big picture? That's usually the point at which I tell young women to ask for a weigh scale when they check into a hotel. There's nothing like business travel to add to your substance."

"Talk to you later."

Evaline couldn't resist trying to think up more ideas for Felicity's poem. John was away so she asked Chris if he had any suggestions and he, too, took the matter seriously.

"How about the importance of having fun?" he asked her. "You're always telling me that if you can't have some fun while you're working then you're in the wrong job."

"I guess that's true – although sometimes we get trapped in jobs where the fun just isn't there. In those cases I guess you have to find another reason for your work, like the trip you'll be able to take with the money you're earning, or the insight you'll have gained into how important it is to go and get qualified for a different job – or even the free muffins you're allowed to eat."

"When I was little I used to like playing with soldiers a lot," mused Chris. "Now I realise that being a soldier is a job, too. Dad's dad was actually killed being a soldier in the war. You sure couldn't call that fun."

"No, you couldn't. I guess that kind of self-sacrifice falls under the category of 'doing the right thing.' And doing the right thing is part of what you should always try to do if you want to be a decent human being."

"Poor granddad. I sure hope he thought it was worth it."

"From everything I know about your granddad, I'm certain that he did."

When Felicity's call came later that evening, Evaline answered after just one ring.

"Any more thoughts, Mom?"

"I've had a couple and Chris has helped me too."

"Oh yeah? What did Chris say?"

"He reminded me that I place a lot of emphasis on having fun and on being happy. And he's right about that. I do think it's important to try to have fun and seek out the things that make you happy."

"Sounds a bit hedonistic – even though I know you don't mean it that way."

"It could be, I guess, if what makes you happy is sex orgies and martinis. I suppose my happiness prescription was formulated with the kind of people in mind who feel happy reading a good book or going to the theatre or creating something beautiful, but I'm willing to embrace those who equate orgies with happiness."

"I notice you didn't include people who are happy running marathons or climbing mountains…"

"Ugh. They don't need me to advocate for them; they can look after themselves. But is *anyone* actually happy doing that kind of thing?"

"I am, but I guess that shows how silly it is to try and be prescriptive about other people's lives. Just look at it this way, Mother Dearest: We're simply trying to give other women some tips about how to identify happiness in the activities life has to offer. They can take them or leave them."

"Okay. Less normative. But I do think you should include a reminder to go home early from work at night and to take your holidays. Everybody needs breaks."

"Me, especially," said Felicity.

"Anyway, I scribbled down a few more thoughts on this crumpled napkin. Let's see if I can read them. 'Give credit to

295

others and take blame yourself.' That's pretty instinctive for a lot of women but it's worth thinking about."

"And I think this one says, 'Pick your bottles' – that's weird. Oh, no, it's 'Pick your *battles*.' Pretty obvious, but it's still probably helpful to point out. For example, you just can't spend your time reacting to every little sexist injustice you encounter or you'll lose your momentum. That doesn't mean they don't matter; it just means they have to wait their turn."

"Pick your battles. Got it. Anything else?"

"This one I can read easily – maybe because I feel it so strongly. It starts 'BE AUTHENTIC' in capital letters, then it says, 'Live your own version of your life. Be you.'"

"Well mom, we've almost come full circle. We're back to Marlo Thomas and 'Free to be... You and Me.'"

"Yes we are. Because, as you know, *there's a land where the children are free...*"

"Night, Mom."

"*...and you and me, are free to be, you and me...* Night, night, sweetie. I hope your slam breaks new ground. Or really hits the audience – in the right way, I mean."

"I hope so too. And thanks."

As she hung up the phone, Evaline could hear "*When mommies were little, they used to be girls*" being sung softly.

Chapter 80: Beauty and the Bard

"Hey, Mom. Did you hear that Felicity's slam poem was a big hit at the women's thing? Apparently one of the attendees compared it favourably to Polonius' advice to his son…"

"Shakespeare, Teddy? Your sister is amazing but I'm not sure she yet merits comparison with The Bard."

"You can see her for yourself; I'm sending you the link to the video."

"Thanks. I'm really pleased it all went well. Where is she now?"

"She's off at an audition for something, but she wanted me to let you know how well it went. She told me to give you a million thanks and a drillion hugs and kisses."

"Got them. So, how are you doing?"

"Great. My new PhD advisor is really hot and she's kindly helping me scope out my thesis topic."

"Somehow I don't think you mean that she needs to turn down the thermostat in her office. Is there some ethical boundary we need to worry about here?"

"No siree. I'm content to worship her from across a radio isotope machine. But you never know – when I've finished my degree…"

"What I really want to hear about is whether you're eating your greens and washing your clothes occasionally."

"Don't worry, Mom, I only smell a little. How are you doing?"

"I'm off to Johannesburg tomorrow, which should be really interesting, but kind of scary. I do admire what that government is telling prospective suppliers about how to win contracts."

"What's that?"

"They've made it clear that if we want to win government business we need to be able to demonstrate that there are significant numbers of black women working for us in senior jobs. They also want us to be able to prove that the women have been working for the company for some time. I think that direction is great, and the men in our South African office have already told me that they're totally committed to doing what the government wants. Last time I was there they sat me down and explained that we couldn't succeed in that market unless we're all totally behind this government initiative."

"Gee – that's almost unbelievable!"

"It sure is. And shame on me for imagining that they'd respond otherwise."

"Anyway, Mom, I was calling you with a question of my own. Or maybe it's a question for both Chris and me. You're always dispensing wisdom and advice to my sisters and to young women at large, but what about your sons? What about all the young men who hope to fall in love with the women you're exhorting to live a full and happy life? What about guys like us who want to love those women and have children and a happy life too? How are we supposed to fit into your gender-balanced brave new world?"

"Oh Teddy, what a good question. Actually, I think that making choices about how to live a happy life can be as hard for boys as it is for girls. The difference is that your gender has a several millennia headstart on some of these issues, and no shortage of spokesmen – and I do mean spokes*men* – and serious thinkers to whom you can look to understand your situation."

Evaline continued, "I do feel that your dad and then John have been excellent role models for you, but now that you ask me I realise that I should have given it more thought. I don't have an easy answer for you, just some half-baked notions about trying to live a happy and fulfilling life. I think it all starts with figuring out who you are and what you want – although I'm a great one to talk; I certainly don't know the answer to either of those questions yet, but I am working on it. My aspirations for all of you are really the same. I want you to feel a sense of accomplishment in your work and to have fun. Gender shouldn't determine your choices for work or fun, and it really is a shame when it's allowed to stand in someone's way."

"I understand. And as one of your finest representatives of my gender, right now I'm going to seek to have fun working."

"Love you, Teddy. Have fun with the isotopes."

"Bye for now."

Chapter 81: Fade to Grey

Evaline started to feel the corporate financial tension late in 2007. Approvals for new initiatives were becoming harder and harder to get from the board, and Solly and his CFO began to share a permanent air of worried distraction.

Things had been going well for Centrepoint Europe, but Evaline knew in her heart that it's easy to look good by consolidating and growing from a relatively small dispersed base. And that was exactly what she had been busy doing for the last several years.

There had been talk about promoting her to a top job in the mother company – although both Evaline and John were hesitant about moving Chris again – but the talk came to nothing and they were saved from having to make the tough decision.

She was feeling at the top of her game, with regular boosts of reward and recognition, the twins squared busy pursuing their interests with varying results (including the production, by Gen, of a magnificent grandchild), John's new book safely at the printers, and Chris off each morning in his suit and tie looking for all the world like a proper English schoolboy instead of the half-colonial import he really was.

As Evaline remarked later, she was a fool not to have realised that it was the calm before the storm.

Solly's flying over to London to talk to her was portent enough, so when he told her over boiled eggs at the Connaught Hotel that he was going to have to divest Centrepoint Europe, she was dismayed but not completely surprised.

As he explained, Centrepoint Limited had over-expanded – particularly in the United States – and the company urgently needed to free up some cash to pay down debt. Solly stressed to Evaline that, in a way, the divestiture of

Centrepoint Europe was her own fault. If she hadn't done such a good job of expanding and developing the business and making it profitable it would not even have been considered for divestment. As it was, some unsolicited offers had already been received and they were serious enough to merit consideration.

She almost cried onto her delicately toasted scone. It had looked for some time like being managing director of Centrepoint Europe might be the pinnacle of her career, and now it appeared that was the case. But it was much, much sooner than she had expected.

When Evaline managed to reach John later that afternoon with her news, he immediately suggested she meet him for dinner at Ozer – a Turkish restaurant on Upper Regent Street. John knew that the ambiance at Ozer was right for a serious conversation at a quiet table, and he knew that Evaline found the lentil soup there very soothing.

"What did Solly tell you about the divestiture timetable?" asked John, after commiserating with his despondent wife on the sudden change in her prospects.

"He and I are going to meet with investment bankers over the next couple of weeks. In the meantime I'll need to tell Martin what's afoot, since he'll be responsible for assembling the data room once initial indications of interest have been received. There are well-defined processes for this kind of sale, so we don't have to do much thinking, just follow the rules."

"What will happen to your employees?"

"Most of them will be fine. They have jobs that are unique to our business. It's the people like Martin and our teams and, of course, yours truly, who are likely to be superfluous. But I suppose it's only fair that the people who earn the big bucks bear the brunt of the big changes."

"You're putting up a brave front, sweetie, but you must be feeling sad."

"Yeah, I am. But you know, I probably would've found it impossible to judge when it was the right time to quit working full time, so maybe it's good that the decision is being be made for me."

"Have you given any thought to what you'll want to do?" asked John.

Evaline laughed. "Sleep? Cuddle? Eat peppermint-filled chocolates? Drink single malt scotch? Read books? Play cards? All of the above?"

"I think that can be arranged."

The sale of Centrepoint Europe was simultaneously quick and slow: The negotiations with everyone who wanted a slice of the process were laborious and labyrinthine, but then, suddenly, Evaline was sitting in the lawyer's elegant offices in the shadow of St. Paul's signing piles of documents alongside the president of the acquiring company, Horizont.

Based in Germany, Horizont already had a strong position in outdoor advertising in continental Europe, with aspirations to integrate both backward into production and forward into programming. Despite the much-touted benefits of the European Union, the regulatory complexity of Horizont's undertaking seemed breathtaking to Evaline and she certainly wished them the best of luck.

"I guess I should be grateful it's not my problem," she muttered to herself.

Concerning her immediate future, Evaline had agreed to spend sixty days briefing the new management and providing insight and experience to their team, then she was free to take her hefty exit package and go.

Solly had offered her a directorship on his board in Canada once the deal closed and Evaline had happily accepted. As she discussed with John, now that she was in the "corporate director phase" of her career, a directorship from a former employer was a sound credential. "It's a vote of confidence. If Solly didn't feel I'd done my best for his company in Europe he never would've offered me a board position, so I'm pleased and relieved that he has. It should be fun to have a chance to think about the various components of Solly's empire from an owner's point of view. Still, I feel a bit wistful about stepping back from active decision-making. I wonder if I'll miss the fray?"

"I thought you told me you're going to sleep and eat chocolates."

"But that's only for the first week. Then what am I going to do?"

"I guess that's your next task, figuring out what to do with the rest of your life."

Chapter 82: Who Am I Anyway?

Evaline hated every dreary second of the sixty-day hand-off. It wasn't the loss of the company she minded so much as the frustration of trying to explain to someone else how to do a job that came naturally to her.

"I'm a doer, not a teacher," she complained during family dinner. "It's not that I don't value teachers, it's just that I don't want to *be* one. It makes me crazy trying to figure out how to describe to someone else what I do intuitively."

"Mr. Alvarez loves teaching," interjected Chris. "He told us that helping 'young minds blossom and bear the fruit of learning' is one of life's greatest joys."

"Remind me, Chris, what subject does Alvarez teach?"

"He's the games master. This term we're playing cricket."

"It figures."

Finally it was done, and a rather large cheque in recognition of Evaline's services was deposited by Centrepoint into her account.

"Is it time to talk about the future now?" asked John over Sunday morning coffee, as they watched Andrew Marr's political guest deliver his carefully rehearsed impromptu partisan message to BBC viewers.

"I think I'd like to go back to university and do a PhD in mediaeval history."

"Mediaeval history? Goodness. That's certainly a surprise. I would have wagered that if you wanted to do something academic it would be around the struggle for women's equality."

"Oh no, I didn't even consider that. The struggle for women's equality is an avocation for me, not a defined area of study. No, I've been thinking about a different kind of struggle – an ancient, enduring and seemingly universal struggle that continues to pit the haves against the have-nots.

In addition to frightening me, the global financial crisis has really got me wondering how our society has arrived at such a dangerous juncture. How could it go all pear-shaped so suddenly? What's wrong with capitalism? It feels as if we've failed to learn anything lasting from history – or even from recent experience."

Evaline mused, "There are no simple answers, of course, but I would like to spend time looking for answers of some kind. Strangely, perhaps because I know so little about it, I really want to learn about the mediaeval period in Britain and Europe to see if that will help me figure out how our economic system has evolved the way it has and why it suddenly seems so flawed."

"Well, it's clear that you've given the subject some serious thought. But the phrase 'out of left field' barely begins to describe it. Where do you think you might start?"

"I've been looking at some of the university materials that Chris has been leaving around the house and I'm beginning to get a notion of where to go, but I'll need a lot of advice as to how to get the proper grounding and how to put my candidacy forward. Despite being an INSEAD grad, I really don't have any idea how one gets into graduate studies in this country, especially if you're old."

She added, "Years ago, back at Cumberland, we had a student club called OTAS, which stood for Older than Average Students. I used to find the notion of the group kind of funny, as well as its name, which just goes to show that you should be careful what you laugh at because it could turn out to be yourself. I suspect I'll need to take make-up courses and, after I've got myself properly qualified to proceed to a PhD, I'll have to throw myself on the mercy of some academic admissions committee with a taste for the older-than-average eccentric. And, naturally, I'll need to buy an entirely new wardrobe."

"New clothes. Now you're talking. There's the old Evaline – or should I start calling you Eva again?"

Chapter 83: Are There Still Battles to be Picked?

"Hi, S-Mom, what are you and your dwindling assortment of dependents or co-dependents up to in London these days?"

"Ah... S-Mom. Now there's an enduring nickname," reflected Evaline. Some years ago a friend had overheard Jo calling her S-Mom and remarked how nice it must be for your children to call you Supermom. "The 'S' doesn't refer to Super," Evaline had corrected her, "it refers to 'Step'."

"I am doing very well, thanks, Jo, but I wonder if your dad might take exception to being described as a co-dependent... Anyway, how about you? Everything going all right?"

"Really great. Last week we started shooting the documentary I told you about – the one about residential schools in the North. It's long hours and surprisingly strenuous, but it's really interesting and fun as well. Most of the members of the crew are quite young, but luckily we do have some veterans to help us out."

"I'm glad you're liking it. You sure worked hard enough to get the job. Wait a minute and I'll call your dad to talk to you."

"Actually, it's you I called to speak to today."

"Oh. What's up?"

"Do you remember that slam poem Felicity wrote for the women's congress a while back? The one with the advice for young women?"

"Of course. It really worked well for her."

"Well, I loved it. And last week I started thinking about the stanza on picking your battles. You know, the part about 'When it's not that sucker's day, walk away.' I asked Felicity about it and she told me she'd got that advice from you, and I was hoping you could help me pick which battle I should fight with the team on the documentary."

"Well, the wording wasn't exactly mine, but I do believe in the message. What or who is confounding you?"

"Like I said, we have some veterans on the documentary team, and mostly they're really helpful in steering us away from beginner's mistakes, but it turns out that working with Dennis, the crew chief, has some drawbacks for me. He treats everyone like a newbie, but he singles me out by calling me 'dear' and 'sweetie' and asking me to run little errands for him. Like in the canteen at lunchtime when we're all at a big table he looks over at me and says in a loud voice: 'Look at that, I forgot to get ketchup for my meat pie. Jo, sweetie, would you mind running over and getting me a couple of those little red-and-white packets?'"

Jo explained, "Of course, I do it, because I don't want to make a fuss, but later the others tease me and call me 'Jo Sweetie' and 'Dennis' gofer.' And he embarrasses me by commenting on my looks in front of the others. Yesterday he said, 'I like that pink scarf on you – makes you look feminine for a change.'"

"You know, Jo, by this time you'd think all the guys like Dennis would have retired or died or realised that the world has changed. But clearly they haven't. What I feel like saying is *plus ca change, plus c'est la meme chose*, or maybe 'You *haven't* come a long way, baby,' but that wouldn't be totally true. In the time since I was getting started, we *have* come a long way – just not as far as we need or intend to go."

Evaline continued, "It's going to be years and years before we quit encountering these alpha particles of sexism that seem to have been sent by some evil force from the past to torment us. Maybe we need a terminator to go back in time and delete their fathers before they have a chance to be conceived... but in the meantime, you're right: dreary as it seems, this is a question of which battle to pick. First of all, I'm becoming a big supporter of the value of visualization. If it helps you at all, try thinking of Dennis as a misshapen sexist alpha particle – or *sap* for short."

Jo chuckled as Evaline went on, "I certainly don't have a simple solution. My approach has been largely trial and error, but what I have learned works best with guys like Dennis is generally to ignore them. Go along with the easy stuff, like getting ketchup, because otherwise you get branded as prickly and uncooperative, but otherwise just pretend you don't hear his old-fashioned comments."

"I'll try that, S-Mom. If you don't mind me asking, when you suggested the "pick your battles" rule to Felicity, were you thinking about a particular situation in your past?"

"Oh, I've had many, many examples to draw on," laughed Evaline, "but there was one silly incident that happened over twenty years ago that I find I still puzzle over."

"Really?"

"Yes. Back when I was a management consultant I was selected to give a particularly important presentation to a manufacturer's association meeting about just-in-time delivery. I dressed carefully in a classically tailored forest-green wool suit and I was well rehearsed. The presentation provoked energetic discussion among the attendees, and at the coffee break one of the young industry rising stars came over to talk to me. I gave him a big welcoming smile, expecting congratulations, but instead what he said was, 'You know, Eva, all the while you were making your presentation I kept wondering how I would feel if it was my wife up there giving that talk. It kind of made me uncomfortable. And I decided that one of the things I should tell you is that you shouldn't put your hands in your jacket pockets, especially when you're speaking – it's just not ladylike. And don't stand with your weight on one hip. It makes you look way too casual.'"

"Wow. What did you say back to him?"

"I don't remember. Probably, 'Oh.' It's possible I even reflexively said 'thank you.' But I still wonder in what universe he thought it was acceptable to tell me to take my hands out of my pockets and stand up straight."

"Well, as you said, thank heaven that behaviour seems to be dying out. I imagine nobody has the nerve to do that sort of thing to you these days?"

"You'd think so, wouldn't you? But fact is, they do. When I joined a board here in the UK recently I looked forward to learning how the other directors and the corporate executives think about women. I'd been forming some unsubstantiated opinions about the social effects of sending young people to single-gender schools, but the men I met during my orientation briefings were engaging and seemingly modern. Then, during a tea break, I found myself standing beside one of the company's so-called global leaders – a man very highly regarded by many… including, as it soon emerged, himself. After listening for a while to him describe his many unique accomplishments, I asked him curiously if his wife worked outside the home. 'Oh no,' he smiled, seeming to relish the question. 'Our family responsibilities are divided quite equally. She's in charge of spending and I'm in charge of earning.' I found it shocking to hear a man – especially a Cambridge-educated one whom the company relies on to understand our customers – casually belittle his wife like that."

"But you didn't confront him?"

"I did chide him gently but I don't think he even noticed. I have no idea how his wife would've reacted. Maybe she'd think his comment was fair – or even funny – and that my feminist reaction was silly. Who knows?

"Anyway, if ignoring him politely doesn't work with Dennis, or he gets a lot worse, you could tell him that if he doesn't shut the F up you're going to cut off his boy bits and make them into a nice pâté with a peppercorn glaze – an old recipe of your stepmom's. I've known that to work."

Chapter 84: Let Me Not to the Marriage of True Minds...

John and Evaline were sitting quietly in their hotel room, holding hands and looking out into the grey twilight across the fast-flowing river Danube over to the ancient city of Buda. While they were both enjoying a local white chardonnay and a snack of cheese dumplings, John was drinking using his left hand, as was his habit when he didn't want to let go of Evaline's hand with his right. Somehow he found her trusting smallish hand clutching three of his fingers a touching contrast to her normally self-contained demeanour.

They had just returned from a bracing walk across the bridge, up the funicular and along to the museum in the Buda Castle, where Evaline had been particularly keen to see the remarkable treasures on display in the Mediaeval Rooms.

"Tiring but satisfying," she sighed.

"A bit chilly for my taste, but very thought-provoking. The world owes much to the artistry intended to glorify religion, yet it has suffered so much death and destruction associated with those same religious passions," summarised John. "You know, I've been thinking a lot about devotion and passion lately, trying to get a sense of a theme for my next series of photographs. I've been pondering the notion of 'love under duress' – the kind of thing you get in the image of an elderly man gently wiping the drool off the face of his stroke-disabled wife, or a wife gently helping her husband with Alzheimer's remember how to dance a waltz. I even have a title in mind – *Love's not Time's Fool.*"

"That's a great title – it's from the sonnet by Shakespeare isn't it? – but don't you think a whole series on the subject might be a bit depressing?"

"Yes, that does worry me. But what I really want to do is concentrate on enduring love between adults, not the forces that act to undermine it. I just don't know how to portray its essence in a photograph. From your considerable experience, what comes to mind when you think about enduring love?"

"Let me think... I used to put my faith in that quotation from *The Alexandria Quartet* that I told you about, the one that claims 'work itself is Love'. But now, having been betrayed by work many times and having loved you for many years, I believe that enduring love for another, if you can achieve it, is more than fair recompense for those of us who've failed to find the solace offered by belief in a higher power – or perhaps it's the other way around. We all want a safe harbour, something that makes the struggle seem worthwhile. Of course, some people are rewarded with both, but they're the exceptionally lucky ones.

"When I think about how hard it is to find enduring love, I feel so fortunate to have found you. My marriage to my True Love was a youthful mistake, and Leo was a kind and good man who didn't live long enough for time's insidious alterations to set in, but somehow, almost miraculously, the timing all worked out and we met when I was ready to meet you on fairly equal terms, which gave our relationship a real chance of succeeding.

"Even now, decades after my false start, it's very difficult for a woman to sort out who she wants to be before feeling the need to settle down with one person and build a life or start a family. And I wonder if I would've been able to find my way into the working world so readily if I'd met you earlier and had to compete with the artistic and travel demands of your career. I feel some sympathy for your ex-wife in that regard in particular, and I know you felt sympathy for her too.

"It would all have been much easier if I'd started out with a clear-cut notion of what I wanted to become. But I didn't. All I ever knew was that I wanted to be more accomplished and more interesting than I was. Looking back, that was an impossibly nebulous aspiration to start with, but in my case luck, some skill, and a fair bit of nonchalance won the day.

However, for me, finding you and loving you, and you loving me back, was the biggest prize of all."

John smiled. Then he said, "I'd like to think I would've given you my full attention and support if I'd met you earlier, but forcing myself to be honest, I'm not so sure. I know I dreamed of making glittering images and exercising glamorous powers, and I was dead set on achieving them. By the time we met I was much more realistic about the joy and fringe benefits that accolades can bring, and I was ready genuinely to share my life and use what ability I have to help someone besides myself win recognition. I guess that was lucky for you."

"Oh, no," laughed Evaline, holding up her empty glass for a refill, "I'm certain that was divine intervention."

Chapter 85: Let the River Run

"Is that you Grandma? I can see you on mommy's big computer screen. She let me push the button. We just got up from sleeping."

"I can see you too, Lockie. You still have bed head. Did you have a good sleep?"

"I think so... Mommy, did I have a good sleep?"

"Yes, you did. Now let Mommy have a turn."

"Hi, Gen, did you have a good sleep, too?"

"Not bad. It does feel good to cuddle up for an afternoon nap beside a little hot body. But the reason I've mobilised myself to call you is that I have some exciting news concerning your struggle for female equality. Last week I was in court to provide moral support for one of my young male patients who was testifying in a rape trial – such a sad case – and I looked around the courtroom and saw something amazing and I knew that I had to tell you about it."

"So what was it that struck you as so remarkable?"

"First of all, this was what they call male-on-male sexual assault, so the accused is male and the victims are male as well. That's not so unusual. But what was unusual was that the judge, the defense lawyer, the prosecuting attorney, the police investigator, the court reporter, and one of the clerks of the court were all female. And the jury was 50/50."

"Wow. That's really interesting. Sometimes I get so frustrated about the pace of change in the battle for equality, and then I learn about something like that."

"I knew you'd be pleased."

"I am. Pleased and hopeful. Would you believe that I found myself singing 'Let the River Run' the other day – you know, the song Carly Simon wrote for the movie *Working Girl,* and when I got to the line, 'Come the new Jerusalem' I started to wonder if it really would ever come?"

"I forget. How does that song go?"

"I hope Lockie's far enough away that he can't hear his grandma's tuneless singing. Here's the part I sing to myself:

It's asking for the taking, Trembling, shaking, Oh my heart is aching
  We're coming to edge, Running on the water, Coming through the fog, Your sons and daughters
    Let the river run, Let all the dreamers Wake the nation, Come, the new Jerusalem."

"I agree that Carly's voice has the edge, but you do good hand gestures, and you're right about the sentiment."

"So how are Lockie and Sarah? Do they like their new nanny?"

"Yes – I think they're beginning to like her better than they like me, but for now that's a price I'm willing to pay if they don't cry when I leave for work."

"And it's certainly better than having them cry if you don't leave for work."

"Yeah, thanks. I think Simon might do that."

"Husbands. They just don't know when they have it good."

Chapter 86: There She Weaves By Night and Day, a Magic Web…

Evaline's reaction to the invitation to her high school reunion was one of ambivalence. On the one hand, she definitely wanted to see how the people who had been her constant companions during the painful progress of her late teens had prospered, and on the other hand she still believed in the poignant truth of Rod McKuen's lament, "Alamo Junction".

As she described it to John, "Alamo Junction" is a chronicle of how the exile, far from where he or she had started out, persists in the belief that when she finally goes home again everyone there will be "pretty surprised to find out just how tall I've grown and oh, how worldly wise.'

"I imagine you're going to tell me that it doesn't work out quite like that?" smiled John, looking from his computer where he was reviewing his most recent photos.

"You got it in one, but you don't get many points for that, it's pretty obvious. As you may have noticed over the years, I do sometimes like to sing songs to myself, or hum them when I'm playing cards – I'll pause here for some ironic laughter – and one of the refrains that features on my interior playlist is that last verse of that ballad."

"My guess is that my husbandly duty at this point in the conversation is to ask you how the ballad ends – although it might be preferable to have you recite, not sing."

"Oh, I'm up for a little dramatic recitation. The last verse goes:

When I got back to Alamo Junction, the town somehow just wasn't the same, all the folks I thought would remember had all but forgotten my name."

"So is that why you're afraid to go to your high school reunion? You're afraid nobody will remember you?"

"Sort of. Sometimes I feel so proud of what I've been able to accomplish, but then I realise maybe I'm just a hero in my own lunchtime."

"You're a hero in my lunchtime, too – and the kids' – but otherwise you could be right. So why does it matter? I thought you wanted to see how your classmates had done."

"And I do. I really do. But I also want them to think that I made something of myself."

"If you don't go you'll never know how they did – or how you did in their eyes either. I think it's worth the risk."

"Will you come with me?"

"No. It's your nostalgia trip, not mine. I already know that no one will know my name, especially since you've disdained to take it."

"Complaints, complaints. I let you be listed as head of household on the census form, didn't I?"

"Not without dispute. You should probably pick a different example."

"Maybe, later."

The long flight of steps up to the party room where the reunion was being held were daunting, but after a very warm greeting and a name tag featuring a photo of her old self, Evaline felt immediately at home. The familiar names, the haunting resemblances, the garbled memories… it was as enjoyable as she had hoped.

There was a little hiccup. A man she vaguely recognised came up and asked her about her 'True Love.' Even hearing his name was a bit of a shock to Evaline.

"Are you two still married? Is he here tonight? I feel like I remember him a bit better than I remember you."

"It didn't last."

"So what's he doing now?"

"I'm not really sure. I did Google him and he appears to own a chain of retirement homes."

"Good for him. I knew he'd be successful."

"Here's my Guinness, talk to you later," said Evaline as she successfully eddied away.

Some of her classmates had careers of renown in politics and the arts, and many were just what Evaline would have hoped they would be – hardworking people who'd lived a fulfilling life.

Poring over the *In Memoriam* book, she was surprised and saddened at how many of her classmates had already died, and she wished she could know more about their stories. Fresh-faced David Caldwell, the first boy she had ever kissed – back in grade 5 – was gone, as was her friend June who had remained close until grad school when they drifted apart. It was hard to believe that June had been dead for almost 30 years and Evaline had not known.

As the evening wound down, Evaline sat in a happy little group, reminiscing about Mr. B's bad breath, and learning, too late to give her the admiration she deserved, of Miss Gimby's remarkable accomplishments.

As she was getting ready to leave, her long-lost friend Anton turned to Evaline and commented warmly: "Who would've thought that the outstanding businessman in our class would turn out to be Evaline Sadlier?"

"Who indeed," she mused as she said her goodbyes. "Certainly not me."

Master Class

Chapter 87: Brutal News

"Hi, José. What's up? I was surprised to hear a message from you on our voicemail; it's usually Carina who calls."

John tilted his head, listening. It was rare to hear from José, Carina's husband. Usually Evaline and Carina were the ones who sustained the relationship between the two couples, emailing and phoning regularly.

"Oh no," he heard Evaline's voice fall. "What's going to happen next? What can I do to help? Should I fly over?"

John became anxious, but there was nothing he could do to help until the call was over. Finally the conversation ended with demands from Evaline to be kept informed.

"Poor Carina, poor José and poor Magdalena," sighed Evaline, close to tears. "Carina has been diagnosed with stage 4 ovarian cancer and she's going to have surgery next week. They just diagnosed her last Monday and the doctor says there's no time to lose. I offered to go to Sao Paulo but José says Magdalena is feeling very protective of her mother and doesn't want anybody there but the three of them right now. I understand, but I really feel helpless."

"Of course you do. It's frightening to have something like this strike a close friend. Quite apart from how much you care for Carina, it's scary to think that serious disease can strike out of the blue like this."

"Yes. José says Carina is in shock right now, but I bet once she gets working on her treatment she'll be all over the disease, researching where it came from and how she may have fallen victim to it. And of course, she'll be worried for Magdalena. So many cancers are traceable to genes these days."

"In the meantime, let's try to figure out what we could send Carina to cheer her up after the surgery and give her something to help her recovery. Maybe Chris could help us load up an iPod with 'get well' music to send to her."

"What a good idea. She would really get a kick out of a selection of inspirational works like 'Climb Every Mountain' and 'Big Girls Don't Cry.'"

Later that evening John noticed that Evaline wasn't reading her novel with her usual intensity; she was just sitting staring off into space.

"What are you thinking about?" he asked softly.

"Oh, just the vagaries of life. In particular, I was thinking about endings, about how we start out all bright and eager and then the shine gets rubbed off by mistakes and accidents and poor timing – and in cases like Carina's, serious illness.

"Remember how we agreed the other day that, especially when one knows the inside story, hardly anybody gets to retire with dignity – not in business, not in sport, not even in life? I must admit that sometimes I've really enjoyed watching the mighty fall, like when Guy was unceremoniously retired by the board of FutureMedia for lying on his résumé about having a graduate degree from Yale. But the truth is, it happens to all of us. One day you're a 'breath of fresh air' and the next you're too something... too sure of yourself or too old or too right or too wrong. Or too expensive. Whatever it is, they've had enough of you, and if you're lucky you may survive to fight another day."

"Evaline, I know that Carina is a special friend and I really hope she gets better. But while what you're saying is true, it's also true that many of us don't know when to leave the arena and have to be pushed out. So if you really think about it, you've already survived to fight another day."

"I sure hope so. I was just thinking that maybe the greatest source of satisfaction is knowing that your work was interesting, that you had fun, and that the number of compromises was kept to a tolerable level. How embarrassing it is to realise that Frank Sinatra said it first!"

~~~~~

Chapter 88: Bearing Witness

"Glad you're home, Mum," said Chris. "Some guy called. They want you to be on the radio again. Something about how you said in some speech that working women shouldn't have to compromise."
"That's not *exactly* what I said. Is there a message?"
"Yeah, he wants you to call. The number's on the table. He said he tried your mobile and you didn't answer. Did you have the ringer too low again?"
"Thanks, Chris. And no, I was in the tube."
"Shit, shit, shit..." Evaline thought. "Why does John have to be off taking pictures in Chile when I need to talk to him? Oh well, I'm a big girl. I can handle this."

"Hello, is this J.J. Singh?"
"Yes, hello. Is that Ms. Sadlier?"
"My son said you called?"
"Sorry for the short notice, but we're looking for a businesswoman to interview on our Friday morning broadcast. There have been several reports recently about progress concerning numbers of women on boards and closing the pay gap – both here and abroad – and the producer was wondering if you might be willing to be interviewed about your career and whether feminism, as you knew it, is an outdated concept. You know, like the suffragettes – a movement that's served its purpose? Or should the struggle still go on?"

"John, I had to say yes. For Jo and Gen and Felicity and Sarah – and Teddy and Chris and Lockie, too. And all the young women who are still trying to understand what their role might be."
"Well, it's brave, Evaline. You know that programme takes great pride in catching out its guests. You got off fairly lightly last time. This will not be a sympathetic interview; it

will certainly not be their intention to provide you with a soapbox for your beliefs. I'm glad I'll be home in time to listen and deliver shoes as required."

"I have no intention of being a 'hollow man' here – or a 'hollow woman' for that matter. And I intend to be more bang than whimper. I think I'll wear my Aussie boots as a statement. It would be difficult to wear only one of them by accident."

"Good luck, sweetie. Just be yourself."

"Has feminism outlived its purpose? I'm here today in the studio with Ms. Evaline Sadlier – a self-described feminist and businesswoman whose career has spanned the Atlantic. May I call you Evaline?"

"Please do. And what should I call you?"

"Oh, please call me Jim. So, much-lauded businesswoman, consultant, non-exec board member, proud mother, PhD candidate... It sounds like you're a real Superwoman."

"Absolutely not."

"Tell us, then, how would you describe yourself?"

"I'm a very lucky woman; a woman who has had the chance to live the life she wanted."

"So you didn't need quotas or rules or burning bras to help you get along?"

"Of course I did. I needed every bit of help I could get. I needed role models and encouragement and legislation and awareness-raising and support from many women and men along the way. I needed every bit of it."

"And is the job done? Are the goals of feminism achieved?"

"Again, absolutely not. We're a long way from gender equality – even in the developed world, much less the parts of the world where women are still treated like slaves or chattels. Feminism is about natural justice and we still have a long way to go."

"But, as you said, you personally have lived the life you wanted. Any regrets?

Dead air... dead air... dead air.
"Come on Evaline," thought John from his perch by the radio, "Say something... anything!"
Dead air... dead air... dead air.
"No. No regrets."
"None at all?
"Well, of course, every life has its highs and lows. I've suffered some painful losses. And I've done some things I wish I hadn't – but who hasn't? I'm the sum of my mistakes as well as my triumphs."
"So that's it? That's how you'd describe yourself?"
"Yes, that's about it."

~~~~

Acknowledgements

First I'd like to acknowledge the triumphs, tragedies and peccadillos of my relatives and friends – even my enemies – who provided inspiration for many of the more remarkable scenes in this book. Strangely, the bizarre episodes actually happened – although sometimes with imaginative variation – to someone of my acquaintance, while the routine had to be made up by extrapolating from the daily modern life of career women I know.

Of course, my husband, William Morgan, encouraged, edited, caveated and succoured me throughout. As always.

Our children also read the first draft and made helpful suggestions.

Barbara Harrison and her daughter Michele took me out for dim sum and helped me believe that even people who are not related to me in any way might think the project worthwhile.

My friend Ines Wichert, author of *Where Have All the Senior Women Gone? 9 Critical Job Assignments for Women Leaders*, not only provided a checklist for Evaline's career, she also read the book and inspired me to keep on improving the narrative.

As did Harvey Schachter, who took the time to fit reading the book into his demanding schedule and then helped me to see that when I get too intense I can be preachy rather than simply helpful.

The insights of Karyn O'Neill, Susan Cornell and Louise Tremblay, all great friends and former colleagues, were vital to me.

My sister Penny Bent and my brother John Whittaker both read near-final drafts of the book and were lovingly supportive.

Ginger Gibson Macdonald, a successful modern young executive and mother, served as 'test market' and rewarded me with a 'You go girl!' after reading the final text.

My good friend Victor Lesk, inventor of the bridge scoring programme BriAn, was kind enough to read the book from the perspective of an enlightened male reader and to give me useful feedback. Margaret McDonagh, a tireless supporter of other women and a remarkable woman in her own right, helped me advance the book whenever I asked. And then there's Faith. Over the years Dr. Faith Gildenhuys and I have shared many of the challenges of what is now called 'work/life balance'. At the point at which I was afraid that I had lost my objectivity, that I was too close to the story and unsure of the power of the narrative, I turned to Faith, a retired professor of English Literature and professional editor, and asked if she would help me. And she did. She gave me the confidence to strengthen the plot and to believe that Evaline's story is worth telling. Symbolic of the importance of Faith's role is the fact that manuscript versions during the revision of the story bear titles ending with 'Have Faith'.

Last on the scene came Georgia Laval, a source of careful plot tracking and my expert in publishing details. Georgia gave crucial momentum to this book and helped Evaline to tell her story.

Thank you all very much.

Also by M. Sheelagh Whittaker: *The Slaidburn Angel* (Dundurn Press), available on Amazon

Made in the USA
Monee, IL
17 January 2021